Thought Bubble

Stories From My Mind

Ethan Thomas

Independently Published

Thought Bubble: Stories From My Mind
Copyright © Ethan Thomas
All rights reserved.

This is a work of fiction.
Any names, characters, places, and events are products of the author's imagination
and are used fictitiously. Any resemblance to persons living or dead is coincidental.
Any opinions expressed are those of the characters and should not be confused with
the author's. No part of this book may be reproduced in any form or by and means,
electronic or mechanical. This includes storage and retrieval systems without written
permission from the author, with the exception of brief quotations in reviews.

Published 2024
ISBN: 979-8-218-43098-6 (Paperback)
ASIN: (eBook)

CONTENTS

When three siblings flee their controlling father to join Mrs. Kettleback's circus, they never expected to inherit a vast fortune. But as they revel in newfound freedom, their joy turns to peril when their aunt dispatches ruthless pursuers to claim the inheritance by any means necessary.

In the whirlwind world of Comic-Con, two souls collide: one timid, one adventurous, both masked by the allure of cosplay. Little do they know, their chance encounter sparks a connection that transcends the convention floor, leading to a serendipitous reunion where love blossoms anew, unmasking their true identities beneath the guise of anonymity.

Embark on a cinematic journey with a group of friends turned filmmakers as they capture the essence of adventure and friendship during a road trip while crafting their very own movie.

INTRODUCTION

Welcome!

Thanks so much for buying my weird little book. Inside this volume you will find a little bit of all kinds of stuff. Not all the stories I write are big enough to be their own book, but the stories that pop into my head still must be written down, otherwise all the people who live in my head scream at me to put them on paper, and until I do they give me headaches. So here you will find flash fiction, short stories, novelettes, and anything else I wanted to put.

I hope you enjoy this book I've put together for all my stories that don't belong anywhere else.

> FLASH FICTION

DEATH BALLOON

The scientist's assistants were preparing his invention. It was supposed to be some sort of flying machine. One of them was setting up some sort of stove while the others laid out a large, very large, piece of cloth,

"Isn't this fascinating Robert?" asked his mother, Martha. They were on their balcony overlooking the park where the demonstration was taking place. The scientist was looking for financing for more of his experiments and as such was preforming for the rich people as well as the crowds of normal people who they spotted tossing coins into an assistant's hat.

Robert, however, was having none of it. He sat on the marble balcony rolling and playing with his new spiked ball. "Honestly James why does he love that thing so?"

"Boys gain fascination with incredibly foolish things until they reach a certain age."

"And what age is that?"

"Whenever their cock starts working,"

Martha patted her husband playfully. She had wanted to get closer to the demonstration, but James had pointed out that if the thing worked, they'd be eye to eye with the scientist and his balloon, "I thought he'd be fascinated with this, Robert come here at once,"

Robert waddled his chubby five-year-old legs over to the balustrades, "Yes?"

"It's starting, don't you want to watch?"

He pondered a moment. "No thank you." Then he went back to playing with his ball. It was a strange thing, small and metal but with small knobby spikes he could push in and out. Livid at her son for not wanting to watch the balloon, Martha grabbed the ball and placed it on the ledge. Robert's face turned red, and he said, "Give me back my ball."

"No, now quiet. The balloon is rising."

All was silent on the balcony while the balloon rose into the sky, getting closer and closer to Martha to the point she felt as if she could reach out and touch it.

Suddenly the balloon was falling. The cloth caught fire and burned quite rapidly. The basket landed with a thud in the dirt. The screams could be heard from the balcony. Martha looked at her husband, "What happened?"

He pointed over her shoulder, and she turned to see Robert, bent over the ledge of a balustrade, looking down to where he had knocked his ball in an attempt to retrieve it. James spoke, "Our son just killed six people."

ENGLISH 101

"Repeat after me, Da ah.." The class repeated the word. "Wonderful. Who wants to try the sentence?"

Haxargh stood up and spoke in his people's tongue, a sound like two pieces of bark rubbing together. "Very well, go ahead. "

He cleared his throat. "Hello Hu-mans, we are here to con-ker you unless you give us your dogs."

"Okay, only a few minor hiccups there, great job. What about the rest of the class?" They all repeated the phrase in varying degrees of English, "And the second part?" In unison the class said, "We do not want to kill them, they are fluffy We like the fluffy. Who is a good boy?"

The portal opened in the wall and everyone picked up their weapons. "Okay class, have a great invasion!"

SIBLING BONDING

"**M**om and Dad fighting again?"

She held up the cigarette she was smoking and said, "The fuck do you think?"

The only time Ibi smoked openly was when they were fighting. They were too busy to notice the smoke. On an ordinary day they were up her ass dusk till dawn, though not always in a bad way. Sometimes it was chores and homework and bullshit, but a lot of the time it was up your ass in that way that you, being seventeen, can't tell your parents that you like, but secretly like all the same. How was your day? Is school going well? Did John Prescott ask you to the winter formal or is he still being a pussy? Do you want me to call his father?

But when they were fighting, boy howdy. The last time they fought she'd almost been caught smoking when the cops showed up. Every fight left her with a full ash tray and an empty pack, sometimes carton, and when the blue and red lights from the driveway illuminated the back porch, she almost shit herself. She'd grabbed the tray and moved back into the shadows, smoking while she cried.

Her brother Desmon walked over and jumped the chain link fence. The dogs crowded him for a second and he paid them all attention in turn, he was like that. He then sat down a couple of steps below her and just, was. They didn't talk, didn't think, they just existed while the night got darker, and their family fell further apart.

The only sounds were Ibi exhaling and screams of what a piece a shit their father was and how he never loved any of them, and the witty retorts of, "You know what? Fuck You!"

"What started it tonight?" Desmon asked.

Ibi shrugged. "Who knows. Dad came home and Mom was pissed. He was pissed when he came home. I was pissed because of what happened at school today, everybody was fuckin' pissed."

She lit another cigarette and Desmon said, "What happened at school today?"

"I don't want to talk about it."

"Okay."

Ibi took two drags and said, "Trisha called me a whore for dating two people so far into the school year and giving hand stuff to seven others."

"She thinks they paid you?"

Ibi's eyes went wide. "I didn't do it!"

"I couldn't give less of a shit if you did. The accusation of prostitution was my issue."

"Yes, I've had two relationships this year, and been on a few dates in between, but I didn't do hand stuff to everyone."

"Did they reciprocate? The ones you did hand stuff with?"

"Why does that matter?"

"Just seems polite if you've got your hands on their hose or up their snatch that they reciprocate."

"Three of them. Okay, I did stuff with three of them, and two of them were nice and reciprocated, but there was just nothing there. And it's only been seven people total this year, I don't know where she got the idea that it was nine."

"Could the issue be you gettin' your feelings hurt, or maybe not owning the slutty side of yourself?"

"What do you mean?" She paused when a window broke, an award their father had won at work landing on the other side of the fence. Ibi turned back to her brother, stood up, retrieved their stashed bottle, and motioned for him to proceed.

"Well, I happen to know that Trisha was giving hand jobs to literally any boy who'd sit still as far back as sixth grade, when she was in my year, so I can't imagine being held back twice and having grown even more hormonal would have tamponed down her libido. Clearly, she is a very sexually hungry girl, It's not like a church girl was calling you out."

"What's your point?" She said passing him the bottle.

He took a swig, "Are your feelings hurt that a huge tramp called you a whore, or is part of you afraid to own your horny side and admit that even if she's right, there is nothing wrong with it?"

"Fuck," she said, mind blown. Another round of exasperated crying came from the window, "I did this,"

"No, you didn't," Desmon said, "He never listens and doesn't care about anyone other than himself,"

"Why do you hate him? It's not like she's perfect,"

"No, she's not. But my issues with her are based on her actions. My issues with Dad are based on who he is as a person,"

Ibi took the bottle from her brother. That was when they got drunk. She'd drink during the week for whatever reason, or sometimes just because she liked the taste, but when they did this, that was when she got truly fucking shitfaced.

She stopped when she'd hit half the bottle. Tomorrow morning would be spent cleaning vomit out of or off something.

"I don't know how much more of this I can take Des,"

"I know. But what 're we gonna do?

'Kill them?"

"If only this were a movie...no I still don't know if I'd do it."

"Why not?"

"Cause why should they get off so easy?"

She laid back, the soft, worn wood of the porch embracing her like an old friend. "You really think I should own it?"

"Why not? You're a big girl, if you 'like suckin' and Fuckin' then why not?"

"So, what, just take her comments?"

"Or fire back with a comment like, 'Don't be bitchy just cause I'm better than you, I know you've had a lot more practice."

Ibi laughed. She could feel the booze start to hit her, the sky getting softer as she was lulled into a more peaceful state by whiskey and nicotine. "I think they might be done." Blue and red lights hit her face. She turned her head and saw the cop getting ready to knock on the door.

"Too late," Desmon said. He jumped up. "Officer. Over here."

Turning back to her he said, "I'm gonna go deal with him so colonel von douche tard doesn't go to jail tonight."

"I'm gonna stay here, drunk and underage."

Her brother hopped the fence, and she looked back up at the sky, wondering why God had put her on earth if it was just to deal with all this fucking bullshit.

ALTERNATE DATING

The tent was not enough for the trip we were on. Why he had failed to pack the heavy duty tent he did not know, Hell, how he had managed to convince the number two actress in the world to come on a camping trip with him was still a mystery.

They had met in a club that his friend brought him to. His friend was honestly not important, a nothing actor trying to work his way up to the point that anyone would know what he looked like let alone his name, but he had gotten a big enough part in one of her movies to be invited to a party on the cast's day off, and he brought him. She had been sitting all alone, having given up serious parting a long time ago. He had never started. They got to talking and before he knew it he was dating her.

"I'm freezing. Take your clothes off." she said. He did as instructed because, well duh. She shimmied into his sleeping bag and their body heat made it nice and toasty, pressure started to rise and before he knew it,

He woke with a start, the lab tech and the doctor standing over him. "Amazing. You actually inhabited the body of you from a parallel universe." The doctor said. "Earth shattering."

He looked away from the doctor into the overhead florescent lights. Earth shattering would have been five more minutes."

WINTER VACATION

"Winter was the only season we could be together." Mom said as they walked through the house. Dad wanted to go away for the holidays, without the rest of the family. Mom hadn't seen her family, or his, in over a year.

"Two of your brothers are overseas, winter is the only time they come back. Carl, Derek, and Melany's tours all miraculously end in time for winter. Your mom can't handle heat, my mom can't handle bugs, all the cousins who aren't in jail have managed to get off at the same time. This is literally the first time that has happened in two years. Everyone we actually like can come to the reunion."

"I wanted to go to the beach. It's my vacation."

"We are going to the beach!" Dad started to speak, and she held up a finger, "And we are only paying for us, our kids, and your parents."

Dad tilted his head as if to say 'Huh'. He kissed her and said, "Fuckin' A let's go."

THE FATE OF THE TELEGRAPH OPPERATOR

The fate of the telegraph operator is sometimes bloody. That's what they'd told Sam when he'd gone to school to learn. They said it pays well and usually comes with side business that's totally accepted, provided you pay a small portion to the company.

What they hadn't told him was just how bloody it was. He'd been in scrap after scrap and thanked his father every day for making him learn how to fight. He'd seen people killed many a time and only by sheer luck was it not his body riddled with holes. Tonight, he was cleaning up before he went to bed when the door opened, and he heard a gun cock. "Shit."

VICTORIAN HAT SHOP

"**W**hy do I need a new hat? Honestly, Mum it's fine."

"No, it's not. We moved to London to make a better life for you and your siblings, and not have you trouncing about the city in that man's rag you have upon your head."

She rolled her eyes. They continued to walk down the aisle of the shop looking for a 'Lady's hat' more befitting the station her parents aspired too. Her mother started looking through a pile of premade hats, even the look on her face yearning for the day her hats would be custom made. She walked into the other aisle, this one holding ties and belts and a few of the stranger styles of men's hats.

She saw a boy at the end of the aisle. She didn't think he saw her, and she pretended to be looking at something while she stared at him out of the comer of her eye. He was quite handsome, dark skin and narrow eyes. He was what her American cousin referred too as a celestial in her letters. Apparently, there were many of them in the states. They were a somewhat rarer sight in London as far as she could tell.

He looked up at her and she panicked, walking quickly into the aisle her mother was in, smacking straight into her as she rounded the comer. "Look at this one, isn't it lovely?"

"Yes, fantastic, let's go."

She was rudely pushing her mother to the counter when the boy walked over and started writing up a ticket. She could feel her face get red and she said nothing to him, just looked at the floor and took her hat when her mother offered it. She didn't breathe easy until they were three blocks away. Though his smile stayed in her mind's eye for weeks.

SITTING ROOM SIREN

Zera was sitting in her room doing homework when she heard a commotion from downstairs. The door opened, her grandmother said hello, and then it was just the faint sounds of two people talking. She couldn't really understand what they were saying, but in this house a single visitor that wasn't for grandpa constituted a commotion. Her friends never came around and Grandma didn't like people other than her quilting circle, and they met at church.

She listened for a few minutes; she knew the voice, but it was masked by the door to Grandma's sitting room. Dear God, that meant that it was one of her friends and that grandma had taken them into the room to...

She stood up quickly from the desk and opened the door the rest of the way. Just as she reached the top of the stairs, she saw her best friend walking up. Zera immediately retreated into her room, holding the door open while Sarah walked in. She was in tears, clutching a dress like it was a life raft. "I told you I'd get it another time." Zera said.

"I know but your date is tonight and it's your favorite dress. Oh God I'm shit."

"What happened?" She asked, though she already knew.

"She went through the reasons why all my life choices were bad, convinced me that Led Zeplin was shit after Bonham died even though I liked the reunions, and I think I promised to attend Mass with her this Sunday. Do you think this skirt makes me look like a chubby slut?"

"No. I think it looks very nice. You really should not have come near her."

"I thought she liked me!"

Zera sighed. "Everybody thinks that until they go into the sitting room."

SILVY SAYS

"The floor tasted like..." He thought for a moment.

I looked at my friends and wondered for the third time in the last few minutes why we were listening to this crap. It wasn't false, as in the story was total crap, no it was crap as in, why was our movie paused why we listened to our super weird friend talk about being bored while at his sister's new house and licking the floor.

"I'm not sure what exactly it tasted like, but it was tart and bitter, and it had kind of a grain to it. Sarah said Josh had spilled a bunch of the baking supplies, so I kind of figured that it was like, baking soda and flour mixed together, but then I tried that when I was in your kitchen a little bit ago, and it wasn't the same."

I was about to tell him to shut the hell up about the second weird thing he'd done when Silvy spoke from the couch. "Was it a bit too bitter? And after you licked the floor did you feel a bit light headed?"

"Yeah." he said with a surprise. "I just kind of thought it was because of how fast I stood up when they brought the TV in."

Silvy looked at me. I nodded and she turned back to him. "Sweetie, uh...Dwight, your sister does coke."

"What?"

"What you are describing, sounds a lot like the taste of Co-caine." Silvy would know.

Dwight sat up and looked horrified. He stood up, saying as he left the room, "I've gotta call my mom."

SIXTY SECONDS UNTIL DOOMSDAY

"Give it to me!" The punch hit his face. The man's blood soaked into the fist of the agent. "Now!" Another punch.

Forty-five seconds to doomsday.

He walked back over to his partner and held his hand out. She put a knife into his waiting hand and he walked back over. "I need that gum to generate an idea on how to save the world. It's the only hope we have left, so you're going to give it to me, or I'm going to make sure you die in the most pain humanly possible. You wanna give it to me?"

The man shook his head.

Seventeen seconds to doomsday.

The agent walked out of the steel and concrete room chewing a stick of gum. His partner followed him out and they met the director in the hallway. "What do you have for me?"

"She's got the code for the virus that will deactivate the nuclear systems worldwide, go!"

She took off running, saying random symbols into her radio. The director and the agent waited for ten silent seconds before it came over the radio.

Doomsday averted.

The director turned to him. "What'd the gum give you?"

"The idea for a multi novel saga that will undoubtedly be popular. Also, cancer, probably. Shit's super toxic."

MARMALADE MAD MAN

J oey walked into the kitchen to find his grandfather ladling goop into a jar. Their kitchen was covered in jars. Big jars, Little jars. Regular shaped jars, spherical jars, even squared jars. They all were in various states of filled with liquids of hundreds of different shades.

Grandpa had been obsessed since Grandma died. He spent every waking hour trying to create the perfect marmalade, or more precisely, recreate his late wife's recipe. There was a dusty jar on a single shelf high on the back wall that was a shrine, to the marmalade, not Joey's grandmother.

It had once contained the last jar of her recipe, long since gone and dissected. Grandpa was now working from her recipe book, which did not contain the recipe for her marmalade but he thought it might lead to clues, and his own notes copiously taken while sampling the last jar under various conditions.

No one had minded at first. It was an old man's way of grieving. But when his duties around the house were neglected, his family ignored, and even his favorite grandson told to leave him alone forever, Joey's dad had come to the same conclusion as everyone else and confronted his wife.

"Mary, your dad's fucking nuts."

AFTER THE FUNERAL

"She liked to fit people into the world like puzzle pieces," Grandma said sitting at the kitchen table.

My mother looked at her. "Mom, we said happy things."

Grandma looked offended, "It is. She could always tell people when they needed to do something, what they needed to do her ability to see the whole picture is what made her amazing," She gripped her cup of tea, "She would have been the best guidance counselor in the world."

Marnie, looking more respectable than I have ever seen her in black cabree pants with black shoes, a plain T-shirt, Purple and white track jacket with her purple highlighted hair in two balls on the top of her head, God, I loved her...

She spoke for the first time all day, "It's true. She told me to start doing my own laundry and three days later my mom and I were able to have a real talk, we haven't had a real fight since."

Grandma motioned to Marnie with her open hand as if to say, 'There you go.'

Marnie hopped off the buffet she had been sitting on and walked out of the room sniffling, I looked after her and then back at my family members gathered around the kitchen. They all looked at me. "What?"

"Go get her idiot," My grandmother said.

"Is it really the time?"

My dad rolled his eyes, "There literally could not be a better time to be there."

I thought about it for a moment and when I looked toward the door, I could have sworn I saw a thumbs up, So I got up and followed Marnie out of the house.

I KEN WHAT YOU DID

T he door frame exploded in a shower of wooden splinters. Marcus fell to the ground and came up, dagger drawn and splinters in his cheek o Crouched in the doorway he saw his wife standing a few paces away holding his flintlock pistol. "What in the bloody hell Dolores?"

"You bastard!" She said and threw a silver pitcher at him. There were several more obscenities and home goods thrown at him in the next several seconds. He fought his way to his wife when she cornered herself in the shack. He took a bible to the temple and yelled, "You foul mouthed bitch, why are you throwing things me?"

"I ken what you did you bloody bastard. I know how many of those foreign women you fucked!"

Marcus knew his face betrayed him. The look of shock would have been readable by a blind man. "What?"

"I know you idiot. The buck some brunette you took aboard ship, she wanted to see the world and when you'd fucked your fill you left her stranded. How could you?"

"How could I what? Fuck her or leave her stranded?"

"Either!"

Marcuse watched as she picked up a heavy iron skillet and threw it with surprising strength. He did not hear her next words.

POLYTHEISM FOR DUMMIES

"There were forty-eight thousand gods in their pantheon and not one dedicated to bisexuals." Martha said.

We were exploring gods and their pantheons because both my friend and I felt a pull towards other religions. We had talked about it before and said that we felt that there had to be multiple gods. The world was such a big place that even if there were only one supreme God, why wouldn't he want some help?

"Two points," I said, "No freaking way you've already looked up all of their specific gods and their domains, and two, there wouldn't have been. They didn't call them bisexuals."

Martha was confused, she tilted her head like a puppy. "What?"

"Yeah, I don't know exactly when, but the term is very modern. Ancient sexuality was all about penetration, so more than likely they would have been called something like, Man who gives and takes,"

She thought for a moment. "Well, there has to be one that would at least work.,."

"How about choose the God who speaks to you the most as your patron instead of trying to find one to fit your modern cultural identifiers."

"That's actually a good point. I did the ceremony best I could last night and Reare was the one who I saw a vision of."

"That makes sense that a forestry death God would be your patron."

"What about you?"

"I don't know. I've been a little nervous to try the ceremony. Does it hurt?"

Martha shrugged. "Not really. I'll help you. I'll grab a needle and some candles, you get naked and go to the back yard."

ROYAL RENDEZVOUS

"His wife was having tea with the king, and he didn't even know about it." She took a drag from her cigarette. "It boggles the mind."

"Not really. He's a banker. They pay attention to very little other than money." He was buttoning his waist coat. He looked around for his watch as he spoke. "The Monarchy used to be the bank, and then they owned the bank, now they must let the bankers think they have power when really they are just moving around the money that the royals want moved.

"Truly?" She asked.

"Yes. The royal family manipulates the markets based on what they need done. Keeps bankers working and distract-ed."

There was a mischievous gleam in her eye. "And why would you need to keep the bankers busy?" She whipped the sheet off her naked body and he spied his watch nestled between her legs.

He smiled at her and crept up the bed. He planted a kiss right on her quim. She shivered. He looked up into her eyes and said, "So we can fuck their wives."

FAIRY FOREST

"So how long has your husband been gone?"

The old lady led her through the house as she spoke. She had not expected to find, someone so deep in this forest, it had been explored only by a handful of people and most of them had died during. She'd had an entire team at the beginning. Peterson had fallen in a quicksand pit, Johnson and Johnson (No relation) had both been stung by something extremely poisonous, the rest were similar tales. One by one they'd all died or turned back and now here she was, three weeks into the most unexplored place in the world, and she finds an old lady in a house.

The old lady sat the hat and coat she had taken from her new guest and sat them on a chair, politely putting the hat on its crown. "My husband has been gone a very long time. He was an explorer like, yourself, we both were. We tried to chart these woods thirty years ago."

"Do you mind if I ask what happened to him?"

"Oh, he had a medical condition that was actually quite treatable, but he refused to take the medication because he said there was no guarantee of it out here. Better to explore new places sick than die healthy never having known, that's what Harold used to say."

"Edith? Who are you talking to dear?"

"No one Harold, just a young lady who came in today. She's an explorer like you."

"Where did she go?"

"Out into the woods, that's where you explorers go. Here, why don't you go and see if she's still around, invite her to dinner. I didn't think of it, silly me." She picked up his hat and coat and handed them to him as he made his way to the door.

VIRIDIAN VIRUS

The sound of the chalk marking the door was earie. Like death waving his scythe across the wood. More than likely that was exactly what was happening, he walked over to the window and looked out at his neighbors' homes. Seven out of the ten or so he could see from the window had marks on their doors.

They would be locked up for seventeen days. They had delivered plenty of food for the whole family, and most of it would go to waste. This virus was unlike anything the world had ever seen. It had a nearly one hundred percent death rate, ninety-nine point seven five to be precise. They were calling it the new plague. Some called it the green death, because eventually it turned the victims a very specific shade of Veridian that idiots on the news had just called 'Green'.

His wife had contacted it somehow. He still didn't get it. They had been quarantined for months, deliveries that were sprayed down, masks when the children played on the roof in the makeshift garden/yard. But she had it. And when it killed her, and eventually all of them, their home would be burnt to the ground to prevent any exposure.

"Daddy, will we be okay?"

He looked down into his little girl's eyes, clutching her favorite toy, and it was then he knew true despair. He spared telling her that the odds were against any of them not catching it in the seventeen-day period that it took to run its course and kill. He didn't explain that he, being an adult male with a good immune system, would watch her die. He simply said, "Yes baby girl, we'll be just fine."

JEREMIAH AND THE TALKING TREE

J erimiah was walking up a hill, trying to get back to town going a way he'd never been before. The idiot had been paying more attention to the girl he'd been visiting in Lockwood, and he'd veered off the path. She was a special kind of girl though, big eyes you could lose yourself in, and huge, 'Thwack' He smacked into a tree in the path and fell down.

"Ow, that hurt."

"You think that hurt? Try having some jackass walk into you while you're just minding your own business being a tree."

"I must have hit my head exceptionally hard. I could swear that tree just spoke."

"I did speak you idiot."

Jerimiah stared at the tree. He thought he was going mad.

Eventually the tree said, "Are you an idiot? You haven't spoken for eight minutes."

"Well, I am in a bit of a shocked state, it's not every day trees talk."

"That depends on the neighborhood."

"What?"

"Nothing."

"Do you have any powers that should know of?"

"I'm a fucking talking tree, how much more powerful do you need?"

"Can you contact other plants?"

"Most of them yes. Ferns are rude and Venus Flytraps only speak German for some reason."

"Would you like to help me spy on people?"

"In exchange for what?"

"Never cutting you down and burying the bodies of my enemies under you for nourishment." "Sure," said the tree.

PLANTATION PANDEMIC

Gretchen was walking into the kitchen as Ivy watched TV. 'They're calling for lockdown and no gatherings of more than ten people, if you absolutely have to gather."

"What're we going to do?"

"Where's Tessa?"

"Putting the kids to bed."

Ivy ran her hands over her face. "The fuck are we gonna do?"

"Half the plantation never goes to town. The other half trusts your word more than the half who never goes to town. We'll follow you."

Ivy thought. She took out a fresh piece of paper and Gretchen watched for twenty minutes as she said the names of each one of her workers, and their children, trying to work out the best plan.

The next day Ivy and Gretchen got up early. When your day normally began at four in the morning early took on a whole new meaning. Two in the morning and they were already knocking on cabin doors. Marcus, one of the workers whose family had been there for generations, answered the door with a yawn. "What's up boss?"

"Sorry to be so early Marcus but we're shutting down for the time being."

His shock was clear. "Really?"

"Because of the pandemic the whole plantation is quarantining. But we're too close down here. You know those two thousand acres we bought last year?"

"Of course."

"Anyone who wants to is going to set up a campsite on a piece of it. Take their family and ride it out. Supplies will be delivered by one of the four of us. Absolutely no one should be allowed within six yards of your camp. Anyone who stays here will be given access to the cabin next door, so you have room to breathe and not lose your shit."

"Good call. These are really just sleeping quarters."

"Right, and now you'll be here all day."

Marcus cocked his head. "Sounds like a good plan. What about pay?"

Ivy mentally braced herself for his reaction. "We're going to put you at half pay in order to stay the storm. We don't know how long it will be and we're shutting down production."

"What about the harvest?" he asked after a moment.

"It's almost finished. The rest will be done by a small crew today."

"Well take me down to quarter pay to help out. I'll head out as soon as I get my stuff packed."

Ivy nodded. "Thank you, Marcus. Stop by the great hall, we have heavy duty tents for everyone."

"Yes mam."

"Thanks Marcus."

Ivy walked to the center of cabin row and met Gretchen walking. "How many are staying?"

"Just enough that we're safe. Only about six people are staying. Most of the families are headed to a campsite."

"So they can send the kids away."

"Right. But they know not to let them into another camp."

They walked up to the laird's table. The 'Great Mill Hall' was a bunch of ancient tables that were really large and standing under a roof that they had only put up last year after a hundred and fifty years of the tables being outside. Josh and his girlfriend Cady were at the ready for when people showed up, the tents ready and masks on. As they walked on Ivy breathed in. She was stressed as hell on a normal day. This was not helping. "Do you have our current balances?" she asked Gretchen.

"Yeah, I brought them." She fished them out of her bag and handed Ivy two books. The bank ledger and the larders.

Ivy looked over the books as she walked. By the time they'd reached the distillery she had made her decision. "We need to increase our larders. Radio Tessa and have her call our customers, tell them we're sorry but we will only be able to deliver on seventy five percent of their order. The remaining twenty five percent would feed us for up to a year."

"I'll tell her to leave that part out."

Ivy laughed. "Smart ass."

Gretchen radioed her wife so she could be ready come seven AM. Then she said, "They'll want a refund."

"We can give them one." Ivy said. "By the end of this we'll be fucked up the ass but we will survive."

She turned and walked into the distillery. David's dad was in the shoe box office up front going over his books. "How much longer do you have left on the still?"

"We literally just put a new batch in."

"Shit can it."

"What?"

"Until further notice we are making hand sanitizer. Keep a skeleton crew of whoever is around, including department heads or me or whomever."

"Why?"

They shared a brief look and Ivy reasserted her position with nothing but a look. "When I get it I'll give you the information on where to send it."

"Yes mam."

"How's everything?"

"Not good. Mary isn't coming home until further notice."

"Lord, that many cases coming in?"

He nodded. "And that is on top of their usual load."

"Where is she staying?"

"They have a room for her in the hospital."

Ivy shook her head. "Unacceptable No."

"Excuse me?"

"Call Mary and tell her the top floor of the Marriot will be reserved for her and the staff of the hospital."

"She was transferred to Atlanta to help out."

"Well then, I'll see what hotel is closest to her. I'll radio you later with the information."

"Can the plantation afford that?" As department head he could ask that without it being rude.

"It'll be fine, but if you must know I'm paying for it, not the family account."

He looked shocked. "You'd do that for us?"

"Frank I'd do that for you even if you weren't my family."

"That's not official."

"I had his baby Frank. You're family even if he's trying to convince me otherwise."

He smiled. "I did the same thing to Mary."

"The women your family marries don't like to be told what to do."

"You know my father warned me about that. He said to look for a woman I could boss around and push away. Bitch fuckin' lied to me."

Ivy laughed. "You'll take care of the sanitizer?"

He nodded. "I will."

She walked out. Her phone buzzed and she made a mental note to ask Josh how to stop the notifications. This shit was going to be hard enough. If she wanted depressing information she would look for it on her own. 'Christ I could use a,-"

"Drink?"

She turned around to find Rose standing there. "I was gonna say cigarette."

Rose dropped her bags and ran. The sisters hugged fiercely and, upon realization, thrust each other back.

"Classes are canceled and the school is closed. So tell me how I can help out."

Ivy sighed. "Come on then, as soon as I figure it out, I'll tell you."

FREAK HOUSE FREAK OUT

"**O**h My God!" Flink yelled. "I am so sick of this house!"

Selina was playing cards with her husband and Clover.

Flink had been confined to the house since the pandemic started and complaining about it ever since. "I am immune to diseases that affect humans!"

"No, you aren't Flink, just most of them. This virus is infecting everyone. Thank God I can so much so we don't have to go out at all."

He was sitting at the counter. Moving his hands dramatically he moaned, "But I like going places! I have been going here and there and wherever I please for thousands of years. Was I ever phased by a pandemic?"

"Yes." Gideon said. Flink looked at him and he continued, "You said you were in Kansas in nineteen eighteen and that you had to stay inside so that you wouldn't be found to be a magic user because they weren't letting anyone leave the town, magically or otherwise."

Flink rolled his eyes. "And to this day I have no idea why a town would have a Gibraltar rock or know how to activate it. But I didn't catch anything!"

"Flink, this won't last forever. You and Rowan can get back to traveling when it is safe. Until then, find an activity."

"I have baked every recipe I know. Your husband and Mort have gained seventeen pounds each."

"Read."

"I have, every book in the house."

"Go for a walk in the woods."

"Your grubby kids are there, and I have already walked in on them enough."

"This is a big house Flink."

"Not big enough for this many people. Lucy and Telulah have commandeered the entire fourth floor."

"For what?"

I have no idea...Telulah threw a curse vial at me when I entered."

"Well then watch a movie."

"Watched them all."

"Christ Flink we're on day seventeen." Clover said.

"Language." Selina said. Turning to Flink she said, "Seriously though."

Flink, a true traveler and wanderer, looked like a junkie on their way to rehab. "What is your deal, you stayed here for way longer before."

"First of all, it feels like I've been here for seventeen centuries. I've stopped using magic just to make the days seem like I have more to do. Secondly, I left Joruk at eighteen, a ridiculously young age. I left because I wanted to. Actually, I left to fight a war and because my mother said I was forbidden to fight in a foreign war. My point is I do what I want."

"Okay then," She said motioning to the doorway that led to the front, "Go with God. And when you are gasping for air, have no magic left -That's if you survive- and are wondering why your death spread the virus to millions of people due to the magic in your body carrying it, think of me."

Flink crossed his arms like a child. "Fine. I'll bake another Goddamned cake."

NASHVILLE PANDEMIC

T hey were parked in a small clearing in a national park. It was supposed to be closed but when the park officials found out that their only other option was a Walmart parking lot they said that so long as they weren't throwing parties that they could quarantine here. They had run out of groceries that night and the next morning Amber and Nya elected to go into town. The little car that they pulled behind Nya's RV would hold enough food and supplies for about two months. They pulled into the parking lot of Walmart and Nya was breathing heavy. "What's wrong with you?" Amber asked.

"I don't fucking know man. I'm not afraid of anything but right now my heart feels like it is gonna fly out of my chest and I'm sweating in my ass crack."

"Do you want to stay here?"

"To hell with that. I'm providing for my family, even if I feel like it may actually kill me."

Nya felt very much like she was preparing for battle. They put on their masks and grabbed wallets and purses and got out of the car. They'd parked at the very end so that they Mill wouldn't be near people. Nya made for a cart at one of the stations and Amber whipped out a wipe like a knife and had the edges sanitized in seconds. "Wow." Nya said. "Couple of rock stars we are,"

"Shut up."

Inside the store was insane. It was like Black Friday with the threat of even more violence. People passed by with carts full of toilet paper. Nya looked at Amber and she said, "Enough for two months. No more, we don't want to hoard. Go!"

Nya ran, eyes scanning the aisles to find the TP. She slid breakfast club style and came up at the right place. There was nothing. Factoring in how often Wade went she grabbed an arm full of over priced hippy toilet paper and a few extra rolls and headed for the end of the aisle. A butch lady ran at her, and she threw herself backward, screaming "Social distancing!" Like a crazy person and running away.

Nya found Amber in the canned food aisle. The cart was full of fresh produce and meat and she was putting canned vegetables and meat in it. Nya dumped the toilet paper and went to grab a case. "What is this?" Amber asked.

"Chef Boyardee. David loves this and so do I."

She picked up a roll. "No, this."

"All they had was hippy stuff and John Wayne toilet paper. I figured if we get desperate then at least we have it,"

"John Wayne Toilet paper?"

"Doesn't take shit off anyone,"

Amber chuckled. A teenager with a mask of started to walk up to them. Nya recognized his purpose with the pad and pen. She held a hand up. "Wow dude."

"Sorry, I just wanted to ask for your autographs."

Nya made a come here motion. "Slide the pad over. We have a pen."

The guy slid the pad like a hockey puck and the girls signed it. Nya also signed the others' names. Sliding it back she said, "I'm totally authorized to sign for them."

"Cool, thanks." The kid said.

They made their way to the check-out lanes and Nya held a broom handle marked at six feet. When a lady tried to crowd them, she held it out. "Back lady. Back."

She moved forward. "No, I want to get out of here."

Nya moved the stick slightly, "Bitch I will knock you out."

The woman backed up and Amber paid.

When the groceries were unloaded, they sprayed the car down and walked to the campsite. All of a sudden Nikki popped out from behind the RV and said, "Wade, move in." The two of them quickly took the grocery bags. When they were out of range Nikki said, "Now!"

From the trees David and Shay threw buckets of water down and Nya and Amber were soaked. "Nikki!" She popped out. "What. The. Fuck."

"It can live in your hair, so we didn't want you coming inside until you were clean. Nice and soapy too."

Nya looked at Amber and they both erupted into laughter.

SEEING HER FOR THE FIRST TIME

By William Francis Channing Mark was walking down the isles of the market when she bumped into him/ Both their groceries went to the ground and he was pissed. He only had so much money. "What the hell? Are you, - "

Then he saw her. She was gorgeous, stunning. The most beautiful girl he had ever seen. She had shoulder length brown hair with a bit of red. She was tall for a girl, which should have made her look like every other girl, weirdly skinny, but she was perfectly proportionate, nice legs and enough of a tummy that he could wrap his arms around and hold her, though she could stand to gain a bit of weight., "Blind?" she said, "Why yes, I am."

He hardly heard her. He was captivated by her face. The slope of her cheek bones leading down to her chin, which led up to her very kissable lips, then to her perfect nose. "Beautiful." he said.

"What?"

He came back to earth. "I...um...you are beautiful."

She blushed. "Thank you, I'm sorry I bumped into you."

"That's fine. In exchange though can I walk with you to get more apples?"

She put a strand of hair behind her ear. "Sure."

They walked along the aisle under a tent. Wooden bins and stands with fruits and vegetables lined either Hi side of them. She moved her cane in front of her, hitting the stand and area in front of her. "You should watch where you're going."

"Huh?"

She laughed. "I can feel you watching me. If you have a question, just ask."

Mark sighed. "How long have you been blind? Can you get around by yourself? What's your name? How old are you? How come you don't have a dog?"

She stopped, ticking them off on her fingers. "Since birth, yes, Zia, fifteen, and It's expensive and I'm allergic."

Mark nodded. "Nice to meet you Zia, I'm Mark."

"Okay my turn," she said. "And I know my question. Do you always tell random girls they're beautiful?" There was a hint of playfulness in her voice.

"Honestly no. I normally would have tried to be cool or stayed back and just look at you like a creeper."

Zia laughed, "What changed?"

"Seeing how utterly gorgeous you are."

She blushed. "Here are the apples."

Mark saw that she was right. He hadn't even noticed. He started to ask when she said, "It's a cliche but it's true. My sense of smell is really good."

They spent the rest of the day walking around and sitting and talking. Mark learned that she lived with her mother, her bad having died in the Army. She was home schooled and incredibly smart, having graduates earlier that year. They talked for hours; he could listen to her forever. But it hadn't taken the full time for him to be in love. It had taken about three seconds. It was dark as he walked her home. They both lived equal distance from the market, just in opposite directions.

As they walked up to the door of her house, a nice blue house with a porch swing, he noticed that she looked beautiful in the porch light. "I had a nice day with you." she said.

"Can I see you again?" he asked hoping desperately for a yes. She smiled. "Absolutely."

NO SPECIAL TREATMENT

Jeffery was watching the boys warm up for practice when the minivan pulled up. He expected the boy's dad to bring him instead of the mom, that wasn't the surprise. The surprise was that the boy was an energetic bouncy twelve-year-old girl.

"Jesus H Christ." Jeffery muttered to himself.

He saw the dad tell the girl to stay put while he walked over, extending his hand. "How's it going? Pete Gamble.

He shook Pete's hand. "Jeffery."

Pete shifted nervously and looked back over at his daughter, waiting patiently. "I know you probably don't want to hear this but-,"

Jeffery uncrossed his arms, his hands doing almost as much talking as his mouth. "I understand that she's probably a great player, but she's not going to be able to play with the boys. I have tried this before."

Pete sighed. "I get it, believe me. All I'm asking for is one practice."

Jeffery knew he would regret this. "Okay, but no parents allowed, and she has to do exactly what the others do."

"Yes sir."

"Okay then, pick her up at four."

"Yes sir, yes sir." Pete walked back, exchanged a few words with his daughter, and continued back to the van.

The girl walked up, and Jeffery asked, "What's your name?"

"Megan."

"Okay Megan," He noticed a few boys had stopped running. "Get back to work!" Turning back to Megan he continued, "Do you know why troll ball games are segregated at your age?"

"Because girls tend to be more mature in magic while boys are more powerful physically."

"Correct. When you get older it won't matter, but right now if you want to be on the boys' team you have to be very good."

"I am."

"I'm sure. Twenty pushups."

Megan got down on her knees and started to do a girl pushup. "No, regular pushups."

"I'm not strong enough."

"Then you're not strong enough to be on this team."

He knew his words hurt. That was the idea. And it worked. He saw the fire burn behind her eyes as she looked up at him. She dropped back down and cranked out fifteen regular pushups. Her arms started to wobble, and Jeffery got down next to her, screaming, "Go! Up down, up down, it's not hard! Go! No special treatment because you're a girl, move!"

Megan collapsed on her final pushup. She stood up looking like she was going to cry, "Very good." Jeffery said. He picked up the whistle on his neck and blew it. "Bring it in boys!"

The whole team hustled in, and a crowd was soon gathered round. "Okay Boys," Jeffery began. "This is Megan. She's going to be trying out today."

"But she's a girl."

"Very observant Theodore. She is still trying out."

"She can't." Said Jack.

"Last I checked this is my team. will choose who is on it."

Another boy laughed, "Will she always be crying?"

Brian, the team leader and by far the nicest boy stepped forward. "Coach makes you cry all the time Davis."

When the laughter died down Jeffery continued, "Now, no pulling your punches. She's trying out just the same as anyone. Let's pick teams and play."

He knew Brian would pick Megan first just to prove a point. Soon they were on either side of the field and he'd blown the whistle to begin, Megan played well, better than most of the boys. She dealt out plenty of magic and hits, but she could also take it. She got blasted across the field and knocked into the goal. In the past, when this had happened to a girl, they had not taken it well, but Megan got up, hobbled to the bench and got a healing potion and was back in the field before it had taken full effect.

As everyone came in at the end of practice Jeffery gave Megan her jersey. He'd added the name during practice when he'd seen her get back in the game so fast.

"Megan," he said. "Welcome to the team."

And the boys echoed him.

MORE THAN SEX

They rolled off each other and laid there panting.

A few minutes later he got up and she stayed there, admiring her claw marks on his ass and the member that had just been inside her. She didn't cover her breasts for two reasons, she was hot and there was a breeze, and fair was fair. If she was staring at him, it was only fair he get to look too.

"That was great." he said.

"Yeah, you've definitely improved since high school." she said making a peace sign and flicking her tongue in between it.

He laughed. "See yeah."

"Bye." She said and he left. Celia laid back and sighed.

She needed to get ready for her date, but she was tired. After a while she pulled herself up and slogged to the shower. She noticed that David had left his flannel over shirt. No matter, he'd be back here at some point. The hot water washed the smell of sex off her as she thought about their arrangement. She and

David had started having sex when they were fifteen. They were friends for a few years before that but had both decided they wanted sex, but they didn't want to slut around and school and ruin their reputations.

So, for the last five years they had somehow managed to keep everyone they knew from knowing that they had sex, in most of the Kamasutra positions. There was no emotion other than euphoria. Even in the hormone filled time that was her teen years David had been just a release. It had actually kept her from blowing up and acting out like her friends did. But recently Celia had started to want more. The sex was still good, but she wanted a guy. She wanted someone to lay with on a lazy Sunday. Not just someone to slap flesh against on Saturday night.

She got out of the shower and toweled off. Something needed to change. And it was probably the friends with benefits situation between her and David. She put on her blue dress with the cap sleeves and went to meet her date at the restaurant. He was a nice guy, really cute, but within about three seconds she knew there was nothing between them.

Celia spent the rest of the date in zombie mode while she wondered if maybe she'd made a mistake. Sure, the sex had been fun, and a great way to deal with the pressure of high school, but had it prevented her from having a real relationship? She had had a boyfriend for a while when she was seventeen, but they hadn't connected well, or lasted long.

The only guy she ever talked to was David, after sex.

When they were done, if one of them didn't have to leave, they would sit in bed and talk. They would also talk as friends when one of them had a boyfriend or girlfriend. She knew a lot about her bang buddy. She loved his little sister, who she baby sat all the time, and his parents were terrific. David's mom loved Celia.

She thought about what she wanted. She wanted a man who loved her. She wanted a man who could go the rest of their lives without sex and still love her. A man to hold her when she was sad. She needed more than a fuck buddy.

When the date was over Celia went into her bedroom and laid down. Then she remembered the dirty bedding and changed out of her dress, put her hair up, and started to clean her entire house while she thought about how to end her friends with benefits relationship with David. And maybe start something new.

It was past six in the morning when she finished. She cleaned when she was upset and she ended up, at one point, scrubbing the kitchen floor. She took a shower, halfheartedly dried off, and got into her fresh bedding without bothering to put anything on.

She woke up around two in the afternoon when David knocked on the door. "Oh Christ." she muttered getting up. She started to answer the door naked, but she decided having their forthcoming conversation would be easier without him eyeing her tits and her bare beaver. She slipped on a pair of pajama shorts and a T-shirt that was loose enough to hide the effects of the cold air on her nipples.

"What's up?" she said opening the door and running a hand through her hair, speaking through a yawn.

"We need to talk." he said looking more serious than she had ever seen him. She let him in, and he proceeded to speak in a hurried, thousand miles an hour way. He spat out everything she had been thinking. He spoke about how he wanted to be with her, and it was his idea for them not to have any sex for a while, until they had made more of a real, public, relationship.

She'd sat there on the couch with her hands in her lap. fighting the fluttering in her heart. "So, what do you say?" he asked when he had finished. She smiled and jumped into his arms and kissed him. And they didn't have sex.

DECISIONS DECISIONS

Love was complicated Arthur had known that forever, even before he'd known what love was. Just watching his big sister's life had taught him as much.

But love had gotten more and more complicated over the last few years. Arthur had managed to fall in love with two people at the same time. James, a really nice and cute boy from school, and his best friend Jane.

They were both wonderful. Jane had been his best friend since his family moved into the house next to hers when they were seven. They had grown up together, even celebrated their birthdays at the same party a few times.

Jane was shorter than him by almost a foot, but she was feisty and fierce. She had long, fluffy brown hair and, since they were thirteen, perfect breasts. The two of them knew each other so well he hadn't even had to come out. They'd been in her bedroom, on the floor watching a movie, when Jane looked over at him and said, "I know you like girls and boys." Then she went back to the movie and from then on it was just a normal thing with them.

James was great too. He was a basketball player, lean athletic body with short hair. He was one of the nicest people in school. Not top tier popular, but popular enough that he could be openly gay and never made fun of for it. It also helped that he had beat the shit out of three guys at once in the seventh grade for an unrelated issue.

Arthur had been partnered up with James on a project and in an almost cliche fashion ended up kissing.

He swore he'd heard at least five country songs like that.

The two of them spent a lot of time together, though they never officially dated. They mostly just made out and talked on the phone. It hadn't taken Arthur long to fall in love, or for James to confess his.

When they were walking down the sidewalk on the way home one day Jane turned to him and said, "I think I'm in love with you." Arthur was shocked to say the least. Jane said how she felt though. She had never been one to hide her feelings or opinions for long. He had started to say something, but she had already left.

He went inside and laid down on his bed, thinking. He loved two people, but didn't he have to love one more? Isn't that how love worked? One person meant more, even if it was by a small margin?

He thought about it for a long time. By the time he had made up his mind it had begun to rain. His heart fluttered and he ran for the front door, taking the stairs three at a time. Arthur had rolled his eyes at the rain, thinking his life was turning into a Nicholas Sparks Movie.

Now he knew why all those rainy love scenes in the rain were in the summer. Because early spring rain still had the icy bite of winter. It bit into his skin and by the time he knocked it felt like his skin had been peeled away by the rain.

The door opened and Arthur said, "I love you too." they kissed.

THE CONTINENTAL

The shop smelled like oil. Oil, and machinery, and old. I walked in and took a look around at all of the machines. My mom didn't get it, but she loved me, and she brought me because she wants me to be happy. My sister stood near the door on her phone, not caring about the sheer amount of history that surrounded her.

I hit the bell on the counter and an old man came out from the back. He looked ancient, like he had been here since the shop opened, which I discovered he had.

"How can I help you young man?" he asked.

"I want to buy a typewriter." I said. "I loved my grandfather's, and I would like one of my own."

The man nodded. "I see, and what are you going to use the machine for?" He walked around the counter and led me over to a shelf of machines. "This one here," he said pointing to a small machine with bright green keys, "Is best for travel, it's quite the typer, but it doesn't do as well as a standard."

I pressed a key and felt the snap of the slug. I turned back to the man and I shook my head, "I don't think so,"

He nodded like he understood. He stepped back, looked at the wall of machines, and then turned to me. "Are you looking for light typing, or are you wanting it for some serious clacking?"

His phrasing made me laugh and I said, "serious clacking. I want to be a writer, and this is the best tool for a real writer."

"So it is." he said with a twinkle in his eye.

He went over to the counter, and he started pulling machines out. I stood there in awe until he had the entire length of the counter covered in machines that he'd taken from the shelves on the walls.

He stood back and motioned for me to come over. I walked over and he showed me the first machine, a dark, dark machine. The green was almost black.

"An Olympia SMJ." The man said.

I touched a key and the slug smacked into the platen. I touched the shift and felt that it was heavy, the entire carriage moving. I looked at the man and said, "I don't like the carriage moving when I shift."

He nodded his understanding again. He motioned to a few of the machines farther on the counter and said, "That will get rid of these, go on and try the next one."

The next machine was small and blue. I pressed down and my large fingers smacked three keys. This time the typewriter man spoke for me. "Too light." he said.

"This," he said, "Is a Royal KM."

I ran ray hand along the side of the big machine. I looked at the glass keytops and I wondered who had touched them before me. Was it a writer I admired? Surely their typewriter hadn't all ended up in museums. "These are meant to be put in one place right? Not carried around?"

He nodded. "Yes, these bad boys are meant to be put on a desk and smacked at forever. They are better for long writing sessions than for travel."

Just as I was about to say something to the man, I saw the typewriter sitting a few machines down.

It said Continental on it, and it had a return lever on either side. I was instantly in love. I ran my hands over the glass tops, and I touched the labels that were in another language. When I looked up from the machine, the typewriter man had a smile on his face. "That one then?" he asked.

I nodded and I could feel my grin spread from ear to ear. The sides of the machine were exposed, so I could see the machinery work when I hit a key. I knew that I would be happy with this machine for a very long time.

The typewriter cost every bit of the four hundred and fifty dollars that I had saved up, but I didn't care. It was fully refurbished and cleaned and ready to type away. As I lifted the enormous machine into the car, my mom asked, "So what are you going to do if you go on a trip or something and that's too heavy to bring?"

I shrugged. "Do what grandpa does, write in a notebook until I can get back to my typewriter."

She looked like she wasn't sure about all this. I had never been the recipient of that look, but I'd seen it dozens of times when my sister did something stupid or Mom thought she was wasting money, which she usually was. I gave mom a hug. "Thanks for letting me do this."

That brightened her face. "You are welcome."

I'd already set up my table. I put it in front of the window in my room so I could look out when I needed to think. The only other things on my table where a lamp, a pad, and a pencil. When I set my machine on the table, I couldn't help but feel like it belonged there, like it had been there for forty years like my grandfather's old underwood.

I sat down and opened the drawer to the table. I took out the stack of paper and put it opposite the pad and pencil. As I put in my first two sheets and made sure they were straight, I couldn't help but smile. I was a writer, I always had been, but now I had my machine.

OUR OLD NEW HOUSE

I t was a large house, not mansion large, but quite large all the same. It reminded him of the kind of house people lived in in old movies and books.

The outside was a brownish gray, and you could see the individual slats that went all around, making the siding. Their moving truck definitely looked out of place in the otherwise eighteenth century looking drive. He grabbed a box and walked towards the house. His younger siblings pushing past him as his mother came back out for another box.

"Don't look so glum," she said. "Your father picked this house for you."

"He did?"

She turned around to look back at the house, standing next to him and motioning like she was a game show model or a tour guide. "Look at it, Fagan, it's a time capsule. This house is three hundred years old, imagine who has lived here before us, who will live here after us? You love books, right? This is the kind of place where books take place."

She was right, he knew that, but he still missed his old room. Fagan was a creature of habit, almost a zoo animal, he didn't like the moving they had done, and he'd hated every house. The worst part was that as soon as he got to where he was at home, they would move again.

He swore his mother knew what he was thinking because she said, "We aren't moving again. I promise you. This house will be our home until your dad and I are gone, and if one of you wants it after that then you can live here."

He looked at her, incredulous, "Really?"

She smiled and walked over to the car. She got in the passenger side and got an envelope out. Walking back over she presented it to Fagan. He read the words and looked inside. It was a bill of sale. "You bought it outright?"

She smiled again. "Yes."

Fagan felt his grin stretch, he looked back at the house that suddenly looked like a castle, the ancestral home of Clan Jones, without another word he took off to investigate his new home.

BEVERLY'S DEMON

F ather Callahan was standing at the door of the church. He was shaking hands and wishing everyone a good week when he saw her. He still felt a pang in his heart when he saw the poor child.

Beverly Rickman was a fourteen-year-old girl who lived in town. She was the sort of girl who managed to be tomboyish and girly at the same time. She had curly hair cut short, framing her face in a way that would have most boys paying more attention to her than the sermon.

But they didn't. No one really looked at her if they could avoid it on account of the scar running down the right side of her face. It was a thick gash that went from her hair line to the very bottom of her chin.

It was three fingers wide. They'd been able to save her vision, but the demon's departing gift had stayed.

Three months ago, Father Callahan had been visited by Beverly's mother. She'd told him her daughter was possessed and he hadn't believed her. He hadn't believed her, but he'd had a horrible dream that night. It was like God had all but told him directly to go see the girl.

He got tip and was knocking on their door at four thirty.

Callahan had been a soldier. He was raised catholic but never truly believed. It was war that made him seek out God. While he was in seminary they'd told them about possession, but most priests believed that demons no longer manifested on earth. If they even believed in literal demons at all.

But when he opened the bedroom door evil hit him in a palpable wave. Beverly was kneeling in front of the wall completely naked, every inch of her covered in blood. A dead rabbit was next to her, and she was drawing on the wall in its blood.

Father Callahan took the mason jar of holy water out of his pocket. When he opened the jar, the pop echoed through the room and Beverly turned to look at him. "Leave here at once Christ Lover."

"I am addressing the entity inside. What is your name?"

"Dave."

"Dave the demon?"

"Did you think we all had names like Belial?"

"Kind of."

In the span of a blink the demon was standing only inches from him. He knew enough not to look away. He stared the demon in the eye. "Like what you see, Father? You priests like 'em young right?"

He didn't respond. He could feel the demon's gaze boring into him. After a moment the demon said, "No then. I have one of the good ones."

"Leave this child," Father Callahan ordered. "Or I will get violent."

The demon laughed in a voice that did not belong to the girl he inhabited. "I believe I'd like to see that." Beverly's hand thrust out and he went flying into the door.

The wood split and he was in the hallway. He struggled to his feet and backed down the hall a few steps. The demon walked out and tried to follow. But he couldn't move. Looking down he saw the trap Father Callahan had drawn. "You crafty son of a bitch." Said the demon.

Father Callahan opened a second bottle of holy water and threw it on the demon. The creature cringed and yelled. The priest began an exorcism.

"Negna terra,cantata dea psallite,"

The demon thrashed while he recited the ancient words.

As he got to the end the beast stopped and looked at him. His calm shook the priest.

"I'll leave with a gift." The demon said. Beverly's long fingernails dug into her face and Callahan watched in horror as the demon clawed a single, thick, gash in the girl's face. Regaining his senses, he quickly spoke the final words of the exorcism. "Benedictus Dea Matrigloria."

The evil vanished. Beverly's body slumped and a black smoke evaporated up through the ceiling.

Father Callahan snapped out of his memories. He realized that he'd been talking on auto pilot, having went through fifteen people without realizing it.

As Beverly approached, he saw that she was wearing a nice yellow sun dress with a white sweater and a big smile. She was whispering to a friend and looking like any normal, happy child.

Beverly was an intuitive child. She must have known what he was thinking because she winked at him when it was her turn, she hugged him. Removing her head from his chest she looked up at him. "Thank you again for saving me."

"I've told you several times my dear, God saved you.

A smile lit up her face. "He sent me you."

A HOMELESS GIRL'S SAVIOR

There were a few people in the park. A jogger, a mom who'd brought her homeschool kids, a fat woman with an equally fat dog. They all looked nice. It was her that looked out of place. Her hair was caked with mud and dirt, her clothes had gone so long without a wash that her shirt was a rag, and her jeans were so stiff they could have walked on their own.

Gia had run away from home a month ago. She had only eaten a handful of times since then. She was disgustingly skinny and, when she got a look in a public bathroom mirror, her face was sunken in and looked like she had had the life sucked out of her.

She was sitting on a park bench watching a lovely young couple having a picnic nearby and absent mindedly thumbing the switchblade in her hand. She'd taken it from her father's old knife collection when she left. She hadn't had the heart to use it for anything besides fending off the occasional rapist, but she was hungry.

She stood up, flicking the blade out, and started to walk towards the couple. When was a few yards away a figure in a hood walked up to her, smashing into her before she had time to react. In an instant the figure had her knife and had her arm bent behind her, forcing her back towards the bench. Gia was pushed down on the bench. She looked towards the young couple, who had noticed nothing.

"Who the fuck are you?" Gia asked, trying to stand.

The figure pushed her back down onto the bench and removed its hood, repealing a girl a few years older than Gia. She reached into her jacket and pulled out a bag of chips, throwing them to Gia.

"Eat."

Gia wanted to say no, but it had been three days since she'd eaten even a little bit. She ripped open the chips and started to throw handfuls into her mouth as the other girl sat down. "What's your name?"

Gia swallowed hard and tried her best to look angry, silently saying "Fuck off." The girl reached into her pocket and took out a soda, holding it out to her. Gia moved to take it and she moved it just out of reach, "What's your name?"

"Gia." She said after huffing in annoyance.

The girl handed her the soda and she snapped it open. As she guzzled it the girl said. "Don't choke."

Gia finished the soda and looked at the other girl, apprehensive. "Who are you?"

"My name's Rey. When'd you run away?" Gia started to protest but Rey held up a hand before she could speak. "Kid, I've been on the streets for a long time. I know you're a runaway. So how about the truth instead of the story you tell cops and adults okay?"

Gia nodded. "I left about a month ago."

"Why'd you leave?"

"My parents want me to be perfect and I can't do that."

Key laughed and Gia looked at her, extremely offended. Rey saw her mistake and held up an apologetic hand. "I'm sorry. I just never thought I'd hear someone with a dumber reason for running away than me."

"Why'd you run away?"

"My parents wouldn't let me bang a nineteen-year-old, so I ran away. Can you believe that?"

"Did you love him?"

"No. He was a douche bag. He drank a lot, and drove with me in the car, cheated on me weekly, I didn't? find this out until later mind you, but at the time," She took a deep breath and I let out a sigh that seemed to be chastising her younger self without words. "At the time I thought he was, 'the one'. He was older and I felt so grown up. I was so fucking stupid. And the bastard didn't even leave with me. I showed up at his house and he told me to go away."

"Why haven't you gone home?"

Rey started to tear up a little bit. "It killed my parents... on the night I left my dad and I had gotten in a fight, and I was so pissed off when my mom took his side, I hated them both so much that I didn't even leave a note. I went back a few months later to find out that my father had gotten depressed and started drinking, a lot. He killed my mom and then himself."

Gia gasped. "Oh my God."

Rey nodded. "Your turn."

Gia sighed. "My parents want me to be a doctor, go to a good school, many a good man, have kids, make a lot of money. They want me to be perfect, my entire life they've wanted me to be perfect and I, -"

"Couldn't take the pressure."

Gia nodded. "Yeah,"

"What do you want?"

"I want to travel; I love to draw and I've thought about being an artist...don't know for sure."

They were both silent for a moment, staring forward. The chips and soda were making Gia's stomach aware of just how empty it was. Rey spoke, "Where do you live?"

"Why?"

Rey stood up, motioning for Gia to come with her. Gia didn't move. "We've got to get you home."

"I'm not going home."

Rey was angry now. She couldn't believe that this kid wasn't getting it. "Yes, you are. You have no idea what it's like to live on the streets kid."

"I've managed to do pretty well so far."

"Pretty well? You're fucking starving to death, and trust me, there is so much worse to come. Do you have any idea what's going to happen when you get really hungry? When you finally do try to rob someone to get food and you get your ass kicked, or you're left bloody on the street? Or..." She took a shaky breath.

"Or when you have to fuck a guy just so he'll buy you a burger? Do you know how hungry you'll be then? You have no idea how bad it is going to get. You are going home now. So come on."

"What about my parents?"

"Who the fuck cares what they want? You need to go home, be a kid until it's time to fight them about college. Study so you have options. Then you tell them what you want. Or you can save money and leave when it's time... it doesn't really matter. But you will not survive here."

Gia looked down at the ground, lost in thought. After several seconds she looked up. "What about you?"

"I'm gone kid. My life is ruined beyond repair. But if I can get you home then maybe I won't go to hell right away."

"Okay."

The two of them were standing across the street from the bus station. Gia was nervous. Neither of them had any money and she didn't know how Rey was going to get a ticket. She worried that they would end up in jail, or worse. "Stay here." Rey said.

Gia nodded as she walked across the street. Gia watched as she walked up to a man and started talking. Rey rose on her tiptoes to whisper something in the man's ear, he handed her a few bills and she walked inside to get a ticket.

A few minutes later they were standing in line for the bus. Rey handed her the ticket and said, "Here, just make sure you get off at the right time, otherwise you'll end up in Florida."

Gia lurched forward to give her a hug, crying. They broke the hug and Rey gave her a good long look. "Promise me that you'll go home."

"I promise."

Rey gave a nod and motioned for her to get on the bus.

She watched as Gia walked back to a seat and settled down. The kid waved at her as the bus pulled away. As it went out of sight the guy she'd gotten the money from walked up, wanting what she'd promised him. "Ready?"

Rey spoke without looking at him, her eyes still on the place where the bus had been. She had £ done right. She just hoped that Gia went home. "Yeah, let's go."

HER FIRST MEETING

He led her down the steps slowly. He knew she didn't want to be here, and he understood. It was awkward, embarrassing, to talk about your problems. "I can't do this." she said backing up the stairs.

"You can," he said, ever so gently pulling her, "You are the one who wanted to get better. This is part of it."

"David I... I'm scared."

"I know. It will be okay, I promise."

She looked awful. Ivy hadn't really slept much in a few days, and she was in the middle of withdrawal. A week ago, he'd found her in a drug house and literally carried her out. Last month she'd ran through a plate glass window while high. That ended with her in the hospital with a scar running up the right edge of her back, and another under her right breast that had almost turned into a mastectomy.

They walked down the rest of the steps and into the basement of the church. Most of the people had not yet arrived. A short, large, black woman was setting up a last chair and turned to see them coming saying "Welcome, welcome!"

"Thank you," David said. "I'm not actually one of...I'm here for her."

The woman nodded, speaking as she came closer. "That's fine, nothing wrong with having help." She looked at Ivy directly, her hands on Ivy's biceps in a comforting manner. "Nothing wrong with asking for help."

Ivy smiled gratefully and David led her over to a couple of chairs in the circle. Before long more people arrived and the woman, who introduced herself as Delia, began the meeting. One by one everyone introduced themselves and talked.

David was shocked hearing the stories the people told about their battles with drugs or alcohol. He was ashamed to admit that before he found out about Ivy, and maybe even after, he'd looked down on addicts as weak. But now he knew there was a lot more to it than that. Everyone had weakness, but some people, these people, had to fight maybe one single moment of weakness for the rest of their lives.

Ivy watched the floor, occasionally looking up for a few seconds at a time. David knew her well, well enough to know that she was gathering her courage.

Just as the meeting was ending, people getting up to leave, Ivy stood up abruptly and suddenly all eyes were on her, "My name is Ivy, and I am an addict."

Everyone sat back down.

MINDING THE STORE

The store wasn't large, but Papa managed to fit a lot into it. They had food, nothing superfluous, but enough to feed a family. There was a tool section, home appliances (a rather small section), books, paper and office supplies, you name it, their store had it.

The store was one building that looked like two. There was the tall part that had their house on top and the body of the store, and the long, short, building that had a really small store section in front and their storage room in the rest of it.

The best part though, was the porch. Papa kept the ice freezer and the coke cooler on the porch, but he also kept a checkerboard on top of a table he'd made from a barrel and a board, with two rocking chairs so kids could play while their folks shopped. Sometimes older people stopped by and sat and played with each other or Papa when he had a break.

Rebecca, or Becky as she was often called, was the eldest child at thirteen. She was Papa's work horse. She did her home-schooling at the end of the counter and oversaw the store when Papa stepped away.

And since Momma died, she was the woman of the house.

"I got paint on me." Came a voice from the door.

Becky turned away from checking out Mrs. McCarthy and saw her youngest brother Ben standing in the open doorway covered head to toe in paint.

"Ben Wilson, you get back outside right now."

"But we're done."

"Then where is Jackson?"

"Still on the roof." Ben said hanging his head.

"Why?"

"He didn't want to show that he's covered in paint... and stuck."

Becky pointed a motherly finger out the door. "Go back outside."

Ben went back outside, and Becky pulled the lever on the cash register that been in the store since her Great Grandfather had opened the store. "Sorry about that." she said to Mrs. McCarthy.

"No trouble dear."

She paid and left, and Becky called upstairs, "Bring the boys some towels." she said.

"Yes ma'am."

Becky walked outside and rounded the corner at the same time that Amanda was coming down the stairs from the house. She took the towels and said, "Thank you, would you mind the store please?"

Amanda lit up. She loved being put in charge. she nodded and ran to sit behind the counter.

Becky sat the towels on a step and walked out to the dirt parking area in front of the store. She put her hand up to shield her eyes from the sun and said, "Why did you get back on the roof?"

"Jackson was up here."

"Both of you get down."

"We can't." They said in unison.

"Why?"

Jackson, the oldest boy at nine, said "I tared myself into a corner and Benny dropped the ladder."

"Don't call me Benny!"

"That's enough out of the both of you," Becky said in the firm voice. "I'll get the ladder for Ben and Jackson; you'll have to jump."

Jackson got a smile on his face and started to jump as Becky yelled, "Wait!" He looked at her and she held up a finger. Jackson watched as Becky walked over to the stairs, temporarily leaving his view, and brought back the old twin mattress from under the stairs.

Dragging it in place she told Jackson, "Jump.," and went to get the ladder for Ben. As he came down, he whispered, "Thanks for not letting me jump."

"No problem." she whispered back.

When Ben and Becky came around the corner she told the boys, "Strip down."

"No!" They complained,

"You're not going inside with paint all over you." She said as she walked over, grabbing the hose and turning the spicket.

The boys, afraid to cross their big sister and even more scared of what she could tell Papa, got naked, holding their hands over their privates.

"Now I can't wash you hunched over like that."

"You'll see us." Ben said.

"I helped Mama bath you both, and I help get you, Ben, dressed every day. Now move aside."

"The cars," Jackson whined.

"They're driving too fast."

The boys still didn't move so Becky just started spraying. The icy water hit the boys and modesty was quickly forgotten as they danced around and yelped. Becky couldn't help but giggle.

She wrapped the boys in towels and sent them to get dressed. inside the store she found the counter laid out with money. "What are you doing?"

Amanda looked up at her like she'd found her watching a movie or some other innocent act. Without waiting for a response Becky gathered up the cash and put it all back in the register. She turned to her sister, "What did Papa tell you?"

"We count money at the end of the day."

"Then why did you do it?"

"I wanted to practice my money."

Becky sighed. "I will have Papa order some play money and you and I will practice, okay?

"Okay."

Becky nodded and, regretting the question she had to ask said, "Did you do anything else?"

Amanda looked like she was gonna cry. "I broke a box of pickles." She blurted out. "Please don't spank me.

Becky sighed. "If it happens again, you're going to get a spanking. There are too many jars in a case, and I have told you it's too heavy. Do you understand me?" Amanda nodded. "Good, because you won't be warned again. Now go upstairs and get to your schoolwork. Make sure the boys do the same."

"What if they say no?"

"Call me."

Amanda ran off and Becky got back to work. She cleaned up the pickle mess and swept up and just generally took care of the store until Papa got home. "Any problems?" he asked coming in.

"I'm sorry Papa," Becky said looking at her hands and fidgeting. "I tripped and I broke a case of pickles."

He sighed and flared his nostrils. "Damn it," he said. "That is wasted food and money in the trash."

"I am so sorry."

He took a deep breath and his face eased up. "Just be more careful okay?"

"I will. I promise."

Her Papa smiled. "Okay then, you are officially off duty. Head up and steal the TV before dinner."

Becky smiled. "Yes sir."

She walked upstairs knowing she would only get a few minutes of TV before her siblings got done with school and she put
on a different tape to keep them busy while she made dinner.

THE WRITER'S ATTIC

Theo hefted his typewriter up the stairs to the attic. The house was big, but there was so much family in the house that this was the only place he could get any peace and quiet. There was a lot of junk in the attic. Trunks, dressers, overturned tables. This was a forgotten place.

Theo righted one of the tables and set his typewriter down on it. He found a chair and retrieved a stack of paper from the top of a dresser, where he'd set it earlier. He sat down, put two sheets into the machine, and stretched. "Finally, I can get some peace and quiet."

"Not likely." He heard from the depths of the attic.

Theo turned to look and saw a girl walking up from the darker side of the room. She had her hair up in a ratty bun and was dressed more or less like a hooker. "Who the hell are you?" he asked.

The girl took a pack of smokes out of her bra and put one to her mouth, not lighting it. "Don't you recognize me, writer boy? I'm the skank!"

"I don't understand."

"That's what you wrote in your notes right? Fiona the skank?" Theo looked ashamed and confused as she walked closer.

"Let's see what I'm known for in the story, sleeping with lots of people, non-discriminately I might add, and oh-yeah, being mean. That's all you have in that brain of yours?" She tapped his forehead with her cigarette. "Think harder!"

"Wait, you're my character?"

Fiona looked at him like he was the dumbest person in the world. "I cannot believe you are # the moron in charge of my destiny."

A guy dressed like a nineteen thirties movie vampire walked out from behind a dresser and said, "What the hell am I? A vampire or just a douche?"

Fiona and Theo spoke in unison. "Vampire."

"Douche."

He walked behind Fiona and perched like a bird on top of a dresser. "Why do I perch like a bird? Do you think this is funny?"

Fiona raised her hand. "I think it's pretty damn funny." She grabbed a chair and sat on it backwards, facing Theo. "Ignoring the bird man, why am I so awful? Can't you come up with a better villain? I'm not even the real villain, I'm just a bitch."

"I haven't really gotten you all the way figured out. I mean, I sort of thought about having you be friends with Amy."

Fiona sighed dramatically. "Why would I be friends with her? I mean, you know what hold on," She turned to the other side of the attic, yelling to the darkness, "Mouse girl, get in here!"

"So now my hallucinations are creating other hallucinations."

Fiona held up a finger without looking at him. "Shush. Amy!"

Amy walked out of the darkness. She looked even more frumpy than he had thought of her. She wore loose, frumpy clothes and had her hair down, all in an effort to go unnoticed. "Yes?" she asked softly.

Fiona stood up and started to pace in front of Amy. Amy looked afraid, like she might pee her k pants. "I mean look at her, she barely talks, she dresses like a twelve year old boy with no mother, and she's just, -" Fiona grunted and moaned loudly, making a gesture like she wanted to throttle Amy.

"I wanted her to be shy, you know, kinda loser."

Then came Fiona's 'You're stupid' look. "Good job."

Theo got up and walked over to Amy. He poked her r in the face to see if she would respond. "Wow, she really won't stick up for herself."

"Grab her boob."

Theo started to obey but stopped a half inch away from Amy's breast. He thought he could feel her body heat. "Dude, she's a figment of your imagination." Fiona said.

Theo was unsure. "No, it still feels weird that she won't do anything."

"Then write her some sort of character traits." She walked over and got in Amy's face. "Emote dammit!"

Amy started to cry, and Fiona threw her arms up, letting them fall on her thigh. "Well, that's not what I meant."

Fiona grabbed Theo by the arm and pulled him back to the typewriter, shoving him down in the seat. "Write. Change her. Add people...do something!"

Theo started to clack on the typewriter and Amy was pulled back into the darkness. The vampire boy was pulled from the other side of the dresser and disappeared from sight. Theo clacked again and said, "One more." Then he got another few sentences and sat back as Amy entered the room. She was still dressed nice, but now it was somewhere between Skank and Frump.

"Thank God, I can actually talk now."

Fiona laughed. "How do you feel frumpy girl?"

"Like smacking you back to the street corner you came from if you ever call me names again.

Fiona looked over at Theo. "I like the new Amy." The two of them started to look around and Fiona said. "Where's Bird boy?"

Theo held up a finger, "Wait a sec." He started to clack on the typewriter again. A few seconds later Fia walked out from the other side of the dresser.

He looked more like a normal person. He was touching his teeth. "I'm still a vampire?"

"It's gonna work, I promise."

Fia shrugged and walked back into the darkness. "Bye bird boy!" Fiona turned back to Theo walking over and sitting in her chair. She stopped and looked into space for a second, then she looked at Theo. "Really, what does that add to the story?"

"You don't like it?"

"In the middle of a chase scene? I don't discriminate, but now I'm stupid?"

"Okay fine, I'll cut it, but I thought it was good."

"If that were true then I wouldn't have a problem with it."

An Indian girl in traditional clothing walked out of the darkness and looked around. "Who is that?" Theo asked.

I haven't got a clue." Fiona said with a shrug.

"Who are you?" Theo asked.

"I'm from chapter seven. I'm a new student."

"Why are you here now?" Fiona asked. "He is on chapter one."

The girl shrugged. "I have no idea."

"Want to leave and come back when he's trying to sleep?" Amy asked.

"Sure."

The two girls walked away, and Fiona looked at Theo. "Really dude? You need a girlfriend."

"Well, I'm clearly crazy, maybe I'll hallucinate one."

"You're not crazy Theodore, you just needed help."

"With a crappy book?"

"That's my life you are insulting."

Theo put his hands up in defense. "Fine, sorry."

Fiona nodded. "Alright then, now let's write."

Theo turned to the typewriter and started to write. Abruptly he stood, knocking his chair over. He was frantic. "I can't do this. I mean, I am a terrible writer."

He started to pace back and forth while Fiona sat in her chair. She leaned back, putting her feet up on the typewriter table. "Dude, chill. Did you see where my ciggarette went?"

Theo stopped and pulled at his hair, looking at Fiona. "Seriously? I'm losing my mind and you are worried about your smokes?"

"I'm fictional, it's not like I'm getting cancer." She pulled a pack out of her bra and put one in her mouth. She replaced the pack and took a lighter out of the other side of her bra. "So, what's the problem, oh magic one?"

"Magic one?" Theo said when he had stopped pulling at his hair.

Fiona shrugged. "You type, it happens in my world. Pretty magic."

"Fair enough." Theo said. "It's my protagonist."

"Amy?"

"Yeah, now that I've met her, even the new her, I just don't know if she's right for the lead."

"Then move her, make someone else the lead, or someone new."

Fiona smoked the cigarette almost gone. Theo watched in silence for a few seconds before rushing over to the typewriter and clacking away. "I know what to do."

Fiona spoke as she lit another cigarette, her voice muffled from the thing in her mouth. "That's what I like to hear."

THE WRONG BREAKUP

Tyler was sitting on the couch watching TV with his sister Ruth when his phone buzzed. "Hand me my phone please."

"Make me." Ruth said in that challenging way that only a little sister can.

Tyler gave her his best older brother look, asking if she really wanted to play this game. After a moment she reached over and got his phone, handing it to him. "Glad you see it my way."

"I just didn't want you to hold me down and fart again," Ruth turned back to the TV and Tyler checked his phone.

It was a text from his girlfriend Beth.

Hey, can you come to the diner?

Tyler put his phone in his pocket and went to the hook on the wall, taking a set of keys off it. "I need you to cover for me." he said. "I have to go see Beth."

Ruthie rolled her eyes. "Fine, but if you come home pregnant, I'm ratting your ass out."

Tyler smiled. "Thanks Ruthie."

Tyler parked his car and walked into the diner. Beth was sitting at their booth, about halfway down the diner. He walked past the other booths in the line and the tables on the other side, as he sat down, Beth reached up to kiss him. "Are you okay?" Tyler asked.

Beth looked sad, it hurt Tyler to see her this way. "Yeah," she said. "I just need to talk to you."

"And it couldn't wait?" Tyler asked. "I mean, not that I'm not happy to see you, I just...you're kind of scaring me."

Beth was silent for a while. Tyler thought that she seemed lost in her own thoughts, and he knew enough to just wait for her to come back. Finally, she spoke. "We have to break up." Tyler felt the wind get knocked out of him. He felt the color drain from his face. "Ty...did you hear me?"

"Why?"

"I'm sorry, I can't tell you."

Tyler was angry now. Three years of a relationship, and the love of his life was breaking up with him for a strange reason and he couldn't even be told what it was? "Why the fuck can't you tell me?" Tyler asked, his voice a little bit too loud.

"Ty please....this isn't easy for me."

"Then why are you doing this?"

Beth started to cry. She wiped a tear from her eyes and said, "I'm not."

Then he understood. He knew who was causing them both this pain and he hated her for it. "You are breaking up with me," he said, and he could hear the pain in his own voice, "Because your mother told you to?"

Beth looked out the window. "Yes."

Tyler clenched his fists. He knew he shouldn't be angry at Beth, and he was trying very hard not to be. "I knew she didn't like me, but this is insane. Why are you listening to her?"

"I don't have a choice, she's my mom."

Tyler sighed. Beth had never learned how to rebel, even in a healthy way. "Please don't do this." he said, his voice shaky.

Beth spoke as she scooted her way out of the booth. "I'm sorry." she said as she left the diner.

Beth rushed out of the diner, trying to get away from here as fast as she could. She was at her car, fiddling with her keys when Tyler came up behind her. She gasped but turned around as he spoke. "I will love you forever. No matter how you feel or how you're told to feel, I will always love you."

"Ty-,"

But she didn't get to finish, because he leaned in and kissed her. After what seemed like hours, he pulled away and walked back to his car.

A week later Beth was still crying. She sat on the couch one day, bawling her eyes out, when her father came into the room holding a book. He sat down in his big leather chair to read, but after only a few seconds, closed it in a huff. "God dammit Beth."

She looked over at him, wiping her eyes on her sleeves, though she knew she was only making room for fresh tears to take their place. "What?" she asked.

He leaned forward, his voice barely above a whisper, "Go to him girl. I'm tired of seeing you like this, I can't stand much more of it baby."

Beth couldn't believe what she was hearing, she motioned to the livingroom door with a hand, "What am I supposed to do about her? She made me break up with him."

Her dad sighed. "I don't know but,-"

"But what Daddy?"

"Sometimes rebelling can be a good, healthy thing baby doll."

Beth straightened up. She wasn't quite sure she understood what was happening. "So, you want me to get back together with Tyler?"

"I want you to do what makes you happy, regardless of what anyone else wants. You haven't been happy for the last week."

"Dad?"

"Yeah Baby?"

"Can I borrow your car?"

Her dad smiled. "Absolutely."

Beth stood up. She knew she didn't exactly look her best, but Tyler wouldn't care. She was wearing sweatpants and a red hoodie. She saw her face in the mirror in the hall and her face was puffy and red from crying. She pulled her hood up and walked out into the rain.

Beth pulled into Tyler's driveway and saw him in the large picture window. He was watching TV, but he didn't seem to be paying much attention. Beth started to walk up to the front door, but she stopped and went back to the car. Before she knew it, she was pacing in the driveway. As she turned around for the fifth or sixth time, she saw Tyler looking at her. He held up a finger and then got up and disappeared. A few seconds later the front door opened.

Tyler came out of the house and met her in the middle of the walkway. Beth tried to decide what she should tell him, and decided to go with the whole, blunt, truth. Tyler started to open his mouth but I Beth started to blurt out everything.

"She thinks we're too close. College is coming up and I stupidly mentioned trying to get into a school that would let me be closer to you and she freaked out. She said I had to break up with you or she would kick me out, wouldn't pay for college. You name it, she threatened me with it. She said she didn't, want me wrecking my life over you."

Tyler sat down on the front steps, he ran his hands through his hair, looking truly exhausted. "I don't want you ruining your life over me either Beth."

"But that's just it, Ty, you can't wreck my life. You are my life."

"Beth, -"

"There's a reason I haven't ever dated anyone else Ty, a reason I've cried nonstop for the last week...I love you."

Tyler stared at her for several seconds until he finally leapt up, taking Beth's face in his hands and kissing her. A couple of minutes later, they broke apart and he said, "I love you too.

HIS FINAL FIGHT

Hyrum stood off to the side of the boxing ring. He didn't like being here, he hated it here, but Marcus like him to be here, at least on the big fights, and tonight was big.

Marcus was still a young boxer. He hadn't had a ton of fights. But he had started to make a decent living, he took care of buying the two of them a house last year, in cash, no mortgage.

Tonight, he was fighting a man that Hyrum did not think fit inside the weight class his boyfriend was in. He didn't know much about boxing, though Marcus had tried to explain it to him, but he knew that the giant black gorilla currently using a tree as a warmup bag, did not seem fit to fight his one hundred-and seventy-five-pound boyfriend.

Okay so maybe the guy wasn't using a tree, but he was sure beating the living shit out of his warm up fight.

Hyrum turned and walked back into the locker room area to find Marcus. His trainers didn't like him being distracted, but he needed to see him. He found Marcus in the locker room, luckily alone. He paused in the door a moment and watched him. His face was so focused, he was staring at a bank of lockers like he was fighting them. His dark skin was glimmering with the Vaseline his trainers put on him. He thrust his gloved fist out and Hyrum saw his thick ropes of muscle stiffen.

Marcus loved boxing. He loved it even more than he did Hyrum, though he would deny it if anybody asked Marcus always said that his very first trainer, Mick, told him that a fighter only has a certain number of fights in him and he needed to know when to get out, otherwise the sport would take more out of him than he took out of it.

That was a code that Marcus lived by, only fighting until his last fight. No matter how bruised or how bad he hurt, when he was offered another fight, he always took a day to think about it and came back saying, "This isn't my last, I'm gonna take it."

Mick had taught him everything he knew. He was an old white man who lived in the inner city before it really was the inner city. When the black people started to move in all Mick said was, "Who gives a fuck? Blacks fight just as good as whites, and they buy crap too." Mick ran a gym and his wife ran a store on the opposite corner.

When crime overtook his part of town, Mick still refused to leave, and after he beat a mugger to death and then three of his gang member friends who came looking for revenge, the gangs in the neighborhood decided that Mick and his kids were not to be fucked with. Marcus wandered into the gym when he was eleven, and within an afternoon he was one of Mick's kids.

When Marcus finished his warmups, he turned and saw Hyrum standing there. "Hey."

"I just wanted to check on you."

Marcus smiled. "I love it when you get nervous. Is he that big?"

"I have no idea what you are talking about."

Marcus smiled. "Yeah right."

Hyrum couldn't tell him. He had started to, that was why he came in here, to ask Marcus to ditch the fight and come home, but he couldn't. He saw that look on Marcus' face, the look that told Hyrum he was truly happy. That look was the reason he stayed with a guy who caused him so much worry, the happiness he saw.

"You're gonna do great." he said. "I just came to congratulate you on your win."

"Isn't that a bit preemptive?"

"Yeah well-,"

Hyrum approached him, but Marcus held his hand out, stopping the approaching kiss. "You know what Mick said."

"Ugh, boxers, The only people more paranoid than baseball players."

"Say what you want, but there's no boom-boom until after the fight."

Before Hyrum could say anything, he saw the trainers coming into the locker room, telling him it was time to fight.

As Marcus was leaving, he turned to Hyrum. "I love you."

"I love you too, now go beat some ass."

Several minutes later, Hyrum couldn't stand to leave the locker room. But he knew that if he didn't go out Marcus would notice, and he also knew that his man got a moral boost from seeing him. So, he went and sat ringside, and he watched the giant pound on his boyfriend. He couldn't help but wince every time Marcus got hit. Hyrum had never been a girly guy, despite being called that more than his fair share because of the gay thing. He could go toe to toe with the manliest of men, but it never mattered who it was, man or woman, watching the person you loved get the shit beat out of them was never easy.

Marcus won the fight. It was close, but he did it. The guy had been warmed up and Marcus had come away battered and bloody, but in the end, he knocked the giant out.

Later, when Marcus was being seen to in the locker room, a reporter asked him to talk and he said okay. The guy asked him what he was going to do now that he was the local champ and had made a bunch of money and everything. Hyrum expected to hear a lot of things, except for what came out of his mouth.

He looked over at Hyrum and said, "I'm going to take my man home. This was my last fight."

POWERED PANDEMIC

W hat can we do?" He asked. "Really? Well do it then. No, I don't care. I have enough cash reserves and equity to last. Well as soon as business picks back up I will make more."

BlackBall was pacing around his kitchen on the phone. He spent a lot of time on the phone these days. It was agreed. that everyone would quarantine at his house since there was more than enough space, it was out of the way, and Juno's parents didn't care enough to know where she was.

"Listen here Margret," he said, her name enunciated like venom, "you are one of my employees, and while I am not your only client, I would feel comfortable guessing that I am a fair amount of your business. So, unless you want to be unable to find any business in this state, and fifteen or twenty others, I suggest you put my goddamned order through and pay these people!" He slammed the phone on the hook and Juno looked at him. She was in a T-shirt and underwear because Juno was one of those people who was always at home, everywhere. Uncomfortably so in a rich guy's house.

"Is that where your name comes from? You have the power to BlackBall people?"

"Mostly. Stupid bitch didn't want to pay my employees. She says that would run me dry."

"Will it?" Derek asked walking in with a yawn.

"Depends on how long this lasts. But I have lots of people who count on my businesses and all my theaters are closed, the restaurants are on a skeleton crew, and the rest of them are somewhere in between."

Katelyn was wide awake, having gotten up at dawn to train. "What about your rental properties?

BlackBall took a bite of a pastry. "Those able are paying their rent, which will go back into paying employees. Those unable are being dealt with in one way or the other, either promises to pay or forgiven depending on circumstance. Single Moms, Dads, etc. are being given a pass. Those who don't need a break or have money but aren't working, the wealthier renters and such, are signing promises to pay when able.

"And these idiots who have decided that they don't owe me my money and are never paying it again, are finding Lawyers and Police showing up and having them sign a document guaranteeing them their unit until this is over, at which time they will be getting the hell out of my apartment, house, condo, or whatever."

Juno seemed to be studying BlackBall. They had all been stressed lately. Patrols had been suspended and Derek and BlackBall had been working from home, so they were all getting a little too close. Juno's training was progressing fast enough that she was right when she said, "You're worried."

BlackBall shot dagger eyes at her. But he soon softened. "Yes. With almost nothing coming in and a metric ton going out we won't be able to make payroll for long. We will be fine in this house because I have stock piles in the cellar. But I worry about the people I employ."

"You're a good man."

BlackBall smiled in thanks. He took another pastry and went to his study to meditate. The pandemic had been hard. There was a small rise in unexplainable crimes throughout the city, but the real struggle was with the powered. Just in their city over one hundred powered individuals had died. Fifty-seven more had been left permeantly de-powdered Doctors still didn't know how it was doing that.

BlackBall kept a running total on a whiteboard in the command room. It normally had a long table and desks on the walls covered in crime data and things pertaining to work. But lately all of it had to do with the pandemic. Thousands of Powered in the US were dead or normalized, tens of thousands around the globe. It was a huge dent when you considered that they were less than one hundredth of a percent of the population.

Katelyn had been training, baking-she had learned to make pastry- and wondering around the house and grounds worrying.

No one knew where it came from. Not the humans. Not the powered. Not even the mysterious people that had pull even BlackBall couldn't reach, people he simply called his 'contacts'.

Katelyn didn't care. If it was China, or Russia, or frickin' aliens she didn't care. She just wanted people to stop dying by the thousands. She wanted it to be over.

A PERFECT FIRST TIME

Colin and Lisa walked slowly up to the chain link fence surrounding the pool. Lisa was kinda scared, they hadn't done anything like this before, breaking and entering, let alone what they were going to do inside.

Colin had his trunks and a T-shirt on, Lisa a bikini underneath her shorts and T-shirt. Colin handed her the small cooler and started to climb the fence. When he was at the top Lisa spoke, "Maybe we should go somewhere else. We could get in trouble."

"We won't, and besides, this is our spot, Remember?"

He knew she did. They both did. As he dropped down, she thought of the time they'd met, a few feet from here.

Three years earlier Colin had taken his little sisters to the pool while his middle sibling, his brother, was being driven to scout camp by his parents. He'd been in the snack line getting the girls something to eat. He'd taken it too them and turned around to go get himself something, when he bumped into a gorgeous girl in a white bikini, an ice cream cone running down her cleavage. Lisa didn't think the boy meant to knock into her. She should have been paying attention. She shivered a little at the vanilla ice cream that was still running down her boobs and making a sweet and sticky pool in her top. Oh my God, are you okay?"

Lisa smiled. "Yeah I'm fine. I should've been paying attention." She took the cone out and threw it in a nearby trash can.

"Here, let me buy you another." Colin said.

Lisa shook her head. "No, that's okay."

He shook his head. "I insist. What kind of guy would I be if I didn't buy a pretty girl an ice cream cone?"

"Okay, but I should get cleaned off first."

"I'll wait here."

Lisa held out her hand. "Come with me."

He looked like he didn't understand, but a few seconds later he took her hand and the two of them ran, jumping into the pool.

They went out officially for the first time after that, to a movie and dinner. But Lisa had to confess when he was dropping her off that she wasn't very comfortable, that she liked it better when they were just them, hanging out, watching his sisters, stuff like that. Thankfully he agreed and from then on they weren't 'dating', they were just together. They took his sisters to the park, and they went to dances at school, occasionally they would go out to eat or something, but it was never awkward again.

Then one night, when his sisters, brother and parents were in bed, Lisa and Colin were on the couch when they started making out. She leaned back and Colin moved his hand up her shirt, first before he cupped her breast she moved back, "Baby stop."

"Did I do something wrong?"

"I'm just not ready." Lisa said, trying not to cry.

Colin did not understand. They'd gone further than this before. "For me to touch your boob?"

Lisa looked at him, her eyes tearing up. Colin hurt for her, he didn't want her to be sad, and he didn't know what to do to make it better, or what he did in the first place. "Sex Colin. I'm not ready for sex."

Colin shrugged. "Okay."

"You mean that?" She asked, crying.

"Babe, as fantastic as your body is, that is not why I love you."

She smiled. "So you're not mad?"

"If I got mad because you won't have sex with me I'm pretty sure that would make me the biggest asshole in the world, or at the very least put me in contention for the title."

Lissa kissed him. "I love you."

"Baby, you alright?"

Lisa was shaken out of her memories by Colin's voice, though he himself looked lost in memories too. "Yeah, I'm okay." She reached the cooler over and climbed the fence. Her heart fluttered a bit when she felt his hand on her butt, helping her off the fence.

They took their stuff to the same old table they had sat at countless times since their first meeting. Colin took off his shirt and trunks and Lisa took off her shorts and T-shirt, leaving her in her black bikini, the one he liked so much. Colin held out his hand and she took it.

They ran and jumped into the pool.

Underwater, they broke apart and came up into the night air, they came together in a kiss. When they broke the kiss Colin asked, "Are you sure you're ready?"

Lisa responded by taking off her top and throwing it outside the pool. Colin was speechless, until Lisa spoke, throwing her bottoms out as well, "I'm sure." A while later they were laying on the concrete, their towels under them to make a cushion. Lisa's head was on Colin's chest. She liked the feeling of being in his arms. She felt safe. His arm was wrapped around her, his hand on her right breast. It had been there so long now she kind of felt like it belonged there, "Thank you." she said.

"For what?"

"For making my first time special."

Colin moved his hand, for a brief moment there was a longing where it had once been, like part of her had left. He turned so that they were facing each other as they laid there. He looked deep into her eyes and saw happiness there.He knew that he would spend the rest of his life with this girl. "Thank you for making my life special."

LOVING A WRITER

The study floor was filled with pages. She didn't seem to have any regard for them whatsoever. The house was silent save for the scribbling of her penciled with blue ink, always blue. He brought her a tray of food and more coffee.

She only drank coffee when she was finishing a book. He sat the tray down and left the room, he wasn't supposed to stay long, though she didn't even notice when he was there. He walked back to the kitchen and thought about when they met. He thought a lot about their past whenever she went into one of these spells and he didn't get to her for days on end.

They had been seniors in high school when he was walking down the sidewalk and she'd hopped down out of the tree she had been sitting in, people watching. He'd thought she was beautiful instantly. She had raven black hair and glasses. Her eyes were brown with specks of other colors. She was slender but he suspected she was stronger than she looked. Her eyes were wild, crazy, but they also looked like they were seeing everything you were but comprehending so much more. She'd told him that she thought he was interesting and she wanted to follow him around and base a character on him.

He'd said yes because she was beautiful.

He'd had no idea what he was getting into. She was crazy, and not just woman crazy or writer crazy. She was woman writer crazy. He would sit in the living room and watch her pacing, muttering to herself, occasionally stopping to jot down a note. They had date nights where he might as well have been alone, she was so focused on her notebook.

Both his parents and hers occasionally commented on not knowing how he could be with her. On top of her writing, she would, from time to time, have depressive fits that used to terrify her parents.

But he'd had a calming effect on her, he knew. For one thing she no longer cut herself when she was depressed. She herself had told him that was because she felt safe in his arms. A month ago he had come home to her trashed study and her in the corner crying. He'd pulled her up and took her into his arms on the couch.

They'd laid there for hours.

He always worried when she went into a frenzy. For days, the longest being nearly five, she hardly moved. Her bladder held herculean amounts of coffee. She went maybe once per pot, not speaking to him on the way to or from the bathroom. During these frenzies she got two or three hundred pages done. But it came at a cost. She slept for days afterwards, suffered migraines, sometimes she got sick from the frenzies.

He'd tried to change her, told her his concerns. She'd yelled and screamed and told him that this was who she was.

And she had been right. This woman, this wild, nutty, woman, was who he loved. The times when she was not writing they had the greatest adventures and the best sex. She was kind, loving, and he couldn't be with anyone else. She just had her quirks.

"Finished" Came a shout. He put his coffee down and ran down the hall. She was already on the couch. He put a blanket over her and kissed her on the cheek. Then he bent down and began picking up the hundreds of handwritten pages with curly, serial killer like, script and started to put them in order

> SHORT STORIES

WE WENT OUT LAST NIGHT

"**A**re you coming out tonight?"

Marybeth looked at her best friend. He was currently laid out on her bed in full over coat and boots and everything, ready to head for the door at a moment's notice. She on the other hand, was standing in front of the closet in knee high socks and her underwear. "I have nothing to wear."

Baxter stood up and walked the three feet to her closet like it was Jesus' trek with the cross. He took down her red sundress that stopped at her knees. "This is the dress."

She knew he was right, she just hated to admit it. It was her favorite dress, and it had been hanging on the open closet door since the last time she'd went out. She grabbed the dress from him and started to put it on as he said, "Lose the socks."

She looked down at them, "Why?"

"Because you are not trying to get fucked tonight. It's okay if that's a happy biproduct, but the purpose of the night is fun with your friends, not penetration."

She held a finger up, "Okay, stop right there, two points, one: Not a good enough reason to use the word penetration. Two: What do knee high socks and fucking have to do with each other?"

"Unless you are on some sort of sports team, knee high socks are fucking socks."

"Are not."

"They are when you wear them with a dress, a dress that stops at the knee leaving just a tiny piece of exposed flesh coincidentally on the way to your vagina. They thicken the cock of every passing man whither they know why or not. Knee high socks say, 'Look at these, right next to the treasure trove, and easily removable.' Ditch. The. Socks."

Marybeth grunted. "Fine. You kinda have a point now that you've laid it all out for me."

"Thank you" he said making-a gesture for her to hand him the socks:

They were soon walking down the sidewalk outside Marybeth's apartment headed to God only knew where. "Where are we going? She asked Baxter made an exasperated poise and put his head down. "Marybeth, you are twenty-six years old living in an incredible city full of the wonderous and phantasmagorical, and while I admire the homebody you normally are the wonderful things you've knitted, once in a, while you need to have an adventure that is not on papers."

She smiled despite herself at the theatrics, and he opened his arms wide., "The city is our oyster!" he shouted.

"Shut the fuck up!" Came a voice from a nearby buildings. They both broke into laughter and started running down the sidewalks. They had walked quite a ways in a direction neither of them normally went, ever, when they came upon a park. It was a small park built in between some buildings and several geese were near the tiny pond. "Give me some crackers." MaryBeth said.

Baxter took a package of crackers out of his ridiculous coat and handed them to her, taking a few for himself. They crossed the street and approached the geese. "Come here babies," Baxter said.

"Here you go little guy." Marybeth said. The geese snapped to attention, honked, and fluttered their wings, and started to chase them. "Aw 'fuck!" Marybeth said' and took off. She rounded the corner of the tiny cement half wall that guarded the park as Baxter passed her.

"I don't think that goose identifies as a guy.'"

Marybeth heard a honk behind her and sped up. "I was just trying to be nice."

They rounded a corner and Baxter noticed a gorgeous looking girl walk into a nearby bar. She was walking away from the streetlight so he only got a glimpse of what had to be the most heavenly ass he had ever seen.

He pointed when she had gotten out of ear shot. "Let's follow her."

"You don't even know what kind of bar that is."

He looked at his friend. "Does it matter?" He held his hands out and moved them up and down like scales. "Liquor, hot chicks, liquor, hot chicks," He leveled them out. "Win win for me."

"Fair do, I could use a drink."

The bar was cozy. Lots of mahogany and leather, a faint smell of smoke indoors which was definitely illegal.

It looked like a comfortable local pub, except for the guys covered in leather dominatrix gear doing unspeakable things in and around the booths that lined the walls, and up against the bar there was a guy, "We need to get the fuck out of here,"

Marybeth turned and walked out of the bar and, as if in a movie, a cab was passing by at the same moment. She whistled and he stopped. She turned around to find Baxter talking out of the bar with a haunted look on his face.

In the cab Baxter said, "That will haunt me forever,"

"Yeah. Where to now?"

"Take us to fourteenth street.' Baxter said to the driver. Turning to her he said, "Silvy and James are working at a new club tonight, I thought we might stop by."

Marybeth shrugged, "Works for me,"

Marybeth looked out the window for about twenty minutes, just watching the people and buildings they passed, wondering what they were doing, how they lived. It was what she liked about living in a city, hundreds of thousands of people each with their own lives, all living within a few feet of another person that could be anyone, a good guy, a bad guy, it was a mystery that she loved to contemplate but didn't want to solve, She liked thinking that in one building several people could be seeing the end of their lives, having lived to a ripe old age, and in the next apartment a couple could be beginning their lives and family.

The cab stopped and they got out, paying the driver as they slid across the seat. He pulled away and it wasn't until he was out of sight that they noticed that they were on nineth street, in the sketchiest part of town, "Fuck me," Marybeth said, "I knew this night was gonna be a mistake,"

"What, you can't walk five blocks?"

They started walking and made it about a block before Baxter got closer to her and whispered, "When I say go, I want you to run."

"Why?"

"Because the bald guys behind us have swastikas on their arms and you're half Mexican and I'm a Jew"

Marybeth's neck hair stood on end and her skin started to crawl. "Hey, let us talk to you a minute." Came a voice from behind her.

Neither of them turned around, Baxter moved to the right of the sidewalk where there was a wall that led up to a small hill and then some small patch of wooded area that the city got a tax break for not developing. He slid his hand along the wall innocently, like he was just out for a stroll. The guy hollered again and called one of them a slur. Baxter moved back over closer to her, looking natural while he did it. "Run."

She took off running while he turned back, flinging the rock he had picked up. Marybeth heard a thud and a "Fuck!" The wind blew her hair back as she ran for her life. Others might consider it leaving a friend behind, but she and Baxter had developed a system for bad guys honed from both being weird in high school and watching entirely too many CW shows. Whoever saw the threat and had a plan would carry it out if they were outnumbered, the other would run in the hopes of getting to help if needed. They'd been in a few fights together, but mostly their approach was to cause enough of a distraction to get away. She'd saved him a month before from a couple of gang bangers that she'd noticed before he did, pepper spraying in their direction before they could do anything.

Baxter was soon behind her. She didn't take her eyes off what was in front of her, but she could feel him running next to her. They ran like the wind, a mixture of adrenaline and fear bringing smiles to their faces when they got the remaining four blocks to the club and walked right up to the black bouncers standing outside who were six-six and six-seven and both looked like they were made entirely of stone.

They weren't very good white supremacists because they were very clearly threatened by the physically superior members of a different race. They ran away like bitches and Marybeth motioned with a finger to the lead bouncer. He bent down and she gave him a kiss on the cheek. As they walked away, she heard another bouncer say, "I have got to work the door more."

The club was loud, like really loud. It was the kind of loud where you forget your own name, the kind of loud where you lose yourself in all the right ways, "You find Silvy and James; and I'll get booze." Baxter said, walking off without waiting for an answer.

Marybeth worked her way through the crowd, A club like this, if they weren't on the dance floor, they would be visible from the staircase that was diagonal to the entrance. Never much of a dancer, unless so drunk she didn't know that she wasn't much of a dancer, Marybeth scooted through the crowd, having her ass groped several times, her tits honked twice, once by a guy. and once by a girl (Neither of which she minded much given the months long dry spell she'd been having.) And she punched one guy in the face when he straight up dragged his hand across her cooch.

She got to the corner, of the dance floor anti saw her friend dancing like a crazy drunken whore, a fairly accurate description of Silvy herself. She was wearing a beautiful silver dress that showed off her body in a way that was alluring, but not overly showy. It allowed for movement and running if need be (she'd told Marybeth of a few times that it had been needed.) and yet she still looked completely beautiful.

Marybeth smiled mischievously and walked up, smacking Silvy as hard as she could on the ass.

Silvy whipped around, "Hey mother-, Oh hey boo."

"Where's your brother?"

Silvy shrugged. "Probably grinding on someone or sitting in our booth sulking."

"Well take me to the booth, Baxter's getting booze."

Silvy got excited and clapped. "Come with me."

Marybeth took her hand when it was offered and Silvy led her to the staircase and up to the weird sort of elongated balcony that she never remembered the proper architectural name of.

They had a back booth, end of the balcony but the best view of the entire club. What it must be like to be rich. James was sitting with Baxter in the booth and judging by the overturned glasses they were a few shots in.

"How are ya now boys?" Silvy asked.

"Fuckin' great and you?" Baxter said.

"Not so bad." she said sitting down next to Baxter.

Marybeth sat on the other side of the booth and noticed a white powder on the table, just a bit of residue. "Are you high?"

Silvy wasn't offended. She shook her head and said, "Nah, that was here when we got here, also James had a donut he brought with him. You know I haven't done coke since like, eighth grade."

"Just checkin'."

"I appreciate it boo."

"What've you guys been up to this fine evening?" Baxter asked. He handed Marybeth a shot. "Here you go kitten."

She did the shot, Tullamore D.E.W., and nodded to James to answer the question and stop smirking at the face Marybeth made when she did shots. "We've been mostly here." Silvy said. "We started off at Kenny's party but it was lame, so we left."

"Why was it lame?"

"He was having a dungeons and dragons party."

Marybeth squinted in confusion. "You fucking love D&D.

"She forgot her stuff." James said.

"I did not forget it. He was playing and he didn't tell me so that I would have to create a new character and I don't want to do that on the spot. I need to have time to get to know a person before we campaign. He is an asshole."

Baxter laughed. "You are like, the hottest nerd ever."

Silvy shimmied. "Thank you."

They hung out in the club for a few hours, drinking, talking, dancing. At one point Baxter joined Marybeth and Silvy on the dance floor and started dancing like such a spaz that people created room for him, and he just went with it, winning the crowd over with sheer enthusiasm.

When Silvy and James had to leave they went with them. The fresh air hit Marybeth's face and it was like a spell that been broken. Inside the club it was as if alcohol had no effect on her, she could drink all night and dance till dawn, but stepping into the air she was giggly and lightheaded and could not stop smiling. A car pulled up and James got in saying goodnight. Sllvy turned around, the open door against her ass. "You guys want a ride?"

"No," Baxter said. "We're in this all night. Not going home like you old people."

Sllvy eyed MaryBeth, an eyebrow raised. She could clearly see in Marybeth's eyes that she very much wanted to already be in bed. "Baxter don't be bitchy."

He approached her, gangly arms outstretched. "I'm sorry, I just love you guys so much and I don't feel like we see each other enough."

"That's because Dad has us working so much. He says he'll fund the parties and lifestyle we like but all of the work has to get done and the company divisions we run have to stay profitable. That's why we're headed to the airport at three am. I have to be in Dubai and James is going to Dublin."

"Your life is so cool." Marybeth said, in that drunken way that you realize too late you've said that thought out loud.

Silvy smiled. "Next week, Friday, movie night like the old days. Your apartment, that okay?"

"My apartment is stupid."

"No honey, your apartment is amazing. You work for it; you are a real adult. I'm a rich kid pretending." She paused and shook her raven black hair. "Sorry, I'm drunk enough to get weird. See you soon?"

Marybeth waved like a giggly child as the car pulled away.

There were a few seconds of awkward silence before she asked, "Where to now?"

Baxter raised his head and looked down the street. "I'm not sure, where would you like to go?"

"I want waffles."

He gave a quick curt nod. "Waffles it is."

They wandered around until they found a twenty-four-hour diner and slipped into a booth. "Are you okay?" Baxter asked.

"Yeah, why?"

"You kinda seemed weird when you were dancing. That guy was up against you, and it seemed like your eyes kinda glossed over for a split second and then you walked away from him. It seemed like you might not be okay."

Marybeth had never been able to hide anything from Baxter. "It's been over a year since I broke up with John and I haven't been, you know, touched, since then. So, when that guy was grinding into my ass I kinda started to like it, then I left because I didn't want to go down that road."

"Why?"

"Why what?"

"Why not go down that road? It's not like he proposed, he just wanted a bit of sexy, dare I say dirty, dancing, and then to part ways. Maybe you screw in the bathroom maybe you don't, but why not see where it leads?"

"It just isn't my style; I don't do that."

"What can I get you?" The waitress asked walking up.

The two of them had been talking normally to each other, but when Marybeth opened her mouth to the waitress it immediately became clear that they were drunk. "We would like some waffles please and thank you ma'am."

"Sure thing." She said writing in on her pad. She rolled her eyes as she walked away, sick of dealing with drunken idiots.

Baxter snapped at her. "Hey, look.at me. I want to make a bet/dare with you."

"Oh lord."

"No no, this will be great. Do you like girls still?"

"Why are you asking that?"

"Just answer the question, Maybeth."

She gave him angry looks at using her nickname from grade school. "Sometimes yes."

"Okay, well I have a bit more booze in this flask,"

He took out a hip flask and sat it on the table, "See that girl over there?" Marybeth looked over her shoulder at a pretty girl at the end of the counter who was drinking coffee and reading the paper. She had dark skin like red clay and gorgeous black hair. She must have felt Marybeth 's eyes on her and looked sideways at her. Marybeth' s head whipped back around, and she saw Baxter smiling.

"You may drink the whiskey if you need it but I bet you three hundred dollars that you won't go over and kiss her, with permission, and get her number. You don't have to get the number I just think that you guys look cute together."

"'This just seems like you want to see two chicks kiss."

"Actually, it's because there are four guys in this room, and I wouldn't do that to you."

Marybeth looked around and saw two greasy truckers with filthy beards and yellow teeth, which she saw because they chewed with their mouths open. Another guy was drunk and passed out in a booth, and the other was a guy at the bar dressed like a dock worker that had visible blood on his clothes. "Fair enough."

Marybeth drank the flask dry and walked over, her heart. beating in her chest. She leaned against the counter next to the girl and slurred, "Heey."

"Hello."

"Listen,"

"I heard, your friend is very loud."

Her face got red. "Oh."

The girl turned on her stool and grabbed Marybeth gently by the back of the neck. She kissed her for what seemed like a hour. Her breath smelled nice, and she tasted like coffee and cherries. When they finally broke, she handed Marybeth a sliver of newspaper and said, "I hope you call. You seem fun."

"Uh...Thanks." Marybeth babbled and slowly walked away. She turned back around in the middle of the diner and said, "Bye."

"Bye," The girl said with a smiles Marybeth sat in the booth and squirmed, excitement rushing through her. Her heart was still fluttering, and she looked at Baxter.

"Isn't that a great feeling?" he asked.

Marybeth was smiling like an idiot and simply nodded. The waitress sat their plates down and poured them some coffee they hadn't asked for, probably hoping it would sober them up a bit. The waffles were light and fluffy, and they drizzled blueberry syrup on them, and they tasted like heaven, or as close to heaven as you can get at three thirty in the morning in a weird part of the city.

They paid the bill and were walking down the street when they heard a ruckus. They passed an alley way and Baxter started forward. Marybeth held him back and he looked down at her, "What the hell, they're beating that guy."

"They're gang members, it's what they do." she said. "It looks like an initiation, and even if it's not, it's none of our business."

"Hey! Stop that!" Baxter yelled and fifteen angry dudes all turned around. Baxter's eyes went wide, and he turned around, pushing Marybeth ahead of him. "Run run run run!"

And then they were running again, this time with a completely different kind of gang chasing them. Baxter turned the corner and they saw Carver bridge, a bridge that was down the river from her apartment building. If they could make it across it was only a couple of miles walk home.

Surely to God they wouldn't chase them across the bridge.

They made it to the bridge and the gang stopped running, seeing no need because they were cornered. The two of them started towards the other side of the bridge and saw that reinforcements had apparently been called. Baxter looked over the edge of the bridge and Marybeth knew what he was thinking. "Do you trust me?" he asked.

"Not after tonight I don't."

"Oh, come on, most of it was great."

"I have been chased by three gangs tonight, Baxter, three separate gangs!"

"The geese so do not count."

"The hell they don't" she said, but she was getting on the railing of the bridge as the gang approached, several of them drawing guns. The morning sun was coming up as Baxter gripped her hand and she said, "I am never going out with you again." Then they jumped.

NO WOMEN NO KIDS

Cameron walked towards the firehouse with the phone to her ear. "Yes sir, I understand, confirm kill. I'm on my way. She hung up and looked across the street. The firehouse had one of the old-fashioned look out towers. It would be perfect.

She walked across the street and tossed a wad of cash to a firefighter. He motioned his head back towards the doorway. Cameron made her way through several back rooms until she was in the belly of the building. There was a staircase leading upwards and she followed it. Halfway up she found the crawlspace and pulled out the green gun bag. She continued up the stairs.

She emerged into the light and felt the cold wind. She wasn't worried about people seeing, no one ever looked up. The wind bit harder the farther she went up. Finally, she made it to the top and unzipped the case. She removed the magazine and checked the rounds, two bullets. She replaced the magazine and jacked a round into the chamber.

She set the weapon in position and looked through the scope. She saw her targets, two kids. Her heart felt uneasy. She'd killed several dozen times, but this went against her code. She followed along with the kids, laughing and goofing off as they went. They started to walk down an alley.

She watched as they disappeared from view. Her phone rang.

"Is it done?" Victor asked.

"I told you. No women, no kids." She threw the phone off the tower.

Cameron was walking down the street as she passed a payphone. When it rang she knew enough to know it was for her. She picked it up and asked, "What do you want? I told you, I'm out."

"Cameron, you're the best killer I have, but you can't beat anyone else."

"Wanna bet?" She asked sarcastically.

"Even Dimitri? You really wanna take him on?"

Uneasiness swept through her. She didn't want that. She hated that she gave Victor what he wanted, but he took the silence as a good sign and continued. "Now, you can kill this kid, as I ordered, and I'll let you walk away. No more hearing from us, I promise. Or you can run and hide and eventually we will catch up to you, and well, you know what we can do."

"I don't kill kids."

Victor was angry now. He yelled into the phone. "You're gonna kill this fucking kid or I'll personally slit your throat."

Cameron knew that more than likely he would have someone else do it, but they would eventually kill her. "Do you understand?" Victor asked.

Cameron let out a shaky sigh. "You piece of shit."

A half hour later the kid was walking down a street and Cameron popped out from the corner. She raked her blade across the poor child's throat and went back around the comer, disappearing as she cried.

.... TWO YEARS LATER...

He walked down the stair into the lower room with several pool tables. There were people scattered around the room as he walked in. He approached a crowd that was around one table, pushing his way through until he saw her leaning over it, taking her last shot as the eight-ball sunk. The crowd cheered and her opponent groaned. The man looked at her angrily. "That's bullshit. You cheated and I ain't paying you."

She gave him a scathing look. "I cheated. At pool? How did I manage that?"

He looked at her, angry and ready to fight. He walked around and got in her face. He poked at her as he spoke.

"I don't know, but you did...bitch."

She grabbed his arm and turned him around, his face on the table. "Pay me my fucking money or I'll break your arm."

He reached into his pocket with the other hand and handed her a wad of bills. "Here, let me go!"

She held him. "This is what happens when you rich kids think you can play, you lose Daddy's money." She released him. "Now go home before you get yourself hurt."

He stood up and she turned around, counting the money.

The man started to throw a punch and she kicked backwards, landing a hard kick to his balls. He fell, banging his head on the table as she walked away to a nearby table, a beer there. The man followed her. He waited a ways away.

"I'm not going to kill you for talking to me," she said. "Though most people around here would tell you different."

He walked over and stood next to the table. "Are you Cameron?"

She looked slightly shocked at him. "Who the hell gave you that name?"

He forgot all fear and sat down quickly, leaning in. "My son was kidnapped. "

"And this is my problem why?"

"I work at the airport, and this young guy who said he worked for...a third-party observer...told me to ignore some cargo that would be coming in off a plane from Spain. I told him I couldn't do that and he said that if I didn't I'd be sorry....I called security and by the time I came home that night my son had been taken."

Cameron listened intently. Third party observer was what they always called Victor when he sent them to intimidate someone. "Why haven't you contacted anyone? There are several Mercs in the area who do things like this all the time."

The man shook his head. "They all said no. They didn't want to go up against these people...one of them referred me to you, said you were the only one who could do it."

Cameron put her elbows on the table and buried her face in her hands. "Was it Charlie smalls?"

"Yes, how did you know?"

Cameron stood up, chugging her drink and grabbing her jacket from the back of her chair. "I knew I should have killed that fucker."

Cameron and Greg sat in a car in the parking lot. She had a bag at her feet. Unzipping it she took out a knife and stuck it in the waistband of her jeans. She took out a pistol and two magazines. She made sure they were loaded and put one in the gun, racking a round in. Greg was looking at her strangely. "What?"

"Don't you need more weapons?"

"You can only fire one at a time accurately."

Greg looked at her for a beat. He faced forward and nodded, not knowing what to say. She opened the door and put one leg on the pavement, turning to Greg she said, "Get in the back seat and scrunch down."

Greg looked at the back seat floor, not wanting to twist his old body down there. "Is that really necessary?"

"Greg?"

"Yes ma'am?"

"Get in the back seat before I stab you." Greg said nothing.

He got down in the back seat and scrunched up. "Good, stay like that in case the car gets shot." She got out of the car and slammed the door.

A young guy was watching the front door. A gun was on the table in front of him. Cameron walked through the door, and he looked up at her. "Hey Cam, what the fuck are you doing here?"

"Working Jimmy." She said, whipping the gun from behind her back and shooting him in the heart. She moved quickly, hiding behind a pillar and squeezing her body small. She peaked out, eyeing all the men.

Upstairs, Victor was sitting in front of a tied-up child.

Two personal guards were standing beside him, one was by the kid, one by the door, and one sitting in the shadowy corner. He heard the gunshots from downstairs and said, "Go."

Everyone except the man in the coiner filed out of the room. That was all he really needed. The men had been talking to the kid all day and Victor enjoyed the sheer terror in his eyes.

A body dropped and Cameron put a bullet in him as she saw Schmitt approaching. He sauntered forward, overconfident as always. "Hey Cam, how the hell are yeah?"

Cameron shot two of the four men. As they fell, she said. "Fine Schmitt, I'm here for the kid."

"Even if you get us both you still have Dimitri."

A brief look of uncertainty flickered across her face and Schmitt smiled. Cameron fired the gun but it clicked, empty. "Shit."

Schmitt advanced and Cameron dived down, bringing the knife out in a sweep. She slashed across his legs, and he fell. As he fell she drove the knife through his brain. She pulled the knife out of his skull and stood up as the other man cowered. "Hey Cam, don't hurt me, I was if just doing my job, okay?"

Cameron picked Schmitt's gun up and took his magazines. "I know Johnny." she said emptying the clip into him. As he fell, she walked up the stairs towards the office.

As she entered the hallway, she saw him come out of the office. They stood far apart as he said, "Hello Cameron."

"So, you're still working for Victor...guess it was stupid to hope you'd left."

"Not all of us have that luxury."

"You fucking bastard. After what he made me do, made you do? You call leaving a luxury? You shove that up your ass."

They were now only a few feet away, having both been slowly walking like they hadn't had the same training and the other might not notice. "Why are you here?"

"I'm taking the kid with me."

"You know I can't let you do that."

"You remember our promise?"

"Of course." Dimitri reached around and took the gun from the small of his back. He dropped the magazine and jacked the round out, dropping the gun. He motioned to Cameron and she did the same with hers. They both put their hands up to fight. "Shall we?" he asked.

"You first."

Dimitri ran at her. She dripped down and slid under his legs, kicking him in the back of the knee. He yelled and spun to keep himself from falling. She spun around and punched Cameron in the face as she tried to stand. She stumbled backwards and he advanced, punching her over and over until she went down. As he stood over her, she kicked him in the balls. He fell down and she rose, small streams of blood going down her face. She straddled him and chopped him in the throat. It briefly reminded her of their first time, which had begun with a sparring match. Dimitri punched upward, uppercutting Cameron and causing her to fall off him. They both stumbled to a stand, and he kicked out, breaking her knee. She cried out and stumbled backward. As he moved forward, she grabbed his leg and pulled. She landed on top of him as he fell and punched him several times. He head butted her and her head flew back. When she looked forward her nose was gushing blood. She grabbed him by the hair and slammed his head into the floor. He groaned loudly.

Cameron reached into her bra and pulled out a knife. Her eyes were full of blood and tears as she put the knife under his chin. "I love you." With a primal scream she thrust the knife through his brain. She got off him and walked over, picking up his gun and magazine.

She loaded the gun and jacked a round in. Walking into the office she saw Victor with a gun to the boy's head. "Hello Cameron."

"Put the gun down Vic."

"You first."

Pure hatred guided her hand as she raised her gun and fired a shot. Victor fell next to the boy and Cameron walked over, cutting him loose. "Who are you?"

"Don't worry about it. Your dad's car is outside. Go home. Now!" The boy ran out of the room and Cameron walked over to Victor, groaning on the floor. "This is what happens when you teach kids to kill people." she said and emptied Dimitri's gun into him.

THE VILLAGE

Maureen was working behind the counter at the store. She only did it on occasion, but Mrs.. Kelly needed to go out for a bit and the old woman was a dear friend. As she was helping one of the Murphey sisters, the oldest women in the village, and the funniest, a man came into the store.

It wasn't a strange for a man to come into the store, though it was true that the women still did most of the shopping in the village, no what was strange was that Maureen had never seen him before.

That was weird. The village hadn't changed much at all since the seventeenth or eighteenth century. Most of the houses had electricity now, and you could get internet in a few places, but for the most part you could have dropped someone from the past into the village and they would have lived much the same. Everyone knew everyone.

Most of the kids had wanted to leave the village.

Maureen had felt a bit of that, she'd even done some traveling when she'd gotten out of University in Dublin, but it wasn't long before the pull of her little village came back, and she settled back home.

She watched the stranger as he began collecting things from the shelves. Mrs.. Murphey laughed a bit when she caught her looking. "And what are you laughing at?" Maureen asked.

"You've been staring at that boy since he walked in. I was just thinking of that look, it was the same look I gave my Harold when I first saw him."

"Oh, hush you. Don't you have soup to make?"

Murphey wagged a finger at her. "Right you are. I'll be seeing you."

"Be seeing you."

The stranger was handsome. He had shaggy dark hair that she could tell was a bit unkempt from what he normally kept it at, and his features were angular and sharp, like a statue that had come to life. His face, she saw when he turned around, was covered in a dark beard she hadn't noticed when he'd walked in. He would raise his head and look around the store every few minutes, like he was keeping tabs on everyone in the room, though it was just the two of them.

Maureen must have been staring again, though she hadn't noticed it, because Mrs.. Kelly had come up behind her and she jumped like she'd been bitten when the older woman spoke. "Ya know, I don't like my customers being stared at while they're trying to shop."

"Sorry, but who is that man? He's new right?"

"Yes. He's American, but his Da was Irish so they gave him his citizenship at birth. He finally decided to use it."

"How'd you know that?" Maureen was thankful they were speaking where the man could not hear them. Her Mum always said that gossip was perfected in Ireland.

"He bought the Walsh farm. Jemma says he plans on making a go of it. Said he's going to retire and live here."

"He's awfully young to retire, isn't he?"

"He's got a pension from the Army or some such."

They broke away as the man came up to the counter. He set his items on the counter. When he spoke, Maureen loved his accent. She'd known some American students in school, but his voice was so deep and gruff, not quite like anything she'd heard before. "Is there any way to start an account so I can pay for things at the end of the month?" he asked.

"Absolutely." Maureen went and got under the counter, the large ledger had been kept when she was a child, and opened it up. "' I already know where you live, I just need your name."

He raised an eyebrow. "Do you now?"

"It's a small village. Everyone knows everything here Mr...?"

"Kiernan. Kiernan Smith."

Maureen wrote his name in the book, along with where he lived. "It's nice to have a new face in the village. I'm Maureen."

"Nice to meet you."

"It's nice to meet you as well."

Kiernan left the store and Mrs. Kelly came back, she claimed to have been stocking things in the back room, but Maureen knew well that she'd been listening to them the whole time. She told her friend she would see her at church and headed home.

She didn't live very far away from the Walsh farm. As she rode her bike past, she saw Kiernan on the roof, fixing the holes brought on by neglect. No one had lived in that place since she was about twelve. She almost ran into the ditch while she was watching him work.

Maureen's home was a small cottage, just big enough for one or two people, and since she was the only one, it was a match made in heaven. There was a small room on the left end of the cottage that was her bedroom, and the right end was another room with an old-fashioned wooden cooking stove, a table, and a sink, which was operated by a pump. It was an inconvenience at times, but she didn't mind mostly.

Her favorite part of the cottage was the center room. It was where she spent most of her time. On the same wall that led to her bedroom was an enormous fireplace that heated most of the house. She had a comfortable couch and a chair by the window. She loved to sit in the summer, when it got slightly warmer, open the windows on the back wall and sit in her chair and read.

Books covered the place. Maureen didn't own a television. She had a record player that she used sometimes, and a radio, but mostly she just read. There were books stacked on the table beside her chair, and on the coffee table that was between the fireplace and the couch. In the winter she curled up with a book and sat on the couch, reading by firelight.

There were books in the kitchen, near the sink and in the cupboards, and all over the kitchen table. The archway that led to the kitchen had built in shelves on either side of it that were stacked with books. It was only when the shelves had been full that she'd started keeping things elsewhere.

Maureen had so many books that she was always lending them to people. The older people in the village that liked to read, the young kids that she taught at the school, and they never betrayed her trust. Every book came back in the same condition that she'd lent it in. She also had a friend from university that was always sending her new books.

She'd had a long day. Before working in the store, she'd been gathering things from her garden all day. Winter was coming and she wanted to get everything in order. She'd spend all day tomorrow canning her vegetables and things, but she didn't mind the work. Hard work was good for you.

She made herself some dinner and ate in front of the fire, a book open on her lap. After she'd done the dishes, she went into the little bathroom off the kitchen that had been added on a decade or so before she'd moved in. She was glad for that because as rustic as she lived, pooping outside was where she drew the line.

She turned on her shower, letting the water get hot while she stayed dressed in her robe. She didn't mind walking around the house naked, it was only her after all, but the bathroom was the exception. When they had added it on, they had not insulated it so being naked in there longer than you absolutely had to was akin to walking through a blizzard completely nude.

While she was in the shower her mind drifted back to Kiernan.

Not in a sexual way, he just intrigued her. She'd always loved a story and she could tell that he had a long, and maybe kind of dark, one. As she was rinsing off the water turned cold. "Christ Almighty!" She screamed as she ran from the shower. She was dripping wet as she grabbed her robe on the way out the door. She was glad she lived alone because she could only imagine how foolish she looked stomping in place naked in front of the fireplace. She certainly felt quite foolish.

When she had successfully gotten her body temperature up, and her robe a bit toasty from hanging on the mantle, she put it on and nestled herself against the warmth. Then she remembered that she hadn't turned the shower off. She went back and turned it off, going out the back door to see the water heater shed. She opened it and saw that it was off.

The flame was out and a part on it did not seem to be in working order, at least, she was pretty sure it hadn't been black before. She knew some about home repair, but she had no idea how to fix this, or even tell if this needed fixing for sure. She decided there wasn't anything to be done about it tonight. So she went into her bedroom, disrobed, and curled up underneath her covers.

The next day she canned. She canned dozens of jars of vegetables and everything else her gran had taught her how to do. She kept quite the large garden, I half her back yard. So, she had enough vegetables and curry and whatever else she grew to feed not just herself, but a few close friends and neighbors as well.

Around one in the afternoon Maureen got a call from Mrs. Bryne, a kind old woman who'd been friends with her Mum before she died. "Hello?" Maureen answered.

"Have you heard about this new man living down from you?" Mrs. Bryne was never one for pleasantries when there was gossip to be had.

"I met him at the store yesterday."

"What she like? I hear tell he's a bit of a shifty one." "you've not even met the man now. Let's give him a chance."

"I don't think I will."

Before Maureen could reply, she heard a crash and the lid blew off one of her canners, glass shards going everywhere. "Dorris I'll have to call you back. I've had a jar blow up on me."

"Careful now. See ya for church this evening."

She hung up the phone and started to walk towards the stove when Kiernan burst through the door. "Is everything okay?"

"Bloody hell! Is home invasion a thing you do for fun in America?"

"I heard an explosion!"

"I had some jars blow up on me. Then you nearly gave me a heart attack ya eejit!"

He started to go. "Sorry."

She ran after him, catching him just as he walked out the front door. "I'm sorry, you just gave me a fright, that's all. Please come in for a bit."

He looked like he didn't want to, but Maureen took his arm. "The older women in town trust me as one o' their own, you'll have an easier time of it if I tell them you were nice."

Kiernan smiled. "Fair enough." He came into the house and sat. Maureen talked while she set to cleaning up the mess she'd made with the canner.

"So, tell me, why this village?"

"I had family that lived here a long time ago. My great grand-parents moved to Dublin and raised their family, and then my dad went to America when he was young and had my family, so when I decided to leave I wanted to close the circle."

"Mind if I ask why you left?"

"I just got sick of it." he said shrugging. "All the bull shit that just doesn't matter. Is Brittney wearing this, did Katy Perry's tits get bigger while she was on vacation? I mean, who gives a crap?"

"Certainly not me." Maureen said as she put the kettle on. "I don't even know those girls."

Kiernan laughed. "They're celebrities."

"Oh, I've never paid much mind to all that. Even when I went to University in Dublin, I mostly studied."

"What did you go to school for?"

"English and teaching. I teach at the school here in the village."

"That's nice. Do you enjoy teaching?"

"I do."

"I had a question, where would I buy livestock? I'm fixing up the farm but when I'm done, I'd like to have maybe a milk cow, some chickens, a few pigs maybe."

Maureen thought for a moment. "I don't know, but you should ask at the store. A lot of the people around here farm and one of them would surely know." The kettle started to whistle and she asked, "Tea?"

"Sure."

She poured two cups and took them to the table. "You wouldn't happen to know anything about water heaters, would you? Mine quit on me last night and that bathroom is not insulated, so cold showers are out of the question."

Kiernan laughed a little bit at that. "I can take a look, where is it?"

Just as Maureen started to speak her other canner went off, signaling that it was time to take the jars out. She spoke as she walked over to the stove. "It's just outside this back door here, the shed bit, should be unlocked.

Kiernan followed where she'd pointed out the back and he was gone for several minutes. She finished up her jars and got a new batch in just as he was coming inside. "You're gonna need a new one." he said. "I tried to get it lit but the part that keeps it lit, where the gas comes in, is fried."

"Like pastry?"

"No, I mean...you know what let's just say it's broken."

Maureen couldn't help but laugh. "I guess I'm out of luck. I'll have to get a new one eventually."

"You can't order it?"

Maureen shook her head. "I've not got the money at the moment, and most places won't deliver this far. Anything too big for the postal truck and you must go get it yourself."

"Well will you be okay?"

Maureen waved that away. "I'll be fine. I've got the tub and I can heat baths up on the stove. I'm all good."

Kiernan nodded. "Well, I'd better be getting back to work. The place was mostly rotted away."

"I'd say so. That place hasn't been lived in since I was a child. It's good that you're taking care of it."

"Yes ma'am. I'll see you around."

"Goodbye."

Kiernan had already gone when it occurred to her to give him a few jars of food. She'd just drop them off on her way to church.

Later on in the day, when she had finished cleaning up from her work, she put on her nicest dress and a coat and set off to walk to church, putting her jars in a basket. Kiernan was her closest neighbor on the way into town, so that was the first place she stopped. He was outside working on the fence. "Good evening, Kiernan," Maureen said. "I've brought you some canned vegetables."

"Okay...why?"

"It's a bit of a thing here. The Kellys share whatever fruit they don't sell, the Murphey sisters knit blankets, and everyone else shares something of theirs. I share veg, and the Brynes always share their extra meat from butchering."

"Well, that's awfully nice. I'll have to come up with something to share when I get this place up and running."

She handed him the jars that were his, and then she looked down the road and back at him. "I was just on my way to church, are you very religious?"

"I am, but I'm not much for church. It's a bit stuffy for me, all the pomp and circumstance, the show boating. You know, I'm better than so and so because of Blah blah blah..."

"American church must be very different."

"Why, is it not like that here?"

Maureen shook her head. "Not at all. You should come some time."

"Maybe I will, but I have some more work I need to get done before the sun goes down."

"That's why my Da always went to this service instead of in the morning. He said wasting daylight was a sin."

"I think I would have liked your Da."

"Yeah, most people did."

They made their goodbyes and Maureen went on her way, stopping at a few more houses to deliver her jars. Most people didn't leave as early as she did because she was one of the farthest houses from the center of town.

As she delivered the jars, she took a few moments at each house to talk up Kiernan to everyone that came to the door. She didn't know why, but it was important to her that he be liked by the village. She wanted to make sure that he became one of them, so she told the women how he'd helped her, come in looking to see if she was okay and having a go at her water heater, and she told their men that he was trying to make the Walsh farm operational. and that he was looking for live stock.

She got promising results. The women thought he was quite chivalrous in coming to see if she needed help, and the men all wanted to know more about how he planned on using the land, though sadly Maureen did not have that information.

By the time she got to church there were several ladies who lived close already there, and they were talking about Kiernan. It was if as Maureen had hoped. The women she'd visited with had called the ones closer and they had spread the news. Even thought there was no over talking during church, she suspected that by the end of mass there wouldn't be anyone left in the village that didn't know about the newcomer and how nice he had been.

She didn't listen to the gossip during church. She sat there and she thought. She thought about Kiernan, his story and his past. It was obvious to someone who had read as many stories as she had that he had one, and that he was running away from something in America. Sure, the stuff he talked about was one of the reasons he'd left, but she could tell that it was only part of the story.

Maureen knew that Father Domonic had heard about Kiernan, because his sermon was about welcoming others and not judging them until you knew them, and even then, reserving judgment for God. It seemed that she was in cahoots with the priest, even though he didn't know it.

When church ended, she said goodbye and started her walk home in the dark. It wasn't a worry. The last crime of any real consequence was a mugging back in nineteen seventy-eight, since then it was one of the safest villages in Ireland, maybe even the whole world. As she walked by Kiernan's house, she thought about stopping in, but she didn't see any lights on, so she assumed he'd gone to bed, and no one liked to be bothered when they were sleeping.

The next several months went by with nothing really occurring, though the same could have been said for the last decade before Kiernan's arrival. Maureen went to school of a morning, and she came home of a night. She would always see Kiernan doing some form of work on his place as she passed by in the mornings and evenings. She didn't know when the man slept. Once she'd gotten up in the middle of the night and she'd heard hammering coming from the direction of his house.

One day, sometime in November, Maureen was sitting by the fire after work reading when she got a knock. She got up to answer the door and saw Kiernan standing outside her cottage. "Long time no see." he said.

"I see you every day."

"I just meant that we haven't talked more than hello and have a nice day in a while." he said.

"That's a fair point, what can I do for you?"

"I've borrowed a trailer and I was wondering if you'd like to accompany me to a livestock sale. It's quite a drive and I don't exactly know where I'm going. Plus, I thought it might be a good time to get your water heater."

In truth Maureen had forgotten about the water heater. She didn't miss the thing at all. She liked the feeling of a warm bath of an evening. "I've decided not to get a water heater, but I'm happy to go with you. It sounds like fun."

Kiernan looked very happy. "I'll pick you up in the morning. I thought we'd better leave early so that we get there on time. Mr. Murphey said it is in Donegal, at six AM."

"We'll need to leave here about four in the morning." she told him. "If I'm not awake when you come to the house feel free to come inside and wake me."

"Are you sure about that?"

Maureen waved that away. "Everyone does it. Every time I play cards with the Murphey sisters I just walk into their house. As long as you have permission it doesn't matter."

Kiernan still looked unsure. "Will you leave your door un-locked?"

She nodded. "People around here seldom lock their doors."

"Well alright, I'll see you at four."

"See you then."

He left and Maureen decided to go ahead and have her dinner so she could get to bed. She skipped the bath because it would take too long, and she wanted to be well rested.

The next morning, she woke up to Kiernan's hand shaking her. She wasn't fully awake, so she jumped back in shock, throwing her bedding off. "Bloody hell!"

"Sorry, I called out several times, but you didn't say anything."

Maureen was calming down. "Yes, I... you just gave me a fright, that's all. She stood on the opposite side of the room, getting off the bed. It was only when she walked around was standing just a few feet away from him, that she realized she was still naked. "I'll be out in a bit." she said.

Kiernan nodded. "Right." He left the room.

Maureen couldn't help but smile when he'd left. She was a bit embarrassed, but it was also kind of funny. It wasn't like she had anything to be ashamed of, she was a young woman, she had a firm bum from lots of walking and riding her bike, good size too. Her chest was a decent size. Her Mum had always said she had a pretty face, and she had brown hair with a tint of ginger, so it wasn't like she wasn't nice to look at, in her opinion anyway.

But that didn't stop her from blushing when she saw Kiernan outside. She'd pulled on some trousers and a flannel work shirt, but both their faces were so red you'd think she came out still in the nude. "I love your truck." She told him. It was American, a Chevy truck that looked really old.

"Thanks. It was my dad's, and I couldn't leave it, so I had it shipped here." The two of them climbed into the cab and they started off down the road. It was the first time Maureen had left the village in over two years. Despite the cold weather, the inside of the truck was very warm. It was close quarters and the added warmth of their bodies mixed with the heater to make the cab actually quite cozy. They had been in the truck for about twenty minutes before Kiernan spoke, "Can I ask you a personal question?

"Sure."

"How come you stayed in the village? It doesn't seem like many young people stayed around."

"I went to University in Dublin, and I traveled around a bit after that was over, but in the end I just felt like this is where I belong."

Kiernan nodded like he understood. He looked down the road and, after being silent for almost three minutes, spoke again, "How has the village survived as long as it has if almost everyone leaves?"

"Most kids go away for several years, but when they want to raise a family of their own, they go back. At least that's how it was for a long time. I don't really know anymore. I think the village might be a bit too laid back for modern folks."

"I think that's exactly what the world needs, a few places that are laid back and not so concerned with the rest of the garbage the world loves."

They talked for a while longer, about lots of things, none of which were very personal. Eventually they stopped talking and drove in silence. Maureen made sure that Kiernan knew where he was going, and then, without realizing it fell asleep.

She woke up to a familiar smell from her childhood... shit. Her Da had farmed and they had enough cows that the entire placed smelled. The smell brought back a lot of memories, and the hundred or so times that she'd slipped in cow shit and gotten it in extremely uncomfortable places.

They went around to several of the stalls to inspect the animals, as they were passing a stall that had an old milk cow in it. Maureen stopped. "Hello girl." Maureen said as she approached the cow. The beast had kind eyes. She looked like she had seen some hard times. She was a bit skinny.

"Her name is Mayble." said a man stepping out of somewhere Maureen hadn't noticed.

"Why are you selling her?"

"She's old and she doesn't produce enough milk to support a family anymore."

"Well Mayble, do you think that you could produce enough milk for just me?"

The cow mooed as if she was answering. Kiernan came up behind her and spoke, "Are you buying her?"

Maureen jumped a little, then said, "Yes, as long as there is room in the trailer."

"Should be. I bought a bull and a heifer and a couple of pigs. I plan on getting some chickens on the way back to the truck."

Maureen looked around, "How long have we been separated?"

"I broke off when you were looking at the calves."

"You sure work fast."

"I don't like crowds. I try and avoid them as much as possible."

"I understand that." Maureen said, thinking that maybe she didn't understand as much as she thought she did. She paid for her cow and led to back to the trailer. Kiernan already had his animals loaded, save for the dozen chickens he bought on the way back, which he loaded into the back of the truck. They got set and headed out for home.

"I'm not even sure where I'm going to put a cow, I haven't got a shed or anything."

"You can keep her in my barn until we build you one."

Maureen looked at him, she couldn't help but feel great admiration for him. "Thank you." she said. "I would really appreciate that."

They stopped at a small place to get something to eat, because they realized neither of them had eaten all day. They got it to go and ate in the truck so they didn't have to leave the animals for I too long. Maureen couldn't help but laugh at Kiernan's inability to talk and chew.

He started to ask her a question but ended up almost choking on his food. "I'm sorry." She laughed. "Are you okay?"

He cleared his throat. "Yeah, I'm fine." A couple of seconds later he started to laugh too. When they died down a bit, he asked his question again. "I was going to say that, if it's okay with you, I'll set them up in my barn tonight and tomorrow I'll come over and start building a pen for old Mayble."

"Thayts very kind of you, but I don't want to keep you from your work."

"It's no big deal, I've got nothing but time now."

They drove in silence for a while before Maureen decided to volunteer a bit of personal information in the hopes that she might make Kiernan comfortable enough to share with her. "I'm not even sure why I bought this cow," She began. "I didn't exactly love the farm growing up."

"Really? I would have pegged you as loving the farm."

"Why is that then?"

"Well, you're like twenty-six and you voluntarily live in a small village in the middle of nowhere Ireland, and you have a garden. That spells farmer in my experience."

"I'm actually twenty five, and I think that gardening is a bit different because you don't have shit everywhere. I use fertilizer but I've never slipped and ended up with shit in my mouth."

Kiernan laughed. "I can see how that would make you not want to farm. But then, why Mayble?"

"I'm not quite sure. I guess she just looked sad, and I wanted to give her a home." Kiernan looked at her with a look she hadn't ever been looked at with before. She wanted to know so badly what he was thinking, but his face hid all but what was on the surface.

They talked a lot on the road home, but again, nothing overtly personal. She'd tried to share something personal, but it ended up not really being personal. It did get him talking about a few things from his past, how he'd grown up in Missouri, on a farm outside a town called Belview. He'd liked the farm, but the desire to get out in the world that befell so many small town kids got ahold of Kiernan too, so he'd joined the Army.

They pulled through the village street, and they saw everyone running in the direction they were driving. They shared a look and Kiernan drove faster, knowing something had to be wrong. They were still a ways away when they saw the smoke.

Kiernan abandoned the truck and trailer, and he ran to his home, the last of which was still a blaze. There was a crowd of people, buckets laying on the ground and a lot of Kiernan's things scattered on the lawn.

Maureen turned the engine off, pocketed the keys, and walked up to the group of women standing in the grass. "What happened?"

"We were walking to the store when we saw the smoke." said one of the Murphcy sisters.

Mrs. Kelly added, "When we got here several of the men set to getting what they could out of the house, and the tried rest to save it, but there was nothing to be done."

"Christ almighty," Maureen said. "I can't believe this. He just bought his animals. He was getting the place fixed up." She felt like she might cry.

"The barn is fine." Mr. Bryne said walking up.

"I suppose that iss something, not much though." His wife said.

"I'll let him sleep on my sofa," Maureen said. "The barn's no place to sleep in the winter." She expected to hear a lot of comments from the women, and she suspected that there would be gossip later, but she didn't give a shite. Kiernan wasn't going to be sleeping in the cold, or on a stranger's floor, when he knew her and she had a couch.

"That's mighty nice of ya child, are you sure you want to put up with the gossip that will bring?"

"Well Mrs. Kelly, given the circumstances you know, will you be gossiping?"

"Not I." she said.

"Nor me." Added both Murphey sisters. Their pledges were followed by the affirmations of her other friends, the women her mother had been friends with, the ones she considered family.

After a while everyone made their way home. Kiernan had set to work getting what things of his had been saved into the barn. Then the two of them got the animals settled, gave them some hay, and were done. Kiernan started to make himself a bed in the barn when Maureen spoke. "Oh no, come on. You're sleeping at my cottage."

"What? No, I'll be fine here. It's plenty warm and,- why are you looking at me like that?"

"Have you ever pissed off an Irish woman that hasn't gotten enough sleep?"

"No."

"Then believe me when I tell you that it is not a good idea."

"Okay then, I'll come with you."

"Damn right you will. I know it's only noon, but I need a bloody nap." Without another word she started towards her house. It was a decent walk from his house, but she a didn't mind. She couldn't see him, and she refused to look back and let him know that she cared whether or not he followed. She happened to see him out of the corner of her eye as she was walking and she smiled to herself, thankful he couldn't see her.

He was still several yards behind her when she went into her house. She entered and went straight to her bedroom, getting some extra blankets out of her trunk. As she walked back into the central room, he entered. She sat the blankets down and started to tell him something but was distracted when she saw him looking at her desk.

Her desk was nice, but nothing really special. It was just a small little desk set against the back wall in front of a window with old fashioned wooded shudders. Right now it was covered in papers she was grading and lesson plans she was working on. But he paid more attention to her typewriter.

It was an ancient thing with a Gaelic keyboard. He touched a key and if the snap of the type slug hitting the paper she'd left in filled the house. "That was my Da's."

"Sorry." He said stepping away from the machine.

"Don't be, I was just saying where it came from." She walked over and touched the machine, it was a big thing, massive. She hadn't moved it hardly at all since she'd moved in. Before that it had sat in the same place in her parent's house since she was a kid. "I love this machine. I use it all the time. When it gets going real fast, and my fingers fly, it's like I can hear me Da working in his study. Boy, could he type fast."

Kiernan spoke as she wiped a single tear from her eye. "I had my mom's typewriter. It's from the, like, twenties. She bought it second hand when she was a kid...I still think of her when I use it...it was the first thing that I looked for in my stuff they saved."

"Did they get it?" He shook his head. "I'm so sorry."

Kiernan shook his head as if he was trying to throw the memory out. "So do you use that one for school?"

"Only for when I teach Irish. For the most I use that one over there." She pointed to where she had left her other typewriter, a small portable Triumph that she had bought in school for papers.

Maureen yawned. "Okay, there are blankets on the couch that you can use, I'm going to bed for a while. Knock before you enter because I will be naked."

"Um...okay."

"Sorry, I've not been able to sleep in pajamas since I got out of school."

Kiernan put his hands up in defense. "Hey, I am not judging. I usually sleep the same way, and I am not about to tell the person nice enough to take me in that they're wrong for what they normally do." Maureen smiled at that, and they both went to their respective places. As soon as she was in her bed, Maureen was asleep.

Apparently she had not slept as good as she'd thought the night before, because it was around six o'clock when she woke. She put her clothes back on and walked out into the central room to see Kiernan reading by the fire. "I hope you don't mind; I just love this book." he said as he looked up and saw her.

"Not at all, I always love when someone gets enjoyment from a book. What are you reading?"

"Pride and Prejudice."

"Not a book that many men would admit to loving." she said.

"A good book is a good book, no matter who it was written for."

Maureen nodded with respect. She liked it when a man could admit to loving an ordinarily female book. She walked through the house and into the kitchen as she spoke, "I thought I would start supper if you're hungry."

"That sounds good. Is there anything I can do to help?"

"I'll be fine, have you checked on the animals?"

"About an hour ago. They're all set up for the night. I don't really know what I'm going to do with them."

"What do you mean?" Maureen asked as she walked back over to Kiernan.

"Well, I am going to have to rebuild my house, that's going to take a long time. I'm not sure if I can do all of it."

"Nonsense. I've seen you work, you're like a horse. Animals in the morning, afternoon on the house, animals in the evening again." Kiernan sat there thinking, apparently not having thought of that. Maureen went to start their dinner.

She made stew for dinner, her Mum's recipe. It wasn't the poshest thing to eat, but it filled you up and kept you hearty. She made a big pot, so they had breakfast as well. They sat at the table eating, each draining two bowls. Maureen made them both tea and they sat there in silence when she asked, "Why did you really leave America?"

"What?"

"I know what you told me has to be part of the reason, but I can tell there is something more to it."

He sat there for a brief moment, like he was trying to decide whether or not he wanted her to know, but he finally spoke. "I got out of the Army, I saw some really horrible shit and I was messed up for a while when I came home. The girl I had, the one I'd written to, the one I was going to propose to, she left me after two months of being home. A few months after I finally got over her, I had another girlfriend who was a total cunt. So, after having my heart smashed several times, and seeing that the country I had fought and almost died for didn't give a shit about me...I decided to leave."

Maureen didn't know what came over her, but she leaned across the table and kissed Kiernan. He started to pull away in shock, but then he leaned into it. He stood up and they walked sideways until they were out of the table and were standing in the kitchen, all without breaking the kiss. Kiernan broke the kiss and looked at her, "Do you?" She nodded. "You're sure?"

She responded by jumping into his arms and kissing him. She still didn't understand what in the hell she was doing, she was not normally this kind of person, but she was tonight. Kiernan walked backwards, turning around in the middle of the room so that Maureen was going first. She kicked her bedroom door open, and he flopped her down on the bed.

Maureen wasn't a virgin. When she'd been going through her 'Get out of here' phase she'd had a few sexual exploits in college, and a few whilst traveling. But none of the five of them had meant all that much. Her only sexual experiences in the almost three years since moving home had been of a self-serving nature.

Kiernan was by far the most amazing person she had ever been with. They made love several times that night, lying there, with his arms wrapped around her, she knew that she didn't ever want to be with anyone but him again. She felt safe in his arms, like she would be protected from whatever the world had to throw at hero The next morning was Sunday, so they slept in... well they didn't actually do much sleeping. They had sex a couple more times and then they just laid there, talking. "You know," Maureen said. "You don't have to rebuild your house. You could always live here, with me."

"Really?"

"I don't want to sound strange, but I've kind of been interested in you since you walked into the store on that first day."

He smiled and kissed her again. "Don't be alarmed, but I've loved you since the first day I came into the store, and I saw you and heard you and Mrs. Kelly talking about me."

"You heard that?"

"Really, that's what you focus on?"

Maureen smiled, laughing. "How come you never said anything?"

"I was afraid to get hurt, and can you imagine how creepy that would have sounded? 'Hi, I just moved here and I'm in love with you.' You would have thought I was crazy."

"You're probably right."

"I did do some stuff though."

"What do you mean?"

"You know how you saw mw working every time you walked by, like every single time for several months?"

"Yeah."

"I learned your schedule so that I was always outside when you would walk by. That way I got to see your smile before you went to school of a morning, and when you came home."

"That is so sweet."

"I also liked to watch you jiggle when you walked by and rode your bike. Your smile and your body made my day.

Maureen laughed, "Right back to perv."

"Can you blame me, really? You've got a glorious chest and the moat perfect arse that the almighty ever put on any girl."

Maureen snuggled into him. "I love you."

"I love you too."

After they laid there for a while longer, just basking in the sheer joy they felt, Maureen decided to make a confession. "I have something to admit."

"What's that?"

"When you were always working, well I would stand off to the side of the road, behind a tree where you couldn't see me, and I would watch you work for a few minutes and think how sexy you looked. My favorite was when you worked on the roof, because I could look at your arse."

"So, you're just as big a pervert then?"

She kissed him. "Yes sir. Now you'd better go see the animals while I make us something to eat."

Maureen stayed in bed, enjoying the look she got at his body as he got up and dressed. When he was gone, she got up and put her robe on. She needed something to protect her from the cold until she got a fire going in the stove, but she didn't want to have too much on when Kiernan got back.

Once the stew was warm and the house was toasty, she disrobed and waited for him to get back. Be brought in a bucket of and milk. he almost dropped it when he saw her sitting at the desk, grading papers naked.

The two of them stayed tangled until Monday morning, when she had to go to work, and he had to start on the plans they had. They were going to fence off what part of his place that time that Kiernan wasn't working on the farm either reading by the fire, or having really loud sex.

There would be times when they were reading by the fire, late at night, when they both would look up from their books, down at Maureen's growing belly, and they would reach out a hand and touch the same spot on her stomach and they would smile at each other.

Feeling like this was true happiness...or at least that's how Maureen felt. And it was the look on Kiernan s face, the same strange look that she had seen on his face that day in the truck, but much deeper and more honest, that made her think he felt the same way.

They named the baby Kierra, and she was the most gorgeous thing they had ever seen. Maureen gave birth on their bed, the village doctor said that Kierra was the healthiest baby he had ever delivered.

Maureen had loved her life before, living alone in a cottage with hundreds of books. But nothing in her life, not University in Dublin nor the scenery in Tibet, compared to how much she loved every second of her husband and daughter. They worked the farm together, read to Kierra at night, they had a perfect life.

Even the bad wasn't that bad. It didn't matter how tired she was, getting to take care of Kierra was okay, and the times that Kiernan would say, "I'll get her" made her love him even more. Kierra would come to school with her Mum, hanging in a purpose all day while she taught. She even fed Kierra in class. She just popped a blanket over her breast and went on with the lesson.

When Kierra got a bit older, she would work the farm with her Da. Few things warmed Maureen's heart more than seeing her little girl waddling after her Poppa as he worked. She was in Maureen's class until it was time to move on. Then she would come home every day proud to tell her parents the new things she had learned. She would run and play with her friends, the village remaining safe enough for them to run all over town, all day long.

And when the day came that Kierra fell sick with the desire to leave the village, they packed their baby girl up, kissed her goodbye, and the two of them, gray haired and shriveled up, settled into the life they'd had two decades before, working their farm, and laying together at night, truly happy.

THE GIRL ON THE BUS

He got on the bus wondering if he was making a mistake. Sure, he was away from his crazy family. His father was in jail, his mother and sister both dead, but he felt as if the new place would just bring about new problems. His friends were gone, abandoned him when he was bleeding in the street, a fight with bikers that had been messing with a girl from the neighborhood, but what was going to happen in the new city, wherever that was? Would he find new people he thought he could trust, only to be betrayed?

The bus was cheap, seventy-five bucks, but the catch was that it made frequent stops all down the east coast and then headed to nearly everywhere else. Unlike most people he hadn't, purchased with a destination in mind, he'd just needed out.

Though now he was thinking maybe he'd get off in North Carolina and drink himself to death.

He was sitting in the farthest back seat, sideways with his head against the seat, trying to get some sleep, when she got on the bus. He could tell instantly that she was one of those people who hadn't yet discovered the horrors of the world, who still thought it was a good place.

She was pretty. Brown hair done up in a ponytail and a sharp, angular A face that had just enough pudge to make her truly pretty instead of model, magazine, pretty walked back through the bus, saying Hello to everyone she passed and looking like she was trying to decide which seat spoke to her. He rolled his eyes at the hippy and went back to hie nightmares. She sat down next to him and said, "Hello."

He said nothing, but she seemed undeterred. "Have you been on the bus long?" He grunted. "I see, I haven't really got a true destination in mind, I think I'm just gonna ride the proverbial rails for a while, see if I like where we end up and settle there."

She went on like that for hours and hours. Asking him questions and him saying nothing, or making a rude remark, but she never faltered in her happiness and friendliness.At some point, he wasn't sure when, he gave up on real sleep and decided to just sit forward with his neck leaned back against the seat, listening to her.

"I'll be right back." she said and walked up to a row of seats on the center of the right isle. He couldn't see who she was talking to as she sat on her knees and looked down into the seat behind hers. He watched her talking, enjoying the way her mouth moved as it formed words, when she suddenly motioned for him to come to her.

He didn't know why his legs were moving up the bus, but they were, and he soon found himself standing next to her, looking down at two kids. One of them was a little girl in a winter hat and an old coat that didn't seem like it kept much & covered or warm. Her bright red hair poked out from under the hat and her mittened hand held onto the hand of a boy who looked to be about four, half her age.

She whispered to him, "Talk to them, ask their story. I'll be right back."

And she walked away, to the next isle, and started talking to an Asian woman in suit pants and a shirt. He turned back to the kids. "So what brings you kids here?"

The girl put a strand of hair behind her ear, giving him a painful reminder of his little sister. "Our parents died, and they are sending us to an orphanage out of state. It is the one that raised our mom until she was adopted so she wanted us to go there if she died."

"Our Dad killded her." The little boy said.

His sister gave him a motherly scolding look. It was the kind of look that she shouldn't have had at that age. Against his better judgement, he found himself caring, feeling very sorry for this poor kid "Trevor, the social lady told you not to tell people that."

"I'm sorry Amy."

"It's okay, why don't you take a nap?"

The little boy nodded and laid down on the seat, his head in his big sister's lap. "I'll, uh,-"

But the girl from before saved him. She appeared at his shoulder and said, "We'll be back, okay? We're going to help you," Without another word she took him by the wrist and led him back to the back of the bus. She sat down and crossed one leg over the other, biting her thumb and staring off into space. "I talked to their social worker. She says that they are going to the orphanage partially because of their mother's wishes, and because they have no family, but also because their state's system is so crowded. She says that they will most likely be split up. Isn't that dreadful?"

"Yeah, he seems to really need her."

"And she needs him, though that proud kid wouldn't ever admit it. They're a family and a family should never be split up if it can be helped."

"I agree, but what can be done to help it?"

The concentration and determination on her face scared him a little bit. She said, "I don't know, but I'm going to figure it out."

Hours later, in the middle of the night, they were both still up. They only spoke every few minutes, though he hadn't spoken in nearly an hour. She did all the talking and he was nodding off. Suddenly she pulled him up and they were making their way to the front of the bus. They sat down rather roughly in a middle seat, next to an old woman. She was a short, squatty woman that looked like she was the one you needed to bet money on if it was her in a fight versus the entirety of the hell's angels biker gang. She looked distraught.

The girl, who he still had not asked the name of, held her hand out. "Nice to meet you."

The woman gave her a distracted look and held out her own hand to shake. "Likewise. Name's Kettleback."

"Nice to meet you Mrs. Kettleback. Where are you coming from, if you don't mind me asking."

"Visiting my husband at Arlington. And yourself?"

"Well as wonderful as a conversation with you would be, I actually wanted to speak of the kids sitting about six seats behind you."

"Oh?"

"Yes, I think that you might be able to help them. They are about to be split up when they go to an orphanage. I hate to see a family separated if they don't have to be."

"That is a tragedy, but what makes you think I can help?"

"Not sure really. I was just sitting in the back there, wondering who could help those kids, who could keep them together, and you struck me as a helper of lost souls."

"I have helped some kids in the past, and half my troupe, well all of it honestly, are folks who've not got many other places to go..." She was silent for what seemed like hours. When he had started to nod off the woman said, "Mayhaps I'll talk to that social worker."

She made to get up and the girl moved her legs out of the aisle. "I think that's enough for today. I'm pretty beat, how about you?"

He nodded sleepily, yawning. They made their way back to their seats. The back seat of the bus took of the entire length, and he moved his bag over to the very left side and laid down, using his bag as a pillow. The girl came over and sat next to his feet. "Thanks for your help. It was a great feeling to help them. Even if it doesn't work out at least we know that we tried, right?"

He looked up at her, filled with rage. "Yeah, it was nice to try and help, but if you think we did anything you're a fool. I've known you for what? Six hours, and already know you're annoying. I don't see you can be so damn happy. Those kids are orphans. You didn't do anything because their parents are still dead. Now go to sleep and wake up with a more accurate world view, please."

He expected it to hurt her. He didn't want it to, but he was so angry that she was in a good mood. That hearing what happened to those kids and trying to fix it still had her in such a good mood. He wanted to hurt her, to make her see that even if she helped everyone on this bus, the world wasn't going to get any better. But that didn't happen. She didn't look hurt, or even upset.

She just calmly said, "You know what, you choose how you see the world and how it affects you. If you want to be a hater and a cynic that is fine, but don't confuse that with being my fault." And with that she picked up her bag and walked to the middle of the bus, taking a new seat.

He woke up to the smell of salt. Before he even had his eyes open, he knew they were at the beach. Opening his eyes confirmed that. He got off the bus starving. The driver told him that there would be an hour before the bus left so he walked to a little surf shack that sold food and bought himself a burger. talking along the boardwalk to the sound of crashing waves he saw her standing at the edge.

He walked up to her and she spoke without turning around, like she had sensed his presence. "You know, I'm not ignorant. I know that bad stuff happens. I know that you've probably been through some really bad stuff. But whatever it is I guarantee someone somewhere went through worse. Some people were abused by their family, in every sense of the word. Some of us ran away and had to do a lot of bad things for a bus ticket and money to eat. Some people know what it is like to be stabbed." She turned to look at him. "But happiness is a choice, it doesn't matter what you see when you close your eyes. How horrible the world really is. You choose whether ornot you will be brought down by it or if you will try to leave it a better place because of you."

She walked away and he was so stunned that he couldn't follow her. He just looked out over the ocean and thought about what she had said until the driver signaled that they would be leaving o He found her in their seat again, looking bummed after having opened up to him. On his way back to the seat he saw a girl crying halfway down the left row of seats. As he got back to the girl he said, "I think I found someone we might be able to help."

"Who?"

"That girl there." he said pointing.

She looked intently, as if studying the girl. "Good idea. Let's go."

They got up and made their way over to the girl who couldn't have been much older than they were. She was crying, but there were few visible tears. It was the kind of crying that you wouldn't notice unless you looked closely, but once you saw you could tell that the person was suffering a great deal.

She sat down next to the woman, and he took the seat in front, looking back at her. "Excuse me, but are you okay?"

"The woman looked forward at her hands in her lap. "I'm fine."

"I'm afraid I don't believe you."

"I just gave my baby up for adoption."

"I see." Was all she said. It took him a moment to realize that she was waiting for the woman.

Finally, she spoke. "I just, I miss her so much already. I'm afraid I made a mistake."

"Why did you give her up in the first place?"

"Because I thought it would be her best chance for survival. I don't have a real way of supporting her, and I'm afraid for her if she would grow up around my family."

"Are your family bad?"

"No, they're just trash. They're good honest working people, but not a damn one amounted to anything. I wanted more for my baby."

"Sounds like you did the right thing." he said.

Both girls looked at him. The woman in shock and her in confusion. "What do you mean?" The crying woman asked.

"Well, if you didn't think that she would have a good life with you, that her best chance was elsewhere, then I think that you made the right choice in giving her to someone that could give her the life that you want her to have."

The woman looked slightly comforted, and the girl said, "He's right."

"I know."

"Where are you headed?"

"Not sure. I was thinking somewhere by the ocean, but maybe farther south."

"Can I tell you what I think that you ought to do?"

The woman nodded and she continued. "I think that you ought to get off the bus in Florida and just start over. Find a job and spend your off days at the beach or something, looking for peace. You did the thing a Momma is supposed to do, gave your baby her best chance. But now it is time that you got yours...promise me you'll at least think about it?"

The woman nodded. "I will."

"Then we'll leave you be, but if you need to talk, we're just there, in the back." They walked back to their seat and sat talking until night.

They didn't talk about anything in particular, the weather, what season was their favorite. His was fall, hers winter. "How can you like winter, it's so cold?"

"I'd rather be cold than hot. I can bundle up great big but there is only so much you can do to cool down, even if you did walk around naked."

At that he looked down at her legs, wondering what that might look like. As if she could read his mind she said, "Eyes up here sailor."

At one o'clock in the morning the bus pulled into a gas station and she said, "Will you get some snacks? I've got to pee really bad."

"Sure."

He made his way into the gas station and walked up and down the aisles picking things out. It was always weird being in a public place when there was virtually no one else in there. It felt empty, like a body without its soul.

He bought some snacks and made his way back to the bus at the same time that she was getting there. She led the way onto the bus, and he stopped at the kid's seats.

"Hey Amy, I got you guys some snacks."

The sleepy little eight-year-old raised her head. "Thank you, sir."

He smiled at her and made his way back to the seat.

He handed her a bag of chips and said, "So where do you think You'll end up?"

"I'm still not sure. I'm thinking of the Midwest. It's got hot summers but some of the most beautiful winters ever."

He nodded like he understood. They talked for another two hours before she put her head on his shoulder started to drift off. After he was sure she was asleep he whispered in her ear, "I think I'm falling in love with you."

The next morning, as they made their way through Georgia, they were sitting in their seats and he was reading a book he'd bought at a little store they stopped at. All of a sudden, she said, "I think I want to help one more person."

He looked over, one more? Was she planning on stopping, or did she just not think that the rest of the people on the bus needed help? "Okay, who?"

"Not sure, but I'm thinking that guy at the front."

He looked to where she was looking and saw a guy in the very front of the bus, on the left row, just behind the driver. The guy was a little older that they were, and he was bent forward, shoulders hunched, his entire vibe being that of despair. "Let's go." he said, getting up.

They walked to the front of the bus and he took her lead. They didn't say anything. They just sat. It seemed like hours before the man spoke. "Can I help you?"

"I just wanted to tell you I'm sorry for your loss." she said.

"How did you know?"

"Your entire posture and aura say that you lost someone."

"I did."

"What was her name?"

"Claire."

"How did it happen?"

"Car accident."

"That's awful."

"Yes."

She looked thoughtful for a moment, seeming like she might cry. "Can I ask you something?"

"Sure."

"What will you do now?"

"I was thinking of killing myself, but I can't do that."

"Cause you promised her not too?" The girl asked.

"How'd you know?"

"Just a gucss."

"Good guess."

"You know what she would want you to do?"

"Yes. She told me to find someone else."

"But you don't want to?" He said.

The guy looked up at him the same time the girl did. The guy looked briefly like he was going to hit him, or curse, but he just sighed. "I can't."

"Why not?"

"How can I just get over her and move on? She was the love of my life."

"Who says you have to move on and forget?" He said, not one hundred percent sure where he was going.

"What do you mean?" The guy asked.

"She said that you need to find somebody else, she didn't say, I'm assuming, she didn't say to forget her and move on from your love."

The guy looked intrigued, as did she. "What would you suggest?" she asked.

"There is a girl back there, in that seat," He pointed. "She is going through a loss of her own. Who's to say that you two couldn't help each other heal. If you get together fine and dandy, but if you don't you would still have found someone else who can do some of the things she did for you and help you too heal while you're still alive."

He didn't know what to say. He sat back and seemed to go catatonic. After ten minutes he said nothing and she looked at him on the other seat, motioning with her head. "Let's go."

When they had walked back to their seat he asked, "Doesn't it seem a bit too easy?"

"What do you mean?"

"Well, we just talk to people and change their life? That guy gets over something the kids get adopted? It kinda seems too easy."

"Just because we talked to them doesn't mean their lives are better. Maybe they will be maybe they won't. Maybe that guy blows his brains out tomorrow. But all people usually need is a seed."

"A seed?"

"A seed of happiness, a seed of health and better-ness. We've planted them and now they will either grow or they won't. But the important ft part is that we tried."

He sat down, contemplating that. He sat there for a long time, both silent. He wasn't sure why she was suddenly so quiet, but soon they were both asleep.

The next morning, he was woken when the bus stopped. His eyes opened and she was standing over him. She leaned down and kissed him. It was a sweet kiss and it stunned him for a moment. When he regained his composure he saw her at the front, getting off the bus. He ran to the front and the bus started pulling away as she walked towards the back. He started hurrying, following her from inside the bus. "Wait!"

She either couldn't hear him or didn't want to. He yelled some more but she kept walking. As he got to their seat, he looked out the back of the bus. She stopped, a bright figure against a dirt road and a relatively dark day. She looked at him and he put his hand on the glass.

She smiled and raised a hand in farewell.

He watched as she faded into dust and blew away on the wind.

TILL DEATH DO US PART?

Jacob was laying on his stomach. He turned over to see her, his beloved, sitting on the table, leg resting on a chair. But he knew her. He knew everything about her, and this wasn't her. "Do you look like her on purpose?" he asked.

"Well you're a smart one aren't ya? Yes, I look like her on purpose. Usually no one notices that I look like their loved one but am not actually. That's a first."

"Is it safe to assume I'm dead?" Jacob asked.

"Yes. You are dead. I am an angel," Her, he had decided it would be easier to call the angel her, wings came out, large bird wings. He could see the texture in them, an off-white color like they had soaked up other colors that had taken them from a pure white to their current color. "I'm here to take you on a little visit to your past, then we will determine whether you go to heaven or hell."

Jacob sat up on the bed, turning his legs to droop over the side. "I'm still confused on the angels being real bit."

"I suppose I can't blame you all that much. You were brought up by the non-religious, and we haven't really been allowed on earth in a very long time. Not since the war ended."

Jacob didn't know what she was talking about, and he decided that it was better if he didn't know. "Well, should I get dressed?"

The angel snapped her fingers and he was dressed. Jacob stood up and looked at the apartment. There were bottles everywhere, he hadn't cleaned in ages, it was a shit hole full of bad memories and pain. "Let's go." She looked surprised. "You don't want to argue? Beg to stay? Take a last look at the house?"

"Um...no, I've hated every moment I was alive for the last two years...let's go."

"Okay, let's go to the first moment." She snapped her wings at him.

Jacob suddenly saw the playground from his elementary school. He saw his younger self playing. He guessed this was around third grade. The angel appeared next to him, though he wasn't shocked. He'd seen enough movies to know more or less how this would go. "So, what do I call you?" he asked.

"My name is Israfiel, angel of the lord."

"I'll just say Israfiel I think."

"Fine by me. Look, here it is." She looked towards his younger self. A pack of grade school kids, the boys doing the bullying and the girls there for their first go at being gang bitches, started to crowd around this other boy. Jacob didn't really remember this, but the other boy looked small and sickly.

He watched as his younger self walked over and stood in front of the smaller boy. When one of the bullies walked up and shoved him Jacob punched him in the eye. That was enough to dissuade the other playground terrorists to go away. Jacob then took the other boy to the swings to play.

Dead Jacob turned to Israfiel, "Why did you show this to me?"

"This is the moment you became a good person. This moment, right here," She pointed one finger in the air and turned it counterclockwise, Jacob watched as the scene rewound.Sud denly they were watching young him from up close, playing in the sandbox as he looked over at the group. He saw the look on his own face as she said, "This is where you decided to stick up for those that couldn't do it for themselves."

"Can I sit?"

She shrugged. "I don't care. You're dead, not like we have a time limits."

"I meant, am I able? We are in the past or my memories or whatever."

"Sure, you can sit down. You just can't interfere. This has happened and we're just visiting."

Jacob nodded and walked over to a green bench near an ancient oak tree. It was a hard metal bench with that weird plastic coating and the metal holes that hurt your butt. He vaguely thought that this might be the spot where he had his first kiss. "So, you are going to show me the good moments of my life?"

"Not all of them. It will be a mixture of the key moments good and bad. I've not got the patience to show you your entire life."

"I don't want to do this."

"Me neither."

"What?"

"I'm a soldier with no war. I'd rather be back in my day. But here we are. Nothing to do about it."

"But you're going to show me, -"

"I know. You still must do it."

Jacob sighed. He stood up and said, "Let's go."

Israfiel stood and snapped her wings out, as they came forward everything melted and then went black.

They stood in the middle of the street. It was a weird feeling as a car ran down the middle of the street and through the both of them. "What did you mean, without a war? Isn't the fight for good and evil still a thing?"

"Not in the same way. "It used to be real war, but these days it is waged in an individual's heart. We aren't even allowed on earth unless it's to escort the dead. Here you are."

They turned to the sidewalk and saw teenage-ish Jacob walk out. "What am I, thirteen?"

"Twelve years, six months, thirteen days." she said.

They watched him steal a candy bar on his way out, walking quickly away. A kid walking out of the store yelled, "Hey, come back here!" The boy ran after Jacob and he picked up a rock, throwing it behind him at the other kid.

Younger him disappeared and they walked closer, watching the bleeding kid on the sidewalk. "Is he dead?"

Israfiel shook her head. "He lives. But he still has severe, mind numbingly painful migraines, to this day."

"And I did that to him?"

"Yes."

"Why did you show me this?"

"You'll find out about that later. Are you ready for the last couple of moments?"

Even though he was dead, Jacob could feel himself exhale. "Let's go."

The music was loud. A couple of drunk people walked through them on their way upstairs. Israfiel extended her wings and knocked a lamp over. It was quickly forgotten by the party goers. Jacob looked at her, shocked, and she said, "On occasion I can influence the past."

He was about to reply when, from across the room, on the left wall, he saw her dancing. She was exactly like he remembered. He saw a twenty-one-year-old him walk from the right part of the room towards her. She was making a loud fuss, because she was only a happy drunk for about twenty minutes until it turned straight to belligerent. Israfiel stood next to him. "Do you want to get closer?"

"No need, I can remember everything.... Hey, come on, let me take you home...No, I'm having fun...well let's have fun on the way home and you can sleep it off....okay, I'll go with you as long as you get me waffles....I will get you waffles..." Younger him started to lead her out."You know, you're kinda cute from back here..."

"How, -" The angel said. "That was every word in perfect cadence."

"This was the best moment of my life; I'd never forget it." Jacob's face dropped. "So, is it safe to assume that the next moment is what I think it is?"

He thought he could hear actual sadness in the angel's cold, impersonal, voice. "The next two are what you think they are."

"Well fuck."

"Wanna post pone? I can give you a few hours of looking in the past."

"Thanks, but I think that this will be less hard if I haven't just relived our relationship. She extended her wings, smacking some guy into a table. She snapped them forward and then everything went black again,

Jacob was twenty-three. He was in their apartment working one day. His sister Piper was about to move to the city. He had lived with his love for about two years.

She walked in that morning and said, "I have news."

"What is it? Everything okay?"

"I'm pregnant."

His face went wide with shock and then contorted in happiness. "That is amazing. I'm gonna be a daddy. Holy shit I've gotta get a higher paying position, or something, I don't know. The apartment is fine for now, but we'll want it to have its own room before long so we should probably start looking. Oh, this is great. I am so excited. We should defiantlyname it after your sister if it's a girl. I mean, that wouldn't upset you, would it? I know you miss her but, -"

"Jacob, I'm not keeping it."

He stopped. "What?"

"I want to live before I have a kid, settle down. You and I have talked about traveling together, visiting all those countries, sex on the beach…"

"So, we put the baby down for a nap and have beach sex while it's asleep."

She tried to suppress a laugh. "I can't. I'm sorry Jacob."

"And I don't get a say? You're going to murder my child; I'm assuming it's mine?"

She looked hurt. "Of course it's yours."

"So, you are going to kill my child and I don't have a say?"

"No, I'm sorry…you don't."

He gave a nod, his teeth clenched. "Then get out."

"What?"

"I love you. I love you more than myself, or anything alive or dead. But I cannot be with someone who would do this."

There was silence. Finally, she said, "I'm sorry, but I have to do this." And she left.

Jacob walked over to the kitchenette area and went into the cabinet. He popped the cap off a bottle of whiskey and walked to the couch, throwing the cap in the bin on his way.

Israfiel looked at him, "Why would you feel guilt over this? That was a perfectly reasonable response."

"I don't feel guilty because I didn't condone our kid's death. I feel guilty because this is the moment I lost her. Right here is when she was gone."

"That's not entirely true" The angel said.

"What do you mean?" And she snapped her wings.

It was evening. They were in the back seat of the car as she drove, on the phone, crying. "Jacob...I couldn't do it. I'm sorry, you were right. This...we ' be okay."

The line went dead, and she tried to call him again. He had the memory of refusing to answer the phone, of turning it off so that no one could get to him. She dialed him again. "Jake, please pick up the phone."

"Don't make me watch this."

"I don't have a choice."

He didn't know that dead people could cry but he was. The tears fell like rain as he realized that he could have been with her. It might have been okay. They could be in a little house right now with their kid, maybe kids, being happy. If he had only picked up the god damned phoned. He knew that she couldn't hear him, but she was there, and he needed to apologize to someone. "Baby I'm sorry. I should have picked up. I'm sorry. Slow down. It's getting dark, it's raining, it's like one big cliche outside. Slow down!" He smacked the seat, and she kept dialing.

"Jacob, I'm keeping the baby. We can talk more about it when I get there, if you still love me."

They hit a bump and her phone fell. She moved to try and get it. Suddenly he and the angel were standing outside the car as it crashed. There was wreckage everywhere. He ran forward and slid like a baseball player, scooping her up. She slid through his fingers, and he looked down at her, she had tears in her eyes and one hand was on her bloody stomach. He swore that she looked right at him as she said, "Jacob." Then her eyes shut, and she was gone.

Israfiel stood over him. "She could see you. Time moves in a ball, and the veil is thinnest right before death. So, you were the last thing she it saw."

He cried, not paying any attention to the angel. She knelt. "It's time to decide. Now. We don't have long," The angel said. "You've reached the apex and the doors will open soon. I showed you these moments because for one reason or another you feel guilty about them. They are your main memories when it comes to guilt."

"And-?"

"And you need to let it go. Your guilt is what will get you put in hell. Once you're down there it is infinitely harder to let it go. And my big brother makes sure that you relive it for eternity. You must let them go. Forgive her, and yourself."

"Did you have this conversation with her?"

"Yes. She had a very hard time about it. It killed her to do what she did, she almost went through with it until she realized that she wanted a life with you, no matter what sacrifices had to be made. She had already begun making alternative plans you three could do as a family."

"How did she let it all go?"

"She said that you would get to heaven. That you were good and no matter what she had to be there when you arrived."

Jacob was kneeling in a fiery wreck. Both literally and figuratively. He was next to the burning car and wreckage that had killed his beloved. And figuratively he had to figure out how to let go of his pain so he could be in heaven with her.

When he looked up there was a door in the middle of the street. 'Open it." He heard. When he touched the doorknob, he felt a millions pounds lighter. He smiled for the first time in years. He opened the door to see his family standing in the doorway of a house. She was holding a baby girl in her arms. "Will she, -"

"Don't worry about it. She is where she is supposed to be now."

"Thank you."

"Happy to help."

Jacob stepped through and the door closed after him.

GETTING BETTER

Katie was in her room, which she had taken to calling her cell when she was in group, mostly to piss off the councilors. She was just looking out the window, hoping he wouldn't come.

She had always been an early riser, but when she'd been sent here, she had started trying to stay awake as long as possible, she would be up all night, sleep for a few hours, and then be up again. That had changed when the therapist found out. She had told Katie that she needed a routine, get up, wash ass, ect. She hadn't wanted to agree, but her schedule was getting to the point that she couldn't even walk without falling over. So since then she went to bed at exactly eight and she got up every morning at five. She liked the schedule. It was the only thing she had actually liked in a long time.

"Shit!" She said out loud, even though she knew the hospital's policies frowned upon bad language because it was 'Unhealthy and not conducive to a healing environment.' But this shit was deserved. She saw him walking up the path to the hospital.

Why was he still coming here? Surely to God he had better things to do with his time than to wait out in the hallway every day.

Heid loved her, she knew that in her heart, but she didn't know how. She was crazy. How could such a great, sweet, guy love someone who was crazy? As he disappeared from her window's view, she hoped once again that he would turn around and leave. When she didn't see him a few seconds later, she turned away from the window.

Katie's room was small, thread bare you could say. They wanted it that way because there was nothing she could use to hurt herself. She touched the scars on her wrists from where she had already, wishing for the thousandth time that month that she had been successful.

Reid had been the one who found her. She hated herself for having put him through that. She hated herself for a lot of things. She took off her clothes, the same white pants and shirt that was only a few shades from a prison uniform. She took a cold shower in her open, suicide proof shower, and put an identical set of clothes on. When the guards came, she was all ready for therapy.

She'd had group for the first few weeks that she had been there, but she caused such a fuss, including making an anorexic boy develop anxiety, that they gave her her very own shrink.

Her name was Doctor Cho, ironically, she wasn't Asian. She had been adopted by Chinese parents. Doctor Cho was a pretty woman. She had brown hair that she kept in a bun, and she wore reading glasses that Katie had accused her of wearing just to achieve the sexy librarian look.

She walked in and Doctor Cho stood up to greet her like she was some sort of nineteenth century gentleman. They both sat back down, and the session started. The office reminded Katie of the one in Good Will Hunting, a movie Reid had made her watch a hundred times. There were books everywhere, crammed into the shoe box that was the room. There were papers everywhere on the three desks that were all between bookshelves, forming a horseshoe around the room, with their area in the middle, two plush chairs and a table. "Why does this place look so much like the office in Good Will Hunting?" Katie asked.

"What?"

"Your office, it isn't sparse like most therapy rooms. It's crowded like Robbin Williams' in that movie."

Doctor Cho moved around to look at the room, seemingly just noticing this. "Huh, you know you're right."

"I thought your therapy space was supposed to be like, sparse and stuff so you didn't excite anyone or make them uncomfortable."

"If people want to be comfortable, they should go somewhere else. Therapy is uncomfortable. I don't want them to be docile, I want them to feel uneasy enough that they don't have the big shields up, just the small ones I can easily get through."

"I kinda get that, confront them while they're vulnerable."

"Exactly." She took her pad and pen out and she looked at Katie. "Now, how about we talk about you?"

"Haven't we been trying this for a while? I don't like to talk about me."

"Then let's talk about the boy who waits outside every day to see you."

"No."

She made a face that was clearly fake sympathy. "Sorry kid, I make the rules here. If you want to make rules, get better and move on to a world where you can."

"I'm not talking about Reid."

"Then I will." She reached to the table next to her and took out a file. "I see that he was the one who found you when you tried to kill yourself."

"Yeah."

"He said that you were supposed to go out to dinner and a movie that night?"

"Yeah."

Doctor Cho looked at her like she had finally figured out her password. "So why did you choose date night to kill yourself?"

"Don't know."

"That's bullshit. I think you chose that night because you love this boy. I think that you chose that night so that he would be the one to find you."

Katie was so mad she thought she was going to throttle this woman. She could feel her eyes doing the only thing they did when she was mad, tearing up. That was the only time she cried. She cried when she wanted to hit something, other than that, her eyes were as dry as a man's ass in the Sahara. "Don't." was all she said.

"Don't talk about how you wanted to say goodbye, but you timed it wrong so that you traumatized your boyfriend?"

Katie jerked out of her seat and started to step towards the doctor, but she stopped before taking a single step, she just stood, clenching her fists. She knew what happened when you attacked your therapist, and it was not good. "Please stop."

"Then sit down and talk to me."

"I don't want to."

"I don't care. I've tried being nice and it didn't work, so either you open yourself up emotionally, or I will."

Katie sighed. She couldn't stand any more of this emotional beating, so she sat down, and she wiped her eyes. "Fine."

Doctor Cho handed her a box of tissues. "Tell me why you tried to take your own life."

It took Katie several more minutes of crying, but finally she spoke. "I tried to kill myself because I wanted to stop hurting."

"What hurts?"

"Everything." Katie said. "It hurts, or I just don't care. It's one or the other, total pain or total apathy. I'm not sure which one is worse."

"When did it start?"

"Before I met Reid. I think I was probably thirteen or four-teen. He helped, for a while."

"Explains what you mean by, he helped for a while."

Katie sighed. She hated talking about herself, yet she also kind of felt like this might be a good thing, but she wasn't about to admit that. "Reid and I have been together for a long time, since I was like, fourteen and a half. And for the first I'd say, two years...it was like I had this weight, pushing me down, and when Reid first came into the picture it was like it was lifted. But then one day it showed back up like, 'Here I am! Fuck you.'"

"So that was sadness, right?"

Katie nodded. "Yeah, the apathy didn't start until later. But at the time, nothing made me happy. Reid started to notice, and God love him he tried to make me happy. I even tried, but nothing worked. It was like every day the weight pushed me just a little further down."

"Do you think that this weight was caused by something? Your parents maybe, or school, or bullies?"

Katie shook her head. "My parents are wonderful, I was actually pretty good at school, and I haven't had a bully since I beat the crap out of one in fifth grade. I think that the sadness, the weight, whatever you call it, it was just in me."

Cho nodded. "I understand what you're saying. When did you stop caring?"

"I can't pinpoint the exact date, it was just like I went to bed sad and the next day I woke up with whatever part of your body that makes you feel ripped out, I didn't care about Reid, or school, or my family, or sex...I just did not care."

Doctor Cho was silent for a long time. It felt like hours to Katie. When she finally spoke, Katie wasn't sure she liked what she heard. "Here's what I want to do, if you're open to it. I want to start to develop a routine for you, some simple things that I think will boost your morale, and maybe lift a little of the weight from your shoulders."

"Like what?"

"First answer me this, do you still love Reid? In those brief moments when you are neither sad or apathetic, do you love him?" Katie nodded. "Then I want you to talk to him today. I'll have a therapy room opened and I want the two of you to talk.

Nothing sexual because I will be monitoring from the other room, I have to, and I don't think that is the best thing right this minute. I just want you to talk through everything."

"I can't do that." Katie said shaking her head. "I want him to forget about me. I want him to move on and be with someone who isn't going to cause him so much pain."

Doctor Cho seemed genuinely sympathetic. "Life is pain. It doesn't matter who! he's with he'll get hurt. The only difference is that when he's with you, he won't mind."

"What do you mean?"

"I mean that, when you're hurt by someone you truly love, and I mean with your entire being and soul, it doesn't matter if they hurt you, because even if they cut your heart out, you'd still be with them."

"Have you talked to Reid?"

"I have, and I think that he really loves you."

"But shouldn't' he want someone life would be easier with?"

Doctor Cho laughed. "Life won't be easy with anyone. You have depression, if he was with another girl, or guy, or whatever, they would have their own crap they had to get through. But we're getting off topic, the question was whether or not you love him."

"Of course I do."

"Then do you want to see him? Go home eventually, be with him?"

"Yes."

"Then what are we doing here? Why are you still in this place if you are serious about getting better? You have been in this place for over a month, and this is the first time you have even seemed interested in going home." Katie sobbed for a long time, she was right, this needed to be taken seriously. She needed to make a commitment to being better. Katie was sure her time had to be about up she had cried so long, but finally, Doctor Cho spoke.

"When you've composed yourself, I will take you to see Reid."

Katie nodded. She forced herself to stop crying, though she was fairly certain that seeing Reid would have them both crying in a few minutes anyway. Finally, they both got up and Doctor Cho showed Katie to a door that was different from the one she had come through. They walked through a part of the hospital that Katie hadn't been to. She was guessing it was because she wasn't allowed. There was color here, stripes that went down either side of the wall in brown with a little bit of orange in the middle. And there were plaques and paintings. This crap would definitely excite the patients.

Doctor Cho led her into a side room that had 'Family Therapy' on the door. It was a nice room, furnished more like what Katie thought a therapy room was supposed to be, just plain furniture, mild decorations, and her boyfriend. She did a double take, "Reid?"

"Hey baby."

Katie rushed forward and hugged her boyfriend. She didn't even realize how much she had missed him until she saw him again. When they broke the hug, she took a bitter look at him. He was wearing a white/brown button-down shirt with jeans, both of which didn't look like they'd had a proper wash in days. His hair needed cut, and he had a disheveled look about him. Reid had never been one to focus on his looks, but he had let himself go even by his standards. "I missed you so much." Katie said.

"Then how come you haven't wanted to see me for over a month?"

Before Katie could say anything, Doctor Cho spoke. "I'm going to leave you two in here, but I'll be just in the other room." She walked out yet another door, what was this place the mansion from Clue? Reid sat down on a couch opposite from Katie and she was suddenly thankful for the coffee table in between them.

"Can I explain?" she asked.

"I really wish you would." He didn't seem angry. He seemed like he just truly didn't understand.

"When I...did what I did," She began, trying not to cry. "I didn't mean to hurt you. I know, -"

"No, you don't."

"What?"

"You have no idea what it is like to get a message from your girlfriend saying, 'Let yourself in' and you come inside the house, expecting to pick her up for a date, only to find...only to find her bleeding to death on the floor. You have no idea what it's like to hold the love of your life in your arms and think that you will see them die. If the nine one one operator hadn't told me what to do to save you until they got there...I'm sorry...you scared me."

Katie couldn't help herself. She started to cry. It was like all the emotions that she had held in, even the ones she didn't let out earlier in therapy, they all came out. The pain leaked out through her eyes along with the shame she felt at causing Reid so much pain. "Can I touch you?" he asked. "I don't know the rules."

Katie nodded without looking up, a moment later she felt Reid on the couch next to her, wrapping his arms around her. She felt safe in his arms, like nothing, not even the weight on her shoulders, could hurt her. But that wasn't a way to live. He couldn't always be there to protect her. She pulled away enough so that she could look up at him. "I'm sorry. I am so sorry. I didn't want to hurt you. Reid, I have problems, I've refused to acknowledge them until today, but there are things wrong with my brain that make me the way I am."

"I've been reading a lot about depression lately." Reid said. "There are a lot of books piled in the waiting room. I had to find something to do while I waited."

She loved him so much. "So, you know that it isn't entirely my fault."

"I do."

"But it is my choice on whether or not to wallow in it. And I don't want to anymore. I want to get better."

He smiled at her. "That's good."

"Will you help me?"

He kissed her. "Absolutely."

"I didn't want you to come see me because I was ashamed of what I'd done, and the pain that it caused you. I wanted you to move on."

He kissed her again, this time just a bit longer. It was only the K second kiss she had had since before she came here, but it was by far the best kiss of her life. Because it said more than any other had before. It said that he loved her and that he was never going to leave her, even when he probably should. "I will never move on from you Katie. This is it. You and me. I'm in it for the long hall Darlin'."

"I love you."

"I love you too."

The next few months were not easy. Katie had to adhere to a strict schedule, therapy, interactions with other patients in a non-hostile manner. It would be dishonest to say that she didn't falter, that there weren't moments where she tried to get a spring out of her mattress to cut her wrists with, but she persevered. She learned things she could do to get better. She learned ways to distract herself from her mood, and even ways to get over and past it. She was a stubborn girl, and when she made the decision to fight her illness, to not let it win, the only thing that was going to stop her was death.

Months later she was released from the hospital. As she walked out of the building, she saw Reid standing at his truck with something in his hands. As she approached, she saw that it was a small pug. He took her bag and handed her the puppy. "Oh, hi sweetie." Katie said as the puppy licked her face.

Reid came back around and opened the truck for her. "I thought maybe she could give you some company and someone to love on when I'm not around, and even when I am I guess."

Katie kissed him and got into the truck, she held her new fur baby on her lap, trying to decide on a name, as Reid came around and got into the truck. As they pulled out of the hospital Katie thought that maybe, just maybe, she would be okay.

OUR FIRST FIGHT

Claire sat against the wall. She wasn't even sure what part of town she was in. She'd just kept walking until she was far enough away. The tears were streaming down her face, and she noticed that her favorite sweater and her nice skirt were getting all soaked with tears and dirt. Her Mom would not be pleased, but at that moment she just did not care.

Kenna was walking down the sidewalk, trying to find out where Claire had gone. She started to tear up more and more as she thought about what had happened earlier.

***

Claire was walking up the path to school when she saw Kenna coming from the other direction. Kenna turned the corner and Claire swallowed hard, gathered her courage, and sped up to catch her. Claire put her arm out and touched Kenna's shoulder as she spoke, "Hey Kenna?"

Kenna turned around, a bit surprised. "Oh, hey Claire, what's up?"

"Um..." Her courage was gone. She'd never done this before! and she was not used to being the outgoing one. She didn't know how long she had been silent before Kenna spoke.

"Claire, are you okay?"

"Yeah, I was wondering if we could talk for a minute?"

"Sure." Kenna led the way to a nearby picnic table where they both sat down, shifting awkwardly in their seats. They didn't normally talk that much. They were friendly, but they were not 'Friends'. "So, what did you want to H talk about?" she asked.

"Um...when we were at Sarah's on Saturday, and we, you know..."

Kenna smiled. "When we kissed?"

"Yeah, urn..."

"That's all? Sorry if I caught you off guard, it was truth or dare and I hate to lose...I'm very competitive."

"That's not what it is, I mean it is, but, -"

Kenna laughed. "Look I'm sorry about the kiss okay?"

Claire looked down, her voice barely above a whisper when she spoke. "I'm not."

"What?"

Claire took a deep breath. "I'm not. I enjoyed it. I was going to say thank you."

"For what?"

"For being my first kiss."

At the memory of telling Kenna that she had been her first kiss Claire started to cry even harder. She was so stupid. How did she think that someone like Kenna could like her?

She was so stupid.

***

Kenna was crying hard as she walked down the street, earning her quite a few looks from the strangers. She looked both ways before crossing the street, having to wipe her eyes in the middle of the road because her tears were clouding her eyes.

She was such a bitch.

Kenna was uncomfortable. She'd been laughing, trying to act cool about the whole thing, but she wasn't. Claire was a beautiful girl, and that made Kenna uncomfortable.

"I was your first kiss?"

"Yeah."

"And you wanted to thank me?"

Claire nodded.

"Have you always been such a dork?" Claire nodded again, this time smiling. "Is that all?" Kenna asked.

"No, I was wondering if you were dating anyone?"

Kenna hoped that the utter terror she felt didn't show on her face. She had been interested in girls before, but she had never really considered dating one, or anyone really. "No," she said trying to get the words out without being mean or showing her discomfort. "Why?"

"I was wondering if you'd like to go out with me."

Kenna stood up rather abruptly. She needed to leave before she got so uncomfortable, she did something stupid, like cry. "I can't I..."

"Don't want to?"

"It's not that, it's just..." Over Claire's shoulder Kenna saw a group of kids coming towards the school. They were looking over at the two of them and Kenna started to feel very cornered.

"Then what is it?" Claire asked.

The group of kids was closer now, looking over at them.

They were probably just wondering what they were doing, but that didn't stop Kenna from feeling like a zoo animal. "I'm not interested in you." she said, much too loudly.

Kenna could tell that Claire was trying not to cry. When she spoke, if it was so soft that she could barely hear her. "Oh."

The crowd had gathered more, increasing Kenna's feeling of being some sort of attraction. She knew they had most likely come over because she was raising her voice like a crazy person, but Kenna was past the point of being rational. "Please leave me alone." She said loudly, in She immediately regretted that. The hurt Claire's eyes cut straight to her soul. Her feelings of being trapped were gone, replaced by a feeling that she was the worst person who ever lived. Claire quickly gathered her things and rushed in the direction that the group of kids had come from. A boy who was a douche on a good day, and a regular piece of garbage in bad times was walking towards school when he passed Kenna. "Nice one Kenna."

"Oh, fuck off Gerald."

Kenna stood still for what seemed like hours but was probably just a few minutes. Then she headed off in the direction Claire had gone.

***

Kenna rounded the corner and saw Claire sitting against the wall. She walked over, stopping a few feet from Claire and earning against the wall. She slid down until she was sitting, she pulled her knees to her chest and sighed. "I'm a bitch."

"No argument here."

Kenna smiled despite herself. "I know it doesn't make it better," she said, "but I'm sorry."

"You're right, it doesn't make it better."

"I'm not one to get scared easy Claire. But I did, I got scared when you asked me out. Then when I saw those kids coming, I got scared and I lashed out. And I am sorry."

Claire looked over at her, wiping her eyes. "The first time I ask someone out and instead of my first date, I get humiliated."

"I am so sorry." Kenna said. She scooted closer to Claire. "And if the offer is still open, I would love to go out with you."

Claire wasn't sure if she could trust what Kenna was saying. "Are you serious, or do you just want to embarrass me again?"

"I didn't mean to humiliate you, Claire. I just got nervous and a little embarrassed myself. I've just never really went out with a girl before."

Claire was confused. "But girls ask you out all the time, I saw Jenna ask you out at lunch Friday, and at the sleepover Aubrey asked you to...you know...do stuff."

Kenna smiled shyly. "Yeah, but I didn't do any of them. I turned Jenna down too."

"So, it's just me you're embarrassed to be asked out by?"

"No, well...yes...see I've liked girls before, but they're all celebrities and stuff. I've never really considered saying yes when girls ask me out, or for sex in Aubrey's case."

Claire couldn't help but laugh at that. "You're really the first girl I've actually thought about going out with."

Claire pushed a stray hair behind her ear. "Really?"

Kenna smiled shyly and nodded. Claire leaned towards Kenna and kissed her, it was wonderful, even better than the first. They got closer and they kissed for several seconds.

When they broke, Claire rested her head on Kenna's shoulder, both of them staring straight ahead. After a long silence Kenna spoke. "Well, I'm glad that's over."

"What's that?"

Kenna smiled. "Our first fight."

THE MAGICIAN'S ASSISTANT

The ancient station wagon pulled up and he got out. It was weird to see a guy wearing a suit (minus jacket) in the middle of a town of mid-western rednecks, but he got out like it was totally normal.

She was sitting on an ice machine, three or four feet off the ground. He thought she looked cute but didn't pay her a whole lot of mind as he went inside. He picked up a basket and started filling it with food and drink. A couple of apples, some snack cakes, a few coffee drinks, some water.

When he was finished, he made his way up to the front and waited in the line of people. The guy behind the counter rang up his purchases and he reached inside his front pocket and found his wallet missing. "What's a matter?" The guy asked.

"Well, it appears that my wallet is missing. I guess I'm not going to be able to pay…sorry."

He walked outside to his car to check and see if his wallet had fallen somewhere, hoping to high heaven that it had. He didn't have time to go back. As he walked out the girl he'd past said, "Nice car."

"Thank you." he said without looking. He opened the door and a thought occurred to him. He looked up and saw her for real for the first time. She had long dark hair and she was tall, nearly as tall as he was. Bodily, she looked terrific. She was lanky like a model, but unlike the stick figure she had a full body, curves in all the right places and enough of a chest to be perfect.

"What's your name?" he asked.

"Mackenna."

"That was an impressive lift, Mackenna." he said playing a gambit.

"Wasn't it though?" It worked. She held up his wallet

"Yes, how would you like to come with me?"

"That's the single creepiest pick-up line I've ever heard."

Doyle laughed. "It's not a line. I'm going to a magician's convention in Las Vegas, and I was wondering if you would like to come with me, as my assistant."

She looked contemplative. "What would I have to do?"

"Well first thing's first, I'm gonna top off the tank, so go inside and pay for the basket on the counter and twenty bucks on pump one. Then meet me at the car."

She gave a nod and hopped down. He took a moment to admire her butt as it swayed and then chastised himself. She was to be his assistant. If something developed it would have to be after the convention. For now, it was magician and assistant, nothing more.

Ten minutes later they were both in the car, headed away from the town and the store. Doyle didn't ask her why she had been so eager to leave and didn't need any clothes or anything, and she appreciated that. Mackenna didn't know him well enough to have that conversation.

As they pulled onto the interstate she asked again, "So what will I have to do?"

"You're the distraction. So, you'll just move things around, like big tricks and things, and you'll help volunteers and generally be an assistant."

"What do you mean I'll be a distraction?"

"That is better explained with a visual aid, but basically they are going to be looking at you while I do the trick. Here," He reached a hand behind him and grabbed a little bag. "Take these and work on them, there's an instruction booklet inside."

As they drove down the interstate, she took one trick out after another and was a genius at magic. She performed the jumping rabbit so well that for a moment he didn't even know how the rabbit got into her other hand.

He saw the sign for their exit and an idea was already forming in his head. "So, you're sure you've never done magic before?"

"Once again, no."

They were at a costume store and Mackenna was in the dressing room trying on the things he brought for her. She came out in a gold sequined dress that made her breasts seem a size or two bigger and her rear end more full. "Why must I dress so slutty?" she asked.

"Because you're the sexy assistant. We need everyone staring at your goodies so that they aren't paying attention to the magic being done."

"So, I'm using T & A to distract from your magic."

"Yes, traditionally speaking. But I want to shake it up a bit."

"What do you mean?"

"Well, the assistant is part of the trick, but on occasion, by which I mean most of the time, I'd like you to be another magician. But no one can know."

"Why?"

"Because if they see me as your boss and you as nothing but a big titty underling, then you remain a secret weapon that we can use when we need it. I know it's not very feminist friendly but,-"

"Well, if you turn into some bullshit feminist, I'm walking so I'd say it's a fine arrangement."

Doyle smiled. "You are one confusing woman, you know that?"

"Yes. Though there isn't anything confusing about this. I want to earn it. Feminists want it handed to them. Got it?"

He raised his hands in defense. "Got it. Any feminism and you walk."

She gave a curt nod. "What's next?"

"I think we'll take the gold, black, red, -"

She interrupted him. "Not the red."

"Why?"

"It rides up so much I felt like it was trying to get me pregnant."

Doyle laughed. "How about the green one then?"

"That's fine, and the blue."

"Sounds good. I'll get two of each and we'll be on our way. The contest is in a month so we'll do some impromptu road shows to work on our act."

"Why are you so early if the contest isn't for a month?"

"I thought I'd have to go looking for an assistant and I wanted to give myself enough time."

They made their way out of the store and went on down the road. He saw a hotel that had a pool like he was needing. There was even a sign that advertised their one-of-a-kind pool. "How long can you hold your breath?"

"Three minutes without trouble, why?"

"No reason." They checked into the room and started rehearsing some easy tricks.

They were in the motel room for the third straight hour. The rehearsing was not going well. Even basic movements had them tripping over each other and knocking bodies, and a lamp, over. "This isn't working." he said in frustration."

"Ya think?"

He looked angrily at her. She went for his notebook, a beat-up leather think that had all his tricks and illusions in it. "There's got to be something better in he- "

He cut her off and snatched the book. "Don't touch that. Ever."

Mackenna put her hands up in defense, "Sorry, jeeze."

Doyle took the book and slipped it into his vest pocket. He gave a big sigh and said, "Sometimes you have to run before you can walk." He turned to Mackenna. "Let's go."

He left the room, and she stared after him, speaking as she followed. "No, you don't that is the exact opposite of how learning to walk works."

Doyle walked out of the room and allowed her to catch up. He started explaining the trick to her as they walked in a hushed tone so that no one else would be able to hear him. Mackenna didn't quite understand what was happening, and when he broke off to go somewhere else and said, "Stay here." She became conscious of everyone looking at her around the pool. She'd been to the pool and even the beach before, but she felt exposed now, wearing more than a swimsuit covered. She'd always worn swimsuits in her size. She'd never worn something designed to be revealing. She put her hands over her breasts and Doyle came out of the door he'd gone into. He whispered in her ear. "There is a pipe running under the pool that leads inside. Only exclusive guests get access and the maid says no one is in there at the moment. Swim through the pipe and ditch your costume, then put on the second one when you've dried off. I bribed the maid to lock the doors except for that one." He looked at her and she knew he could read the insecurity on her face. "What's wrong?"

She didn't tell him, but he must have guessed. He pulled her hands away, and when she put them back, he did the same, more firmly but not ungently. "Listen, you have to be confident, or this isn't going to work. You have to have so much confidence that if you walked over there completely naked, they would be the ones that felt award and exposed. Can you do that? Or at least fake it?"

Mackenna gave a weak nod. She felt stronger with him there. She gave another, surer, nod and said, "Let's do this."

They walked back over to the pool area and Mckenna saw Doyle put on his showman face. "Ladies and gentlemen, gather round, my name is Doyle, and this is my lovely assistant Mckenna. Today we would like to do a couple of tricks for you."

Mckenna got closer, just like he'd shown her. They did a few basic card tricks, including one where she had the card and used her distractive-ness to move it into the pocket of a boy of about fifteen. His eyes were so glued to her she could have robbed him blind and he wouldn't have noticed. But she'd promised Doyle not to steal from any audience members. When they got through all of the small tricks they'd practiced they moved on to their final bit, the one Doyle had just put together.

"For our last trick I will show you Mckenna's impressive mermaid ability." Without another word he spun around and pushed her into the pool.

The water was colder than expected. It shocked her system more than she had thought it would. She swam around for a long time, having taken the early signal from Doyle and taken a big breath. She saw them looking at her from underwater and she swim toward the tunnel. As a distraction, when she was in the tunnel and away from eyes, she slipped out of her costume.

She swam up and came out of a shallow pond type pool, before it went out into a bigger one. She hurried over, feeling even more exposed but not minding it as much as before. She stepped into a giant, hair dryer type thing and was dry in a few seconds. She slipped on the second costume and hurried to the door. She walked back through the bushes, emerging at the right time with a flourish.

It warmed her heart when the crowd cheered. It appeared that one woman had fainted when her costume came up without her. Someone passed around a bowler hat as a boy of about seventeen walked up to her. "How did you do that?"

"I'm afraid I can't reveal my master's tricks, though the swimming was really just my mermaid side."

"I think we both know that's crap. But I can't figure out how you got to the other end of the parking lot, dry. I never even saw you leave the pool."

"You play dungeons and dragons a lot don't you?"

The boy scoffed. "What does that have to do with anything?"

Mackenna saw Doyle motioning to her to come along. "Nothing." she said and walked away.

She joined Doyle in the parking lot, and he started putting money in his vest. "We made fifty bucks off that show."

"Wow, what are you going to do with the hat?"

He looked down as if just realizing that he had the hat still. He started to throw it away and then put it on his head. It somehow managed to look good when most guys who weren't a thousand-year-old Irishmen looked gay, and not in the homosexual sense of the word, but in the flamboyant annoying sense of the word. "How's it look?"

She reached up and straightened it on his head. "I think you should keep it. It adds a bit to your character."

Doyle looked at his reflection in a car window. "I agree."

They worked a few different places on the way to Vegas. Over the course of a week, they managed to get to know each other very well and to work even better. They still never talked about families and home. It was like they both had silently agreed that their lives began in partnership, and nothing had happened before.

They had made enough money preforming a street show that afternoon, in which Mckenna disappeared out of a box and back into the crowd, appearing as an audience member complaining about the trick, to pay for a few drinks at a local bar.

It was a nice, seedy, little place. It was full of dark wood and smoke and people playing pool, and everyone looked like they had killed at least three people in their life time. Mckenna looked the proper pervert wearing a shoulder to ankle trench coat that was tied shut. She looked like she was about to flash the whole bar at any second.

She got their second or was it their third? round and brought it to a booth on the far side of the bar, where Doyle was scribbling in his notebook. He looked up and said, "Thank you." He took a drink of the whisky as she sat down.

Mckenna was drinking a deep, smoky scotch that she had had only a few times before. It burnt as it went down her throat. She blew air out of her mouth with the burn and said, "Are you an alcoholic?"

He looked up. "No, why are you?"

"No, I just don't understand how you can drink whisky without at least a little bit of a burn noise coming out. My Dad's drank whisky for thirty years and even he does it on occasion."

Doyle picked up his glass and offered it to her. She took a drink. It was hard to describe the taste. It was like an oak board covered in honey. Sharp and strong, with enough of sweetness to make it the best drink she'd ever tasted. "What is this?"

"Tullamore Dew, best whisky Ireland makes. The burn isn't enough to be audible most of the time, and it has a much smoother taste than scotch or bourbon."

"I like it." She downed his glass and said, "I'm going to get more."

She stood up and made for the bar, but she started to falter. Doyle's arm was there in an instant. He pulled her up and said, "Let's call it a night."

"But I wanna try the dew."

"I'll buy you a case after the convention."

She shook her head, conscious of the fact that she went side to side five or six extra times, "No."

Boyle put a ten-dollar bill on a nearby empty table. "Get it without stumbling or falling down and you can have it."

She gave a big nod and took an over exaggerated step and fell down. "I'm finnneee." She started to giggle.

Doyle, who didn't seem all that strong with his more cat like muscles, bent down and hoisted her over his shoulder. He tossed some money on the bar, and they went out into the night. "You have a nice ass." Mckenna said.

In the motel room he flopped her down on the bed. He went to the bathroom and came out after brushing his teeth. "Why are you naked?"

"Cause I wanna get laid!" she said. "Will you lay me?"

Mckenna looked, amazing, naked. "No." He said, though his literal entire body said yes.

"Why? I'm not drunked enough for it to be weird and you have the bad feels. I's just drunked enough for fun."

"Yes, that is true. But we're partners, and this would only complicate things."

The naked Mckenna folded her arms over her boobs, missing the point and lifting them to set on her crossed arms. "You're a dick."

"Yes, and you can't have any." Doyle said suppressing a laugh. He led Mckenna back to her bed and opened the covers. She snuggled down in and was asleep by the time he got the comforter over her. He took one last look at a beautiful naked woman and covered her up. He got into hhis bed and was asleep as soon as his head hit the pillow.

They didn't get on the road until the late afternoon. Doyle was up at his normal time and saw that Mckenna was still passed out asleep, no chance of rousing her, so he took the chance and went back to bed.

She finally stirred at three o'clock and they were out of the parking lot by three thirty. Neither of them said anything for several hundred miles. Finally, just as it was getting dark, Mckenna spoke, "You know I don't think it was called for, what you did last night."

Doyle eyed her from the corner of his eye. "This oughtta be good."

She turned more sideways so that she could look at him. "You carried me out of that bar like a disruptive child."

Doyle chuckled to himself. "Do you have any memory of the proceeding events?"

"No, but I don't see,-"

He cut her off. "You tripped and knocked things over, you were slurring your words. You looked more like a baby deer than you did a person."

"That can't be true."

He cocked his head and looked directly at her. "You also stripped yourself while I was brushing my teeth and asked me to lay you."

Mckenna looked down at her body like it was a foreign entity. "Did you?"

"No, and that angered you very much."

Mckenna rubbed her hand over her face. "I'm sorry. I get weird when I drink."

"You think?"

"Thank you for getting me to bed. If I don't go to sleep, I flitter between violent, horny, and violently horny for the rest of the night. I appreciate it."

"Any time."

"Did you at least get a peak? You deserved something for the trouble."

Doyle was about to answer when Mckenna screamed. He turned his head at the last second and saw the other car.

Doyle woke up in the hospital with a doctor standing over him. He couldn't move his neck and his dry mouth was making speaking very difficult. He watched as the doctor left and he felt something on his hand. He flicked his eyes and saw a giant cast on his right hand. To the other side he saw Mckenna sitting next to the bed. "Water." He choked out.

A second later Mckenna came into better view. She had a black eye and a nasty cut on her forehead. "You've got to be still; you have a severe concussion."

"What about my hand?"

"It went straight into the dashboard. Your ring finger is broken, as well as some tiny bones in your wrist."

"Magic?"

"They said that it will heal eventually, and that you should be able to do magic, it will just take time."

"You?"

"My head hit the dash and I got pretty beat up but all in all I'm fine. I didn't get anything near what you did."

Doyle didn't know what to say. He thought about the competition and how they were definitely not going to be able to do it now. He started to cry, and almost immediately got angry. "This is your fault."

"I know."

"If we hadn't been talking about your stupid drunkenness, we would still be able to make the competition."

Mckenna looked like she was about to cry. "I know, I'm more sorry than you can imagine,,"

Doyle looked as if he was going to say something else hurtful, so Mckenna decided to do what she did best, hurt the other person before they hurt her. "Well, I guess there's nothing more to be said. It was fun messing around with you and doing this stuff. Hope to see you again, maybe in hell."

It was supposed to be her dramatic exit. But she walked back in and said, "I forgot, you're being released. I'll help you out front."

They were both completely silent as she wheeled him through the halls. She helped him stand up and they both stood on the sidewalk outside the hospital. "Be seeing you." Mckenna said and walked one way. Doyle nodded and walked the other, looking for the closest liquor store.

Two weeks later, only a day and a half before the convention and competition, Mckenna was in line for a bus. It had taken her a long time to hustle enough money to get a ticket. An ancient looking Mexican woman got on the bus, and she was just behind her. As she stepped her foot up onto the stair, she was hit with a flash of the memories she had preforming magic and how it made her feel.

She traced her steps back to the hospital and followed the direction Doyle had gone. It took some detective work and asking around, but she finally found where he was staying. It was like real resolve came over her. She wanted to do this and she wanted to win.

Doyle had been fortunate enough that Mckenna had used her money to pay for the hospital, because that left him with enough money to pay for a month in a motel, and enough booze to have him piss drunk the entire time.

He was sitting at the pool, jean legs rolled up to let his feet in the water. He was drinking whisky straight from the bottle and trying to figure out how long it would take him to drown if he jumped in with his clothes on and full of whisky. He saw Mckenna walk in and for a brief second thought he was imagining her. She walked over and said, "I want to win."

He stood up, wabbling back and forth, and said, "What did you have in mind?" He waved his cast for effect

"First thing's first...sobriety." she said and pushed him in.

When he was sober enough to comprehend that she was really there, Mckenna explained her plan to win. All of Doyle's big props and magic acts had been in the wreck. They had to work on what they could do with limited props and no money. They had to avoid eating one day and bought a strait jacket from a Goodwill in town. They never went back because they didn't really want to shop at any store that would sell a strait jacket used.

The day arrived and they headed to the convention center to get registered. As Doyle was signing them in, he saw a friend at the registry table. "Hey Carmen, when did you guys get back in the country?"

"Weeks ago. Everyone is taking a bit of a break for the off season, so Neil and I are working the contest and convention. Ricky's around here somewhere, incase you'll need tricks designed when you win."

"Thanks for the vote of confidence."

She spoke as she handed him their numbers, "Not a vote. I've seen you perform, and I know you'll be great. Even with the hand, though I must admit I'm curious as to how you're going to do that."

"Never reveal the secrets, right?" he said with a smile.

Carmen smiled back. "Never reveal the secrets."

They said their goodbyes, with promises to have dinner or something so they could all catch up. Doyle walked back over to Mckenna and gave her her number. "Okay, so I guess we mingle and stuff. Meet backstage when it's time."

"Yes, sir boss."

Mckenna made her way to a group of girls in trench coats just like hers. It looked like they were having a stripper's conference. "Hi." she said to no one in particular. A girl a few years older than Mckenna with carmel colored skin and a gigantic rack said, "Hi, you new?"

"What do you mean?"

"Well, they have this convention, and the contest attracts a lot of amateurs, you sort look like a professional, but you haven't been here before."

"Damn sherlock." Mckenna said. "Yes, I'm new. My boss just hired me as his assistant." She held out her hand. "Mckenna."

"Nanzi." she said.

"Hello." Mckenna thought for a moment. "You wouldn't happen to have any tips, would you?"

"Your magician send you over here to get secrets?"

"What? No, I meant about being an assistant. I've only done a few roadside performances and I don't really know how to do this on like, a stage. Do they really send assistants to spy on each other?"

"Oh yeah. Some of the bigger guys will actually hire someone to go undercover and be someone else's assistant just to have a double agent in someone else's camp."

"That is intense."

"Yeah, but what do you need help with?"

"Just anything you can give me, like my walk or hand flourishes, whatever."

"Sure, I can show you how to walk for a big stage." Nanzi took her coat off and the completely straight Mckenna was momentarily distracted it by her memorizing hips and an ass that had Mckenna believing that maybe God wasn't completely fair. She showed her how to more her hips and walk right and how to move quickly across a stage, but still make it look like she was moving sexy and slow. She even showed her how to stand to the side looking sexy and mysterious while the magician was doing something with a volunteer and didn't need her.

Doyle and Mckenna were on late in the afternoon. They knew they would have to be extra special for the judges, who'd seen a thousand other acts that day, to even register that they were there.

They took the stage and Doyle clapped loudly. "Hello Ladies and Gentlemen. My name is Doyle and today I will do some card tricks, and one escapement for you." He took out a deck of cards and Mckenna straightened herself and made for the audience as he talked. "I will be in need of a volunteer. As you can see my hand isn't in the best of shapes, to be more accurate it's in three pieces and the shape is more of a U."

The judges laughed. Mckenna reached them and looked around. She walked around, touching each one in turn. Finally, she got to the end, a female judge in a pants suit. "Aw, it seems my wonderful assistant has chosen a volunteer, and the most attractive judge to be sure. Madam, would you be so kind?"

Mckenna removed the card from between her butt cheeks and patted the next judge on the chest. She leaned over to expose a lot of breasts and said, "Maybe next time." She replaced his wallet without him seeing and caught up with the female judge and walked her to the stage. She did the sexy hip walk over to Doyle's other side and watched the rest of the trick.

"Now madam, if you would take a card from the pile."

The judge took a card and Doyle said, "When you're ready, return it."

The judge returned the card to the pile and Doyle turned, throwing the deck of cards at the judges. I am afraid I cannot continue with the trick. This woman's card been stolen." He pointed to the male judge. You sir, allow us to see the contents of your wallet."

The judge opened his wallet and picked up a card. The four of hearts. Doyle turned back to the female judge. "Is that your card?"

The woman gave an astonished nod. "It is."

There was applause from the judges as well as the audience. They did their other tricks, the bit with the straight jacket, and then they left. They went to a little restaurant inside the convention center and bought food that neither of them seemed the least bit interested in eating. "That was amazing." Mckenna said.

"It really was. You did excellent."

"Can I ask you something?"

"Sure."

"What if we don't win?"

"If we don't win, I am still going to do magic. We'll get a car or van or whatever and book whatever we can, do street shows. When I'm old, I'll teach the next generation how to do magic."

"So, you're saying you still want me around, as an assistant?"

"As what we discussed earlier." he said, knowing they couldn't discuss being partners in public.

McKenna smiled. She had found a partner and a purpose. She and Doyle would be just fine.

> NOVELETTES

MRS. KETTLEBACK'S CIRCUS

When three siblings flee their controlling father to join Mrs. Kettleback's circus, they never expected to inherit a vast fortune. But as they revel in newfound freedom, their joy turns to peril when their aunt dispatches ruthless pursuers to claim the inheritance by any means necessary.

PROLOGUE

The story I am about to tell you is strange. It involves four kids, billions of dollars, and a cyclops tiger named Nico. It is a bittersweet story that will delight at times and cause you to streak tears at others.

The story is dear to my heart. It is something that know as fact, though you may see it in another way, or not at all if you aren't reading this, though I think we both know that you are because you just read that last line. I wish you the best of luck in reading this story.

I have spent a great deal of time with it and am now passing it on. Here goes...

CHAPTER ONE

David Bingley had done a bad thing that night, in a legal sense. In a moral sense he was perfectly fine. He had spiked the scotch he made for his father with Benadryl. They were leaving tonight.

Sophia was younger than David by just a year. At sixteen she was more grown up than any kid her age should have to be. While other girls her age were spending that night talking about boys or wondering what color to paint their nails, she was getting the kids ready to go, begging them to be quiet.

When their father had finished half the bottle of scotch he passed out. The man had an Olympian tolerance earned from years of drinking, so it took him half a bottle and what amounted to half a case of Benadryl to pass out. Even still they were careful not to make noise. Both of their hearts fluttered as they got out of the door. But it wasn't over.

They walked down the street holding a kid apiece and as much food and clothing as they could fit into a backpack. David was a strong boy, very athletic, but even so after seven miles his body ached under the weight of the food and his little brother Ryan. He couldn't imagine how Sophie was doing .

Sophia was ready to fall over. Ruthie couldn't have weighted more than thirty pounds, but the clothes on her back added onto her made it hurt a lot. But she had to get away, as far away from her father as she could. Their father had hurt them for a long time. He'd hurt their mom even more. But after David was big enough to hit back that had stopped for a while.

After their mother died and they had to get jobs he had started to hurt them again, and she wasn't about to stay long enough for her father to keep hurting Ruthie. They walked until they were out of town. They saw the old fair grounds coming up and Sophia said, "David I need to stop."

"Yeah," He breathed. "Me too." They walked over to the dirt area where cars would park, though it was empty. The entire place had just been broken down like they were leaving. There were a bunch of trucks and RVs around. David led them over to one and sat Ryan down as he opened the back. They both cringed as the door creaked.

No one came though, David sat Ryan in the truck and climbed up. He took Ruthie as she said, "Shhh, it's okay stay quiet." When they were inside, he reached down to help Sophia up. They closed the door and ventured a little into the truck. They had a flashlight with them, and they saw that there were costumes all around, even a few makeup tables, like this was where everyone got ready.

Sophia expressed her worry about being found and David assured her that they would not be, they would get up before the truck pulled away and be on their way with a decent night's sleep. They found boxes of material and sat each of the twins in one, they then sat on the cushions they found and rested their heads. Within seconds all of the Bingley children were asleep.

CHAPTER TWO

"Marco, get Neil and Mrs. Kettleback." Came a feminine voice, Sophia opened her eyes and saw a girl who looked to be about twenty. She jerked up into a sitting position and looked around for Ruthie and Ryan. They were where they had been left, awake and looking at the girl. Sophia kicked David awake and he jumped like someone had shocked him. They all stared at each other.

Just as David was about to speak in defense of himself and his siblings a short, squat woman in a skirt and sweater walked up a ramp and into the trailer. "Who're you?" she asked sternly. "Come on, out with it."

Looking back years later, Sophia had no idea why David told the truth, but she would forever be glad he did. "My name is David Bingley and I, along with my sister, stowed away from our abusive father before he started hurting them like he did us. We walked seven miles with them, food, and all the clothes we could carry. We slept here because we were ready to fall over."

The woman, who had wrinkles on her face that spoke of years of experience and wear, gave a curt nod and spoke as she turned around, "Well then come and get some food."

They followed her out and saw a bunch of people standing around. There was a large man in a kilt with a beard, and an Armenian looking man with gray hair and a close-cropped beard standing next to a woman who they assumed was his wife. There were a handful of people who looked to be around their age. Farther off some kids were playing.

A man stepped up. He was tall and lanky with blonde hair that was cropped close. He had a calm demeanor, but powerful. Like he didn't need to show off, he just owned the room. "Mary? What's happened?"

"I'm taking these kids to get some food, is the stew ready?"

"Yes."

He turned on his heals and started to lead them to where four RVs were set up in a semi-circle, with a camp in between them and a large cast iron pot over a fire. The smells coming from it made them realize how hungry they were.

Bridget, the girl who had found them, bent down and whispered in David's ear. "That's Neil, he's the ringmaster and magician, He is the only one who calls her Mary. Everybody else calls her Mrs. Kettleback."

David didn't know what to say so he just nodded. They were led over and given spots around the fire and bowls of stew. After scarfing down a bowl David asked, "Where are we exactly?"

"North Dakota, about halfway between Fargo and Bismarck." she said. "But we have more pressing matters to discuss."

"What are those?" Sophia asked.

"Well, I don't cotton to free loaders, -"

"Be nice Mary." Neil warned.

"Oh hush." She turned back to Sophia and David. "I don't cotton to freeloaders, so if you want someone can drive you to Bismarck and drop you off, but if you want jobs in my circus then you're welcome to them."

David and Sophia were close. They were as close as any two people who go through trauma are like to be. So, they only had to exchange a look when they heard this to both know what the next two things to be said were. Sophia was first. "Why would you do that? You met us five minutes ago."

Mrs. Kettleback smiled. "My Dad was shite as his job. My mother wasn't much either. Those of us who're emotional orphans have to stick together."

Then it was David's turn. "What would having a job in the cirrus entail?"'

Mrs. Kettleback looked impressed, and she was. She had been working and traveling for decades and she hated how unintelligent young people seemed at every new location. When she found young people who were smart enough to ask the right questions, it made her smile. "Well, you'd find somewhere that made you happy and you'd learn to work that job. You'd also help set up and break down. Everyone here does the job of a crew."

The Bingleys looked at each other again, and then back at Mrs. Kettleback. "We'd love to join the cirrus." They said in unison.

"Wonderful." she said. "Stand up and let me have a look at ya" She pointed to Sophia, and she stood, twirling as prompted.

Mrs. Kettleback ordered her to sit down and she turned to one of the RVs, "Jazz!"

A girl of about fifteen popped her head out of the window of the RV. "Yes ma'am?"

"Is the trapeze set up yet?"

"Yes ma'am, we set it up when we got in last night so that we had time to rehearse, I was just headed there now."

"Take, what is your name?"

"Sophia."

"Take Sophia and see how she likes it."

A smile spread across Jazz's face. "Yes ma'am." she said, disappearing through the window and popping out of the door a second later in baggy pants and a jacket.

Jazz was tall and lean. She reminded Sophia of a cat, all lean muscle that could pounce at any moment. She took Sophia by the hand and led her towards the large tent that she hadn't noticed until that moment.

Mrs. Kettleback told David to stand. He spun for her, and she told him to sit down. She thought for a moment. Finally, she said," You know, I'm not one hundred percent sure so I'm going to have you float a bit...but let's start you out with Bridget."

The cute blonde girl that had found them stepped forward and put a strand of her short hair behind her ear. "I'll get my gear and meet you back here." She walked towards the same RV that Jazz had come out of.

David looked at Mrs. Kettleback. "What about my siblings?"

She smiled at the two toddlers with stew on their faces. "I shall guard them with my life."

David believed her. He shouldn't have trusted her...but he did. He knew that if anyone came around looking for them, this woman would die, or kill, to protect the twins.

CHAPTER THREE

Jazz talked the entire way to the tent. She told her all about the circus and their family and her parents being third generation acrobats and how she and her brother were following them into the business and had been doing things for years and years already. She told her all about the circus and suggested that they be friends.

Something to know about Sophia Bingley. She had never had a friend. In all her sixteen years no one had ever tried to be her friend. She was a shy girl who was not out going in the slightest. So, she was very uncomfortable around Jazz. But sometimes in life what a person needs the most is exactly what makes them uncomfortable.

The tent was enormous, it seemed to not have an end. But what seemed even more daunting was the trapeze. Jazz led her over to a ladder that was ten or a hundred times the size of the high dive she had jumped off as a kid. Sophia had never been afraid of heights before, but even still she had a catch in her throat.

Jazz must have seen her apprehension. "Do you like girls?"

"Excuse me?"

"Do you like girls...you know, like attraction?"

Sophia could feel her face getting red. "Honestly I've never thought about it...I don't think so."

"Oh, I was just going to suggest you look at my butt while we climb. My Mom said that was how she got my dad to do it the first time. She was the trapeze, and my dad was an acrobat, so when he did his first run up there, she had him stare at her butt until they were at the top, that way he didn't think about how high it was." She turned around and started to climb. She got down and said, "Why don't you go first. I'll catch you if you fall."

Sophia nodded and put her hand on the cold rung of the ladder. She climbed, focusing on putting one hand after the other until she pulled herself up to the top.

When they were both at the top Jazz unclipped a bar that was hooked to two wires. A looked of realization dawned on her face. "I forgot a harness...oh well, you don't need it." She grabbed the bar and swung out into the air and was soon upside down, looking at Sophia. "You shouldn't try this at first, but it's really fun."

She swung back in and said, "This is uncomfortable." She took off her sweats and jacket to reveal a leotard that had bright orange and pink flames on it. "That's better." She offered the bar to Sophia.

"What if I fall?" she asked, looking over the edge.

"There is a net to catch you."

Sophia looked back at her. "I'm afraid. It looks like a lot of fun, but I don't know if I can do it."

"Look, I know we're not friends yet, but do you trust me enough to help you?"

"Okay..." Sophia said hesitantly. And with that Jazz pushed her with both hands off the platform.

Sophia felt the wind rush out of her and she fell through the air like an asteroid hurtling towards earth.

Just when she thought she was going to hit the ground, she landed on a cushion of net and bounced a little before finally landing safely, an enormous smile plastered on her face. She laid there for a moment laughing before Jazz cupped her hands around her mouth and shouted, "How did that feel?"

"Amazing!" Sophia called out.

Sophia watched as Jazz swung out with the bar and did a flip in midair before gracefully falling and landing on the other side of the net. She stood up and walked over to the other side and offered Sophia a hand.

"Sorry about that. It was how my mom taught me to not be afraid and I thought it would work for you."

Sophia was still smiling. "Mission accomplished." She said taking the hand and getting up. Jazz showed her how to get out of the net and they started their climb back to the top.

While she was having a bunch of fun, David was outside the tent. Behind it to be more precise. Bridget had set up a small wooden stand with several targets, facing the direction of the woods where no one would be harmed by her bullets, though she was more worried about David's. Bridget was a master with a gun. She? had spent most of her life trying to live up to the likes of her hero, Annie Oakley. She could cut a hang man's rope, shoot while looking through a mirror, or do the famous cigarette trick.

She twirled her pistol and handed it butt first to David. "Have you ever held a gun before?" David shook his head. His mother had gotten rid of all the guns in the house under the pretense of paying for his father's liquor, the good stuff. But really, she hadn't wanted him to have access to a firearm during one of his benders.

"Okay," Bridget said moving closer to him, aiming for him. He liked the smell of her as she guided his hand, like pine and the same oil he smelled on the gun. "Close your left eye and run your right down the barrel, when you have your target picked make sure that your sight is just a bit under it and squeeze the trigger."

She let him go and he took aim. The gun was an old-fashioned revolver, like David had seen in the westerns his father liked. He thought you were supposed to hold a gun with two hands but since she had only used one, he decided maybe that was what he was supposed to do with this kind of gun.

When he had picked a target, an old brown whiskey bottle, he pulled the trigger. The bullet hit just below the bottle, sinking into the wood. David was disheartened but Bridget assured him that time would make him better. "How good are you?" he asked, prompting a smile from her.

"Take that bottle there and stack two more on top of it." David did as instructed and Bridget unwrapped the bandana she had on her wrist. She ordered him to step back aways and he did. Bridget wrapped the bandana around her eyes and walked quite aways away. David was confused, but he held his tongue and watched as Bridget fired a shot.

The middle bottle shattered in a way that made the other two stay where they were, only the top bottle replacing the broken one. Next, she fired another shot, murdering the bottom bottle so that the top one was the only one left. She walked closer to him and maintained eye contact as she fired over and hit the last bottle, never once looking anywhere near it. "I'm that good."

David clapped. His jaw dropped and he was speechless in awe.

I should now tell you about Lilly. She was a vile woman, average height and with pleasing facial features for a woman of nearly fifty. She would have had a nice life with a husband who loved her, were that possible. You see, Lilly of the Valley as her Father used to call her, was a pretty girl who's pleasurable features had for all her life been mitigated by the fact that she was loud, rude, and constantly jealous if anyone but her had the attention or was even remotely happy.

At the same moment the Bingley children were having a wonderful day with their new jobs, Lilly was waiting for her father's will to be read. The man who would be reading the will was small, frail, and had been her father's lawyer since they were young. He straightened his tie, sat down, straightened it again, and cleared his throat.

"Now to read the Will of Charley Aberworth." He scanned the typewritten page as Lilly waited impatiently, tapping her foot. "The entirety of Mr. Aberworth's estate will be granted to the children of his youngest daughter Martha, should she have any."

Lilly's eyes filled with rage. "What?"

CHAPTER FOUR

Over the course of several days Sophia and David started to let themselves hope that they had found a home with the circus. They got to know everyone. Bear, the giant Scotsman who was worthy of his name. He had a knife throwing act. They met the tiger act, Leo and his wife/assistant Beth. They met the head clown and his twin daughters, also clowns, Brittney and Taylor. Sophia found Kenneth, the juggler and unicyclist and worker, very cute, and he looked to be about her age.

One night Sophia noticed a man walking by who she had seen around but to whom she had never spoken. He wore a barrette and had a sad look about him. She watched him from a little ways away as he started to care for the animals. He was an older guy, fifty at least by her reckoning. He seemed more comfortable here than with the humans. "You know, if you're going to stand there you could at least help."

That shocked Sophia awake and she strolled over to him. He handed her a bucket of what looked like mashed up branches and bark. "Cash hasn't got the best teeth so we feed him his food partially broken up."

Sophia nodded. While she walked over to the elephants, two of them, she remembered reading a book about circuses and how they made their animals obey. "Can I ask you a question sir?"

"I work for a living. My name's Jacque." he said. "But sure."

"Do you hurt the animals to make them listen? I've read that some circuses have and do that sort of thing."

Jacque looked at her like she had just smacked him in the face. "I would never. Look at that beast." He pointed to an elephant. "That beast is smarter than you and I combined. It doesn't need to be hurt, only taught. The only reason to ever hurt ah animal is when their trainer is too stupid to do anything correctly. And even then, it's not an excuse to hurt the animal." He grunted at the thought.

"I'm very glad to hear that." Sophia said walking over to the tigers. She pointed to one that seemed to have only one eye and started to speak, but Jacque was already explaining. "That's Nico. He had a bad eye, but he was so sweet and smart that we decided to save him."

"Where do you get all these animals?"

"Save 'em," he said. "Nico, we found when the government cracked down on an animal smuggling ring. That's actually how we got him and his sister Nicky. The third one, Louise, we rescued her from a farm half starved to death."

"Wouldn't it be better to return them to the wild?"

He shook his head. "That would be a death sentence. None of them were raised in the wild and they didn't have mothers to teach them. If we took them out into the wild, they wouldn't last more than a few days before something got them."

Sophia looked at them, the animals, and thought that she knew how they felt. They hadn't been able to have a normal life and they were here, being given a second chance.

David was by the fire that everyone ate near. Neil sat next to him on a large log and David looked at him, nervous. Neil was kinda big around here. Being the ring master as well as a friend of the owner gave him considerable influence. "You can ask me whatever you want." Neil said in a surprisingly friendly tone. "I don't bite and you're part of the team now."

"Well," David asked hesitantly. "I was just going to ask how you came to work with the circus"

Neil had a sad look in his eyes as he set his bowl on the ground. "I've wanted to be a magician since I was three." he said. "I tried to make it in Vegas, but it didn't go well. I met Logan, my husband, and he brought me here. I've been here ever since, even after Logan was gone."

It took David a moment to realize that he'd lost his husband. "I'm sorry."

Neil had a forlorn look in his eyes, and he spoke softly. "Me too, he was a great man who died doing what he loved."

"What did he love?"

"Climbing. He loved to climb mountains and he would always climb whatever was nearby. One day it didn't go as planned."

Before he could say anything else a beautiful woman who looked to be about twenty-five walked over to them. She had cannel colored skin and large, perfect breasts. Her name was

Carmen, and she was Neil's assistant. "I can't get the cabinet to lock." she said.

"I'll get it. I rebuilt it this morning so it would be easier to get out of, but that made it trickier to get into."

Neil walked away and Carmen started to follow, but David touched her hand. "Can I ask you a question?"

"Sure."

"Well, I've watched your guys' act a couple of times now in rehearsal, but I can't figure out what you do. Especially in the parts where he says an audience member will be part of the trick."

Carmen laughed. "I'm the distraction. I help get things ready and I contort and stuff, but mainly people look at these," She motioned to her breasts. "While the actual magic is happening."

"Wow. That's smart."

She laughed. "Tomorrow, I'll show you some of the even smarter parts of the act."

The set up for sleeping arrangements was nice. Those who drove the big trucks had cabins in the backs and they slept there. Neil, Mrs. Kettleback, and Carmen had one RV, Adults, their spouses and younger kids lived in the other two, and the last was for the teens and younger adults.

There wasn't an inch of unused space. When not traveling the seats in the front were swiveled to allow someone to sleep there. The back bed was shared by Brittney and Taylor. In the hall to the back there were crew bunks where most everyone else slept. David was given a bunk on the bottom, opposite Sophia's top bunk. Jazz was across from her and when the curtain was open, she could see that Jazz's bunk was personalized with photos and a small bookshelf packed with paperback novels.

The kitchenette and dining table were always being used by someone whether fer a midnight snack or to do homework. Someone had bolted a bookshelf where there was extra space and it was packed with novels and books of all kinds that the Bingleys were given to read whenever they wanted, saying that it was a house library.

Ruthie and Ryan shared the bunk just under Sophia so that they were close enough to get to if they needed. Thankfully they were young enough that they didn't really understand what had happened, only now they lived with the circus and that seemed to be all they needed to know.

Early Saturday morning, or maybe Friday night they couldn't tell it was so dark, David and Sophia were woken by Jazz and her brother Mark. "Mrs. Kettleback wants you in the show." they said.

"Is the show early?" Sophia asked.

"No silly," Jazz laughed. "The matinee is in six hours and we have a lot of work to do before then."

Mary, Bear's wife, was a pretty woman with blonde hair that stopped at her chin. She could have been Bridget sister if Bridget hadn't denied it. She was sitting at the dining room table with a book and said to them as they passed, "I'll take good care of the kids."

They thanked her and they were led out of the RV, which Jazz told them was named Dorne. They were led in opposite directions, Sophia to the costume truck and David to Bridget. "Why is it called Dorne?" she asked as they walked up the ramp.

"Cause it's where the weirdest people in Westeros are from."

"Huh?"

"I'll lend you the books. But for now, you need a costume."

Jazz had spent all her life in the circus. She had been walking a tightrope when she was eight, trapezing at eleven, she knew her way around. But the talent that she had which was more of a god given, and not a learned ability, was finding the right costume for the right person.

Jazz moved with awe inspiring speed as she went from rack to rack, pile to pile, searching. Occasionally she would hold something up towards Sophia and then throw it down. The other performers came in and got ready.

Marko slipped into his costume and then put a track suit over it to keep warm. The dancers and miscellaneous assistants, Lana, Tiffany, and Olivia, came in with sweats and tank tops on and started to gather quick change outfits for later use in the show.

Finally, after about a half an hour, Jazz brought forth a blue leotard with silver lightning bolts on it. "This is perfect," she said. As they were getting Sophia into the costume and Jazz sprayed hairspray on her bum she asked, "Are you sure I'm ready? I've only trained for a few days."

"You're gonna do great." Jazz said standing up. "Marko and I do most of the hard stuff, we're mostly going to flip you between us and then drop you when it's time."

Sophia's eyes went wide. "Really?"

"Yeah, you've gotten really good at flips, you're gonna do great...oh and by the way, the lights are going to make it look like there isn't a net, but there is. I promise it will catch you."

Sophia nodded, but she wasn't so sure.

David was given an old west style costume and it would be his job to stand there while Bridget shot things off his head. He stood there, in the field, while she aimed, trying not to pee himself. He was trying his best not to move because he knew any movement whatsoever would get him killed. He heard the bullet leave the gun and less than a heartbeat later sugar glass was falling down around him. The crack seemed to echo in his ears. "Great job!" Bridget called out.

Their first show was at noon. The crowd packed in as they all took their places. Neil was wearing a red Victorian style coat, though he wasn't the only one. There was a man in the crowd who seemed to be wearing an older, more worn version of what Neil was, though his seemed not to be a costume, simply what he wore on a daily basis.

Neil owned the room. He walked around, talking to everyone and no one in particular as he announced, "Ladies and Gentlemen, boys and girls, for your entertainment this afternoon I present, the most dangerous Scotsman you've ever seen, the Mighty Highland Bear."

Bear and one of the dancers, it looked like Lana, started his knife throwing. Sophia was high up, but even so she still winced every time he threw a knife and it almost hit Lana. He threw one so far in the air that it felt like it would hit the platform they were standing on.

Soon enough it was their turn. Jazz got on the bar as she was introduced and sat upside down. "And our newest performer, the lightning bolt."

Sophia grabbed Jazz's hands as she swung in and she let her feet off the platform, once again happy that she had peed before the show. She was in a crouch just like she had been taught and she looked up at Jazz as the other girl spoke, "Are you ready?"

Sophia gave a weak nod. Jazz swung back and let go. Sophia tucked her body, scrunched her abs and did a flip, looking for Marko's hand as she came out of it. Her heart flew from her chest as she started to fall, only to be caught at the last second by Marko.

Sophia was so focused on staying in the air as the siblings played ball with her seventy feet up, that she didn't hear Neil tell everyone that she had never done this before. Nor did she take notice of her awe inspired big brother who was standing at the bottom behind a curtain, watching her with both worry and amazement.

When it was time Neil announced that she would do a straight dive to the net. The crowd gasped and she was passed to Jazz another time. "There is a net.

She swung Sophia back out and she did another flip in the air, coming around and falling headfirst towards what appeared to be nothing. She trusted that the net would be there, not that she had much of an option at this point.

She was beyond help even if there wasn't a net. At the last second, she threw herself backwards and landed on her butt in the safety of the net. She heard the crowd cheer, and she was giddy Smiling she rolled over to the edge and flipped out of the net. Not long after the other two followed. Jazz was all smiled as she rushed over to Sophia, "You did great. I told you you would be good at this!" Sophia smiled and they went to wipe the face paint they had on off before they were needed somewhere if else as different performers.

The Bingleys would look back on that first performance in later years as one of the defining moments of their lives. It was the moment, at the end, when they all did a circle through the tent as the crowd cheered, that they knew for the first time in their lives that they were right where they belonged.

Unfortunately for them a private detective named Raymond Figgis was in the audience. He was a brutish man who valued money over the lives of his fellow people. No doubt you yourself have met someone like this at certain points. Those who value money more than anything are always the worst, because their pursuit of material gain makes them smarter than they have any right to be, and more powerful than is safe.

After the show, when the grounds had cleared, all of the performers were finishing lunch when Figgis walked back to where the RVs were parked. Mrs. Kettleback stood up saying, "I'm sorry sir, this area is not for the public."

"I understand mam but see, I'm not the public. I am looking for four children, the Bingleys. You see ,they ran away and they have a lawyer looking for them."

"Why is that?" Neil asked.

"They are the sole heirs to their grandfather, Charles Aberworth."

Several eyes went wide around the camp. "The billionaire?" Someone asked.

"That'd be the one."

"Well," Mrs. Kettleback said, "Sorry to say that the kids aren't here anymore. Bridget drove them to Bismarck days ago and dropped them off."

Being the bright children that they were, David and Sophia realized that this was a code, because without the detective seeing, Bridget drew and cocked her pistol behind her back.

"Well, it strikes me as weird," The detective said, "That they came through here, and now you have new performers."

"Mr. I don't much care what strikes you as weird. I would like you to leave."

The detective drew a gun and a second later it was somewhere in the grass, shot out of his hand by Bridget. She cocked another round in the chamber and said, "She asked you to leave."

Raymond put his hands up and started to back away. "This isn't over." He turned around and ran away from the camp.

Something flew from his pocket, but he kept going. Mrs. Kettleback walked over and retrieved what he had dropped. She took a small flip phone out of her cardigan and dialed the number on the business card. She stayed over where she was out of ear shot to the rest of them. Sophia watched intently, trying to figure out what was going on.

Finally, she walked back over and ordered all the kids to be taken away. Mary led them off, knowing that Bear would fill her in later. When the young ones were gone Mrs. Kettleback said, "Turns out he was hired by the lawyer, but when I told him about the guy pulling a gun, he said he suspects that the man is working for your aunt."

"We have an aunt?" The Bingleys said in unison.

"Apparently. See, when David turns eighteen you all will have access to billions of dollars from the estate of your grandfather. The lawyer says that he and your mother were estranged for some reason II years and years ago. but he left it all to the four of you to make up for not being in your lives." She took a deep breath and continued.

"Your aunt is going to try and have you killed. So, we need to keep you all safe until David turns eighteen."

She looked at David. "When is your birthday?"

"November fourteenth."

"So just over six months then."

Everyone was silent for a while, thinking. The circus was a close family and they had already, in just a few days, adopted them and every one of them wanted to keep their friends safe. At last, someone spoke, "What about fake names and masks or paint?"

Everyone looked at Tiffany. "What do you mean?" Neill asked.

"Well Sophia wore face paint and makeup and went by a fake name...what if they just do it that whenever we're around the public? Make sure we all know their fake stories so that no one slips up."

There was more silence before Neil looked at Mrs. Kettleback and said, "I like it."

She gave a curt, approving nod. "Me too."

CHAPTER FIVE

I t was the last performance of North Dakota. They hadn't had any sign of the detective since that first time, but that didn't mean he didn't have other people around watching them. Sophia was going by the name Carol, or thunderbolt during the act. She wore the same silver paint with a blue bolt but changed her face paint into different patterns for different acts to match whatever costume she wore for that particular act.

David was going by the name Elliot, and he had since begun helping both Bear and Neil, learning all he could about magic and sleight of hand, as well as throwing knives and how to care for them. He wore a wig and was starting to grow a beard and mustache, so he began to look older and different.

No one would know what the twins looked like because their dad had gotten rid of all the pictures of them, what few there were. But there were still plenty of David and Sophia, so they had to hide. They were on alert at all times. Preforming was the only time they had anything else to worry about. That night

David got to throw his first knife in the show, actually managing to hit the target, and Sophia flew through the air, getting better and better every time.

Unfortunately for them, when they were tired and sore from preforming, they were told that they needed to start breaking down the circus. Sophia helped Jacque get the elephants in the truck, where they had a wonderful space to sleep. As Leo was bringing the tigers into the truck Nico stopped, looking at her. She wasn't sure if she should move so she just stood there. Nico pawed the air in front of her and Leo said, "Put your hand up."

She put her hand up and Nico gave her a high five, eliciting giggles from her. "He likes you." Jacque said.

Outside everyone was breaking camp. It took everyone to get the tent down. The middle pole came down and was brought into the truck while everyone took the stakes out. They all had their directions to walk and fold and after a half an hour it was finally in a small enough shape that they could carry it to the costume truck, which held a little bit of everything really.

It was one thirty in the morning when they were finally finished. Everyone climbed into the trucks and RVs. When they climbed aboard Dorn everyone, but Jazz started towards their beds. Marko brought out his bed from the couch. Jazz walked over and got a travel mug down that was big enough for the rest of the coffee in the pot.

She walked over and stepped down into the cockpit.

"Are we leaving already?" David asked.

"Yep." She yawned. "And I have first shift driving."

David gave her a thumbs up and walked back to put the twins to bed. Sophia walked down into the cockpit and asked, "Mind if I sit with you?"

"Sure, do you know how to drive?"

"No, do you have a license?"

Jazz shook her head. "No, but don't tell anyone. You can keep me company until Taylor's shift."

Sophia nestled into the large cushiony seat, and they pulled out of the fair ground after the adult's RV in front of them. A while later they were cruising down the highway. They talked about a lot of stuff, but Jazz didn't pry. That was what made Sophia think she could be friends with Jazz. When she said she didn't want to talk about her family all Jazz said was, "Okay."

"So how am I doing, honestly?"

"At trapeze?"

"At all of this in general." she said motioning around them.

"For the fact that it's not even been two weeks I think you're doing great."

"Really?"

"Honestly I think you're a natural, and so does my mom. And she's been doing this for decades. She didn't stop preforming until her body quit on her a few years ago."

"So, what does she do now? I haven't seen her in any of the shows."

"She and My Dad are in charge of the dancers and acrobats and all that. They choreograph our parts in the show."

"Um...," Sophia said, trying to think of something to talk about. She didn't have any experience so she thought she should just go with the classics. "What about boys? There don't seem to be many around. I count one that you aren't related too."

"Yeah, but he's still like a brother." Jazz said. "I don't really date. I mostly just work. Once in a while when I meet someone exceptionally cute I'll have a quick day date and make out with them a bit. But that's it."

"No sex?"

Jazz shook her head. "I would never risk getting pregnant and being unable to perform for that long. Not to mention the fact that I'm far too young to have a kid."

Sophia's face showed that she was impressed by this attitude. She had gotten more than her desired share of bad TV while waiting for her father to come home from a bender, worrying about what would happen if she wasn't awake to meet him and take a beating, and all that TV had kids on it who wanted nothing more than sex, but then were completely unfit to deal with the consequences. (This is in fact a public announcement against Teen sex. She and Jazz made me put it in here as a condition of using their conversation. It's completely true though.)

It was around four thirty when they stopped for gas. It is always a strange feeling, being at a truck stop in the hours when night is ending but day has not yet begun. There are only a few people there, travelers, vagrants, and the workers who desperately want to be somewhere else. Jazz sent Sophia inside for some drinks and to book them a couple of showers while she got Taylor up. She got the stuff and met Jaz, who had gotten their Pajamas, at the showers. They put their clothes behind a divider and started to shower. Sophia was hesitant at first, but Jazz told her, Taylor will leave us, so I'd hurry."

They showered, changed into pajamas, and ran bach to the w with their drinks and bundied up dirty clothes just as Taylor was pulling away with the rest of the convoy. Sophia didn't think she would be able to sleep after the shower woke her up, but as soon as her head hit the Pillow she was out.

CHAPTER SIX

A circus does not travel the same as a normal convoy. There are many people, all of whom have to go to the bathroom at different times, and it is never a good idea to go number two in an RV. There are also animals that must be tended to. There are any number of reasons why it took twenty-seven hours to get to Arizona for their next set of shows, but none of them are very important.

As any of you who have been to Arizona or lived there for any amount of time know, there is not really more than one season in Arizona. It is more like there are two modes, hot and cold. When the sun is up, it is hot. The tent was up, and everyone tried to find a reason to do their work under its shade. However, when Jacque came in saying that the elephants needed a lot of water to stay cool, it became the job of everyone who wasn't an adult to carry large buckets of water over to where the pens were.

David was surprised at how strong Bridget was. But even more so at the dancers, Lana, Tiffany, and Olivia were all carrying two buckets for every one of the rest of them. While they were filling up David asked Bridget, "How are they so strong?"

"What'd you expect? They spend all day holding their bodies up by a finger or a toe." They both laughed and started to carry their buckets to the inflatable pool that Jacque had set up so the elephants could spray water on themselves.

They were all in the costume truck when the cop showed up. There was a guy behind him, long and skinny. He looked more like a basketball player who had let himself go than a private detective who had called local authorities for help.

The officer on the other hand, he was the real deal. He was over six feet tall with a buzz cut, thick boots that looked like they could break concrete, and so much muscle that he didn't probably need the forty-five on his hip in most situations. "I'm looking for the new performers." he said.

Luckily Sophia had her face paint on and David his wig. "That would be me." she said. "How can I help you?"

"When did you join the circus?"

"In the last town."

"And what is your name?"

"Carol, sir."

He looked around at everyone in the truck. "Have any of you seen two older teens with two twin three-year-olds? This gentleman is looking for them for his boss. Apparently, they have inherited billions from their grandfather or something."

"Sorry officer, we haven't seen them since the last town. They asked for jobs but we'd already filled the position with Carol and Elliot. Bridget drove them into Bismarck, and they went on their way."

"And no one thought it weird that they were just walking around? Didn't anyone ask any questions?"

Taylor stepped forward. She was tall, gorgeous, and muscular from all the dancing. She put a strand of brown hair behind her ear and asked, "Officer, have you ever been stabbed?"

"No."

"Have Mrs. Kettleback tell you about the time she was stabbed and then you will know why circus folk don't ask questions."

The officer seemed to understand that. He looked at the lot of them and said, "Thank you. I will alert Bismarck PD and let you get back to your work."

As they were leaving the detective gave them all a sneer and followed the policeman out of the truck. Lana went to the edge of the truck and watched them drive away. She gave the all-clear and everyone breathed a sigh of relief. "We're going to have a problem." Taylor said.

"What do you mean?" David asked.

"That guy is going to come back, and I would bet money that he'll have people in Houston."

"I don't understand."

Jazz finished Sophia's makeup and started to fill him in. "Houston is the biggest venue we do. It makes us like, most of our money...only it is a joint thing with a carnival that Mrs. Kettleback doesn't control. Usually, it is a lot of fun, but it's also a perfect place to cause a problem and go unnoticed by most of the people."

Sophia was filled with worry, as was David. They started to hyperventilate silently, hoping no one would notice. They felt hands on their shoulders, and both looked up to see Bridget. "I promise," she said. "I've got a bullet for each and every one of them sons of bitches that try to take them kid."

They smiled at her and in unison said, "Thank you."

Mrs. Kettleback walked up the ramp and looked around. "I need some of you to go shopping," There were cheers and volunteers before she said, "but only for supplies."

A half an hour later one of the RVs was pulling out of the fairgrounds with Taylor, Jazz, Kenneth, and Olivia on board. David checked on Ruthie and Ryan, who were playing with Jake and Janie, two of Leo and Beth's kids. When he saw that Mary was looking after them, he went and found Bridget by the fire with some weird looking equipment. "What are you doing?"

"Making bullets, wanna help?"

David shrugged. "Sure."

She showed him how to fill a casing with powder and put in the primer while she molded the projectile from hot lead that she heated in the fire and put into ani iron mold. "So how did you get into trick shooting?" David asked. "Did you learn it from your dad?"

"I read a book about Annie Oakley when I was a kid and I thought she was so cool, and I wanted to be just like her. My Dad knew how to shoot, and he got me into guns, but I mostly learned the tricks on my own."

"Wow...so why an old west revolver?"

"I'm actually related to a bounty hunter from the eighteen hundreds." She took her gun out of the holster and handed it to him, butt first. He saw that it had a brown handle with several letters carved into it, worn from age. "That was her husband's gun, then hers, then her daughter and on through the generations until it came to me."

"That is amazing. " David said. "Is that why you have to make your own bullets?"

She nodded. "Modern ammunition isn't good for it."

They didn't have a lot to do that afternoon, so they made bullets until they were out of supplies. Then they sent word to the others to pick up some more while they were out.

It would probably do to tell you how the twins were doing at that moment. The Bingley kids had never been like other kids, and as such they comprehended things that you and I didn't until we were much older. Like David and Sophia, both twins were reading by age two, and by age five would understand big words like fiduciary. (I'm still not entirely sure what that one means.)

The twins knew why they didn't see much of their siblings during the day. They knew that they had taken them away from their evil father and a life of getting beaten, or worse, every day. So, they were trying to make the best of what was happening. They had a semi large play area that was set up in front of one of the RVs that Mary would sit in with them. When the other kids weren't working on snacks or selling them during shows then they would play with the twins while Mary read nearby.

Mostly the twins came up with games that they played together. They, since learning to speak, had started to develop a language that was all their own, as so many sets of twins do. And many afternoons while the others were practicing being in the circus, they would sit or lay in the grass and work on new words for their language.

That night, after everyone had come back from town and dinner had been eaten, they all retired to their homes. The twins were in bed, as were the dancers, while the rest of them were either reading or watching a movie.

There were sudden screams from the bunks and Sophia was there in an instant. Ruthie was tossing and turning and yelling. She put her hand on her and Ruthie looked at her, crying. Those of you who have ever had someone who comforted you when if you were sad, or had a nightmare, or just needed holding, know how it feels to melt into someone when you feel like you can no longer stand or breath on your own. Like you are finally safe and sound. For those of you who don't know what that feels like, I am truly sorry, and I recommend finding someone who makes you feel safe.

Ruthie melted into Sophia's chest, crying and telling her of the dread she'd had. "It's okay," Sophia whispered. "He isn't here. He's gone and you never have to see him again."

The others, who had been watching from the doorway, slowly backed up and went back to where they had been. David felt a pang in his heart that she had a nightmare. The others were in a bit of a daze and silently thanked every god they could think of that they had grown up with good parents. They made mental notes to thank their parents and apologize for every fight they'd ever had.

Sophia held her sister close until she got back to sleep, and even for a while after that. When she was sure that Ruthie wouldn't wake up, she started to cry. She had been hoping her sister would repress these memories.

CHAPTER SEVEN

David watched Sophia dive down through the air and sighed as he fumbled the magic trick for the seventh time. Neil smiled at him, "What's on your mind?"

"I don't think I'm cut out for magic."

"Yeah, me neither."

David's shock showed on his face and Neil said, "What? Would you rather I lied to you, and you spend a bunch of time on something that you are not good and don't enjoy? I would prefer you find something that you like and might be better at."

David sighed again. "Me too. But I don't think I have a thing. I mean, Carol is great at the trapeze and stuff, but I've not got anything I'm even good at. I throw knives worse than I shoot, and I am very bad at shooting."

Neil looked contemplative. He sat down on a box and put his chin on his fist. Finally, he said, "Have you thought about not preforming?"

"What?"

"Maybe your mind is for business and things. Mary hasn't performed in years and years and yet she is the most important part of the circus. Who do you think books the venues and makes sure that we get paid? Shops for deal on feed so that we can keep the animals in good health and maybe save a bit of money, travel expenses, etc. We might be what they come to see, but Mrs. Kettleback is how we get here and why they come to see us."

David sat there wondering while Neil got up to continue his rehearsal. He had thought about preforming the entire time they had been here. He had been silently wondering when he would find what his thing was...maybe this was it? He needed to find Bridget and see what she thought.

David rushed out of the tent as Leo was bringing in the tigers. Jazz stopped and looked down at them. She flipped up to look at Sophia who was sitting on the platform.

"Wanna watch?"

"Sure." she said and Jazz swung towards her. Sophia swung outwards and Jazz caught her hands They both let go and fell, doing flips at the same time and crashing into the net at the same moment to watch the tigers rehearse.

Leo held a stool in the air while he backed one of the tigers into a corner. "Isn't that kind of mean?"

"It only looks like he's threatening him." Jazz said. "He's actually just confusing him. See, the tigers are just big house cats, and their eyes want to look at every leg at the same time, so they focus more on stool and less on eating anyone."

Sophia nodded, understanding. Leo turned his back to the tigers as he spoke to the audience that wasn't there, "Ladies and gentlemen, these are the best-behaved tigers in the world. Allow me to introduce them." He motioned to one of the girls. "This is Louise, say hello Louise."

Louise roared and pawed at. the air, looking like she was waving.

"This lovely thing is Nicky, say hi to the people Nicky."

Nicky did a flip and seemed to be waving her tail at the stands. "And now," Leo said. "The king of the jungle, the wild cat who lost his eye to a fierce rival, the mighty Nicol"Nico gave a roar that could be heard outside the tent, and he pawed at the crowd.

Sophia and Jazz sat in the net watching this spectacle for the umpteenth time, yet for them it never got old. Sophia looked at Jaz and asked, "When can I learn the tight rope?"

Jazz looked confused. "Have we not? Huh, I could have sworn that we already...yeah, let's go."

They went to the edge of the net and flipped down.

As they climbed down Jazz said, "My parents are working on a new routine for the three of us, you know...something special now that you're a permanent part of the team."

"That's so nice." Sophia said.

David walked out of the tent and around the back to where Bridget had been shooting, but he didn't find her. He walked back to the RVs and found her at the picnic table cleaning her gun. "Hey," she said. "Is everything okay?" "Yes, I was just look-ing for you because I wanted to ask your opinion of something."

"Shoot." she said smiling and holding up her gun. "Get it?"

David laughed and said, "You know how I'm not very good at everything around here?"

"You-yeah, I do."

"Thank you for not pretending." David said sincerely. "I was talking to Neil, and he suggested that I think about learning the business side, you know, like Mrs. Kettleback does...what do you think?"

Bridget looked thoughtful. David didn't know what she was thinking, but I can tell you. She was thinking that he would be excellent at that. She was also thinking about how she hoped they stayed around. She didn't have many friends. The other people her age in the circus were friends, but they had a certain separation because of their acts. Bridget got along better with Bear and Leo than she did the dancers or acrobats. And for most of her life guys had not wanted to be around her when they found out that she could outshoot them and was generally better at guy stuff. That didn't seem to bother David. Finally, she said, "I think you'd be really good at it. You seem pretty smart to me."

David blushed at the praise. "I just....I wish I was talented."

"Who said you weren't?"

"Huh?"

"Do you have any idea what I would do if it was my job to run this outfit?" She held up a bullet. "One of these would enter my brain shortly after I got the job. I don't know how to do it. I could never hope to learn. And without Mrs. Kettleback and Neil to run this outfit we would all be out of jobs, and I would have to resort to prop bets outside a shooting range or being a bank robber."

David laughed. "I guess you've got a point there. What are prop bets?"

"I used to make small, totally fixed bets with people and trick them into paying for range time as well as getting all their cash."

"You will never stop being intriguing, will you?"

She smiled at him. "No sir."

CHAPTER EIGHT

At the same time that the performers were getting ready for their shows in Arizona, Lilly Aberworth was throwing things around her office in frustration. "Where are they?" She screamed as her detective dodged a flower pot.

"We think they are in the circus but we can't get past the other people. When I went on near them, one of them shot my gun out of my hand, and when I had Mickey go with a cop they just convinced the cop to leave." He hoped she was out of projectiles.

"Well then," she said in a tone that was frighteningly calm. "Perhaps you should remove your head from your rectum and start acting like a proper henchman"

"Do you think you're a bond villain?"

She threw a letter opener at the detective, and he barely missed it. It sunk into the wall and Lilly said, "I think that I am paying you five million dollars to bring me those children, so if I want to call you a sack of monkey dung, then I can. Now, go. Find. Me. Those. Kids!"

"How would you suggest I do that?!".

"Well let's see, if you can't get the big ones...maybe the small ones?"

The detective left the office wondering if he was in the wrong business and maybe if he should have joined that house painter's union that his father offered to get him into.

Rehearsals were one thing, but the sounds and smells of a crowd at the circus was an almost heavenly experience. The kids selling popcorn, the trapeze rosin, the people in the audience waiting for the show to start. This was their church.

David was still going to assist Bridget and she had worked on some new shots. Sophia had spent the last three days trying to learn the tightrope. She wasn't great but they were all going to be using it tonight. She sat on the platform in the dark, watching everyone, and thinking about how she hopped that this went well.

The show was great. It seemed like even though it could get repetitive, it didn't. They all kept up their performances and changed them enough to keep themselves alert. Neil was a master at working a crowd and he could switch tricks and suddenly be on a whole different show if he felt like the crowd wasn't responsive enough. He and Carmen rehearsed three entire shows regularly and they mixed and matched tricks and illusions from all of them.

Then it was time for the tightrope! walk. Marko stepped out onto the wire like he belonged there. He started by walking across, then Jazz walked across, then they both walked out and leaned to the sides, passing each other. When she got tack to the other side Jazz looked at Sophia, "Are you ready?"

Sophia nodded and as Jazz left, she walked out onto line, trying to remember what Louis, Jazz's mom, had told her. She needed to remain calm and try not to think much about the rope, just about! keeping balance. One foot at a time.

Soon they were all three on the line at the same time. They passed each other, Marko smiling to her as he moved around her. When they were at the end of it, they all three fell in unison down to the net.

And they fell. When the weight of the three of them hit the net, it snapped, and they hit the ground at a rate that was slowed down, but still fast enough to bruise. The audience gasped and the three trapeze performers looked at the sides of the net to see it on fire.

They jumped up and started to look all around them. The entire tent was on fire, People started to scream and the whole world erupted into chaos. Sophia was looking for her brother and she found him next to the flap in the tent making sure that everyone was getting out safe.

The stampede didn't last long and soon everyone was out. The people ran for their oars while the circus members tried to get what they could from around the tent.

The fire department was too late, but they came anyway and made sure that nothing else would catch fire. They pulled away at five in the morning as all the members of the circus stood around in a stunned silence, watching the piles of ash that used to be their livelihoods. Nearly all of Nell's magic equipment was gone. The trapeze rig, all the small tools and props they used like little boxes and stools for the animals to stand on and the box of things to juggle with. Most of the costumes, which had been in a large box and on a rack for easy access during the shew, were gone.

Finally, after what seemed like days, Neil and Mrs. Kettleback both stood up and shot into action at the same moment. They both went to their RV, which functioned like an office and had phones that they hooked up whenever they stopped at a new place. Mrs. Kettleback pulled one of the phones through an open window and started to spin the dial.

The rest of them watched in silence as they went through call after call. When they were done, they walked over and Mrs. Kettleback said, "Bear, Jacob, Marko and Leo are going to go with me and get a new tent in Missouri."

Neil added, "Carmen, David, and Kenneth are coming with me to Vegas to get magic supplies and the other props."

Mrs. Kettleback's turn, "Mary, Beth, Louis and Mickey, and the kids are going to make a camp of sorts at the first rest stop in Texas. Off of I-thirty-five. We will all meet up there."

Jazz raised a hand, "What about the rest of us?"

Mrs. Kettleback held up a hand, silencing her. She walked over to Mickey and Louis and whispered amongst them. When she turned back to the rest of them, she said, "The rest of you will go to Oregon and get the new trapeze set up and the costumes. Now don't dally and be safe. You all need to be at the rest stop on Texas in three days if we want to get to Houston. We leave in five.

Everyone broke off to go to their respective RVs for the trips. Sophia saw David, break away from Neil and. they met mid. stride. "I just asked," he said, answering her question before she had time to get it out. "Since they have people looking for us, they thought if we were all in different places then we could hide easier."

"Do you trust these people with the twins?"

His sincerity shocked her a bit. "Yes, I really do."

"Okay then, see you in Texas."

He smiled. "Love you sis."

"You too."

Sophia walked to Dorne just as Jazz was getting there. Her friend had a proud look on her face as she said, without prompting, "They trust us enough to get the rig!"

"What?"

"My parents trust me enough to get the rig. It's a big responsibility and they just said that they were staying behind because they trust me and Marko enough to do it. That's huge!"

Sophia smiled and congratulated her friend. They climbed aboard and Taylor elected to take the first shift driving, so the rest of them went to get some sleep. Mrs. Kettleback knocked on a window and Sophia opened it. "Yes ma'am?"

"Here, this is for the rigging. Find costumes and it everything as cheap as you can with the rest."

"Yes mam, thank you."

"Yeah yeah, now get goin'." She said with a smile.

Sophia walked back and pulled herself into her bunk. She hadn't realized how tired she was until her head hit the pillow she fell into a thankfully dreamless sleep.

David noticed that the inside of the RV he was in did not match the other one. It looked older, less space. But it seemed to have a lot of character. The young people RV seemed more like a college apartment shared by too many people. This seemed like a family home. There were some doodles on a wall in crayon, toys on the floor, he thought this was what their house should have looked like.

CHAPTER NINE

The twins cried and moaned some at not having their older siblings. But they were mostly fine waiting in Texas. The rest stop had a playground that they were allowed to spend all the time they wanted on for the next three days.

Sophia and Jazz had the late-night driving shift, and they were the ones who were driving when they pulled into the place at five o'clock in the morning. Jazz yawned great big and went to make coffee. Marko was woken and soon they were going to meet the man when he arrived. Sophia watched from the window as they went into the warehouse.

The man didn't look like the kind of guy you would expect to be in this type of business. He had bushy gray hair, despite looking young, and he had jeans, a sweatshirt, boots and a ball cap. He looked more like he would work for a rodeo.

They disappeared inside the tan and blue warehouse as Tiffany sat down in the driver's seat next to her. "You know, we don't blame you...well Olivia does but she's a bitch."

Sophia Looked at her confused. "For what?"

"The fire. We figured one of the people after you started it. I just wanted to tell you that no one blames you... except for Olivia."

"Maybe you should blame us...we brought this trouble down on all of you."

She waved that away. "Trouble's always around a corner. Whether it's this or the next. I can't really blame you for wanting to get your little siblings out of the situation you were in...do you want to talk about it?" Sophia shook her head. Tiffany smiled shyly and said, "If you ever change your mind." She looked out the window and saw Marko motioning for them to come help with the stuff. Tiffany turned to the rest of the RV and screamed, "Get up' There's work to be done."

Las Vegas looked grand as they drove in. There were hundreds of lights and displays. There was so much that you could look for a year and not see everything. David wondered which of the many places they would be going to, but they didn't. They drove on until they were in an older part. It looked like it was Vegas without the lights. Smaller, Grand, but not as ostentatious.

Neil told Carmen where to drive and she did. They went down an alleyway that was almost too small for the RV to fit through. "Stop." Neil said when they were at the back of a building that was a deep pink, almost red, brick. Even the door.

"I haven't been here." Carmen said.

"I've not been in an emergency for a long time. I usually pick things up from his other place."

"So, it's Ricky?"

"Yep," He turned to the others, including Bridget, who had gotten put on their RV at the last secondo "Come on guys, let's go." They got out of the RV and Neil banged on the door three quick times followed by a fourth one that seemed longer. A second later it opened and a bald man with glasses that had tape in the middle poked his head out. "Hello Ricky." Neil said.

"Hey Neil, come on in." His words were nice, but his tone was suspicious as he eyed the other three that he didn't know. Ricky moved back and they all walked in. Carmen turned around in the doorway to talk to the other three,

"Don't mind Ricky," she whispered. "He is very secretive of his tricks that he sells...he's also paranoid and mildly schizophrenic." She smiled and turned around before they could tell if she was kidding. Bridget's hand rested on ger gun as she walked in last.

The shop was a dark place. There were strange objects hanging from the ceiling, racks of weapons David suspected did not function like real weapons. There was an entire section that was taken up by large boxes, some clear, some wood, metal, with slats, in pieces. He didn't know what any of this stuff did, but he got the feeling it was a magician's paradise.

They walked through what seemed to be storage and past a small, waist high wall. This area seemed more for work. It was longer whereas the other section seemed wide. There were work benches and things and what looked to be failed tricks in pieces mi farther in the room. Carmen and Neil seemed right at home. Carmen jumped up and sat on the wall while Neil and Ricky discussed what the package he had included and a lot of other jargon.

The rest of them stood awkwardly with that same feeling you get when you are in a new person's house, and you feel like you are an intruder instead of an invited guest. Carmen was eating fries that she found on a table while Ricky spoke. "This has three full shows, it's mostly what you had, though some of it's new. I also included a sword box modified to use real swords, and this." He showed Neil a notebook he had on a bench while he looked over at the other three like they might kill him and take it.

Neil looked to be genuinely impressed. "This is amazing Ricky. Carmen come here." She hopped off the wall and walked over to them, taking the notebook without asking.

Her eyes went wide. "How exactly am I...oh I get it...very nice mole rat."

"I hate that nickname."

"No, you don't."

"Alright then..." Neil said.

They bought the large box that was said to contain all the magic tricks. As well as some fortified boxes and things that would hold an elephant's weight, but make it look like it couldn't. When they had all of the supplies loaded up, they headed out of town.

In Oregon, Sophia was waiting outside the dressing room of a thrift store with Jazz. The two of them had found all the costumes they needed within a half an hour. The last three had been spent waiting for the Dancers and Marko to pick through the large supply of used dancewear while the two of them bought a few books and personal things and waited for them.

The dancers and Marko had wanted to go to a new store, but they were persuaded by the rest of them to go to this place. Brittney and Taylor had gone somewhere to get some new Clown makeup, because some things you just don't buy used. Lana walked out of one of the dressing rooms and gave a twirl. Jazz said, "Too slutty."

"Is not."

Sophia looked up and saw that it was indeed. 'It rode so high that hairspray wasn't going to keep it from getting stuck to her butt, and it was cut so that not much was left to the imagination, and most of Lana's offsets were on display. "Fine," Jazz said. "Dance. Spin a bit like you would during 'a show,"

Lana spun and was about to smugly say that she was getting it when she noticed that both of her breasts were out of the top. "Fine, something else then."

She stomped back into the dressing room and Jazz flipped a page in her book. "Thank you...this is a family show after all."

When they were finally finished and had enough costumes for three different shows, they paid and left the store. They stopped at a Walmart on their way out of the state in order to get some food and drinks for the road and a movie for whoever wasn't driving. While they were looking through the DVDs, Sophia went to get some snacks. She pushed the cart along the aisle and out of the corner of her eye saw a guy that looked a little too interested in her. She acted as if she was turning right and. then turned left. He followed. She tried to get going faster and then stop suddenly, he kept his distance so as not to alarm her.

Finally, she got ahead enough that she lost him and she turned in the aisle so that she would be facing him when he went by. He saw her and started to walk towards her. "Hi there," he said. "I work for your aunt; she'd really like to meet you."

Sophia shoved the cart at him and ran, not waiting to see if it hit him. She heard a groan and thought it probably did. She ran as hard as she could. Luckily the exercise from preforming and training had her in better shape than she had once been in. Jazz was standing at an endcap as she ran up on the electronics section. She just yelled, "Guy chasing me, we have to go." As she ran by, she turned a corner for the exit and saw her friends running after her.

They hit the RV door and Olivia dove for the driver's seat. She had the engine on, and they were pulling away even before Marko had caught up. He dove inside and they slammed the door as they pulled out of the parking lot.

Everyone made it to Texas within the three days. Dorn was last, arriving late in the night. They exchanged inventory lists, and everyone noted that they had gotten everything for the circus o The new tent seemed to be a bit larger than the old one. And it was a deep crimson color instead of the old gray. They ate and slept for a long time, and when it was time to go, they headed for the largest show of the year. As they were going down the road on their way to Houston, Sophia asked, "Do you guys think I'm good enough for such a big show? I don't want to screw up so that you'd have to give someone their money back or something…"

Marko waved that away. "Stop it, you'll do fine. Honestly, you're getting better than I am."

"And that means something coming from him," Taylor said, "He's always had an over inflated ego."

They all started laughing and Sophia went to check dm the twins. She was lucky that no one had known where they were. She didn't mind people coming after her, preferred it, as long as they left her family alone.

CHAPTER TEN

There had been no exaggeration about Houston. They had been the first ones there, set up the tent and animal pens, and waited for everyone to get there. Within three hours there were enough booths and game owners on the grounds they could have populated a small town.

At noon people started to come, raising the amount of people there to a few thousand. The crowd at the tent was the largest the Bingleys had ever seen, and they were turning them over almost faster than possible.

From noon to seven they did six shows, with more to follow the next day and the day after.

When the last show of the day was finished and the tent area cleaned up, they were all going to head to bed when Mary ran into the tent. Her face was beaten, and blood had poured from her nose and dried as it went down her face. "The...they took Ruthie." She said before passing out.

Bear rushed to look after his wife as Sophia and David felt their hearts leave their chests. "Where is Ryan?" David asked.

Mary had regained consciousness and she said, "Timmy had taken him to the bathroom when they came. He's fine."

Sophia began to breath heavily. Ruthie was gone. She had done all of this to protect her sister and then she was taken while she was doing stupid trapeze. What if her aunt killed her? What if they sent her back to their father, all alone? "We have to go after them." she said. "What do they look like?"

The man who came the first time, three women with guns, and a man with arms the size of trees, also with a gun."

Jazz and Marko stepped forward and Marko said, "Let's go."

"No, you can't." Their Dad said. But they were already out the door. They were closely followed by Sophia, David, and Bridget. They pulled out going far too fast for an RV to handle. When they were going fast Marko moved over to let David drive and Bridget got into the passenger seat. The acrobats went up to the roof and looked for the car. Finally, they found it when the rest of the cars turned to a large highway and a blue sedan turned down a country road. As they got closer, they saw Ruthie looking out the back and a man trying to pull her down.

"Get closer!" Jazz shouted above the wind.

David got as close as he could. One of the women with a gun saw them and started to fire. Bridget opened her window and shot the woman' s gun out of her hand. The woman pulled another, and Bridget's shot missed. David was shocked by this, but he didn't think it appropriate to mention given the circumstances. Bridget cursed. "I'm out of practice while moving. I have to do better." Her anger must have made her shoot better because the next three shots killed the women with guns.

They started to slow as the RV sped up and the acrobats jumped on the roof and caught Sophia as she started to slip. Bridget, having reloaded, started to shoot as the three of them slipped into the back and front seat.

Marko slapped the driver in the ears and took the wheels jerking them off into the ditch. The men struggled out of the car and got up ready to shoot it up when Bridget killed them both. Sophia held Ruthie close as they got out of the car. She and Jazz had blood on them, thankfully not their own. They all looked at the dead people in the car and on the ground. They were silent for what seemed like hours before Jazz said, "You know, if people find out about this it will set circus folk back like, a hundred years."

"What?" Bridget asked.

"Well, everyone thinks we're murderers and weirdoes. It's only been in the last few decades that we haven't been looked at like vagrants."

The other four all looked at her like she was nuts. Bridget said, "I say we set the car to explode and go home."

"Why do we have to do that?" Sophia asked.

"Cause otherwise there is a good chance we will all go to jail and that child will go to foster care or the aunt trying to kill her."

That convinced everyone. Sophia dropped Ruthie in the RV and got a lighter while the others put the bodies in the positions they had been sitting in. They punctured the gas tank and damaged the engine. Then they used a rag Sophie had brought as a fuse and they lit it and. drove away. Sophia covered Ruthie's head as the car exploded in the distance.

CHAPTER ELEVEN

T he next morning a police officer knocked on the RV door. He ordered everyone out and they saw that the rest of the circus was already standing around, looking as cool as cucumbers in the fridge. "My name is officer Danko and this is Officer Reagan."

The man said introducing the female officer that was interviewing Bear nearby, "We are just asking questions about a car that exploded up the road and we were wondering if you had any information."

Jazz yawned and ran a hand through her hair, "Was it a sedan? Three women, two men?"

"The bodies were burned beyond recognition, but it was a sedan yes."

"Aw...they were here. They stayed longer than they were supposed to. They bought a bunch of alcohol from the beer cart during the fair and they stayed late drinking. After the vendors had all shut down and it was just us here we asked them to leave and they just drove off."

"Did you offer to call them a cab?"

"No sir, but Mary did, that woman there." She pointed over to the bruised Mary. "That's when the larger man decided to hurt her. They drove out of here rather quickly when they saw her husband coming."

"That is the large Scottish gentleman?"

"Yes sir."

"I see... did anything seam off to you?"

"Apart from drunkenness and willingness to hit a woman, no sir."

It was Taylor's turn, "When I was in the parking lot, I saw a sedan looking car with bullet holes in the back of it."

The cop eyed her suspiciously. "Why were you in the parking lot?"

"What do you mean?" She asked evasively.

"Well, you live here, and you work up here, what reason did you have to be in the parking lot?"

She looked around, eyeing her father standing near Mrs. Kettleback. She moved closer to the cop. "Promise not to tell my Dad?"

"Yes."

Taylor looked shyly again. "I was there twice. Once I was flirting with and ended up making out with the hot dog vendor boy, and the second time was I with the girl working the cotton candy booth."

The cop looked a bit strangely at her, but he seemed to shake it out of his head. "How do you know what bullet holes look like in a car?"

"Bridget."

The cop looked around and Bridget stepped forward. "A few years ago, we had a car donated for one of our shows and I did trick shots on it. Including one where Taylor was my assistant and I put her in the trunk and shot around her."

"That sounds pretty cool. I might have to get a ticket and see what else you can do."

They went on like that for the next several hours. They told the cops the story that they had all discussed over and over again.

They ruled the deaths an accident and wished them a good day They all breathed a sigh of relief and got ready for the shows they had to do that day.

CHAPTER TWELVE

The season was over at the end of August. They head to Mrs. Kettleback's land in New Mexico and set up camp, albeit a more permanent one. The entire place was about eighty acres with two areas fenced in for the animals.

The Elephants had twenty acres and the Tigers twenty to run and hunt and do whatever they liked. Though Jacque still fed them. They set up the RVs in the same way, but with more I space apart. The first morning Bear went to a storage shed and brought out a five foot across cast iron skillet. He and Mary woke everyone up with an enormous breakfast.

Mrs. Kettleback handed out the last of the season's pay saying that everyone had understandable pay cuts thanks to having the fire and having to replace everything. Everyone talked about maybe going somewhere for a vacation while the season was over. Jacob and Leo talked about a fishing trip, and the dancers and Brittney and Taylor were thinking of going to the beach in Florida.

The Bingleys were thinking about how for the next three months they could hide here and wouldn't have to deal with their crazy aunt. Mrs. Kettleback said that she stayed here for almost the entire time she was not on the road and that a lot of the rest of them did too. Jazz and Marko set up the rig so that they could stay in shape and learn new routines.

There was a minivan in a shed on the property that those who were leaving got in and went on their way. With Brittney and Taylor gone the big bed was open, and immediately claimed by Jazz. The first night that she slept there the rest of them were still sleeping in their bunks. But when they got up Jazz saw them and called to Sophia, "Hey, come here."

Sophia walked back to the bed and found Ruthie and Ryan cuddled up next to Jazz to the point that she couldn't move. "They weren't here when I went to bed were they?"

Sophia shook her head. "No, they weren't." she said trying to suppress a laugh.

Jazz smiled. "They look comfortable, so I think we're just gonna lay here for a while."

"Thank you."

And she did, they all laid there for another three hours until the twins got up on their own. Everyone was just happy to see that they had made it through the night without any nightmares. That hadn't happened in a while.

It does not help our story for me to tell you the events of the next two months. Not a lot of things happened except for a feeling of home that happened to come over the Bingleys. There were a lot of rehearsals and training and David asked Mrs. Kettleback to teach him how to run the business side and the two of them worked on booking shows for the next year. No, the final part of our story starts in the beginning of November, two weeks before David turned eighteen. They were contacted by the lawyer saying he needed them to make their way to Milwaukee by the fifteenth so that they could sign the money and assets over to David. On the second, one of the RVs pulled out of the property containing David, Sophia, Bridget, Jazz and Marko. The twins gave a slightly teary goodbye, I but they stayed behind because it was decided that they could be better protected there and without a doubt the rest of them were going to struggle through more attackers and more of their aunt trying to step them.

The twins weren't all that hurt. They said their goodbyes and ran off into the field to play with the other kids, Sophia had a harder time saying goodbye. She couldn't help but feel like she was turning her back on them after all she had done to protect them, but she knew that they would be safer without her and David around for a while.

And trouble they got. It wasn't long before they had to stop for gas, and they saw two men in a big red car watching them. Then when they pulled away that car followed them. It drove alongside them and motioned for them to pull over, Marko, who was driving, looked in the rearview mirror at the others, "Guys, I've got someone telling me to pull over,"

Bridget rushed up to the front, she slid behind the driver's seat so that she could get a look at the car. "Flip them off."

"What?"

"I wanna see how they react." Marko flipped the car off and the next thing they produced a small gun and started to shoot at the RV. Bridget popped up and shot out their gas tank and then a tire, car started to slow and then stopped. Bridget sighed relief and Marko yelled, "Ow!"

"What?"

"What? You hurt my ear!"

"Oh, sorry."

They switched shifts and things, and they didn't see trouble again until they were in Oklahoma. They were at a rest stop and saw a car that had been following them for some time. They had expected it to be more people working for their aunt, maybe even their aunt herself, one last ditch effort before her chance at their grandfather's money was gone.

They did not, however, expect to see their father.

He looked cleaner than the last time they had seen him. He was no longer wearing his grimy work clothes and it looked like he had bothered to shower. But he still looked skeevy. His hair was slicked back with a jell he hadn't owned when they lived at home, and he was wearing a suit jacket with jeans and a button up shirt. He held flowers in one hand and a box in the other.

David stopped dead in his tracks, causing Marko to bump into him. As Sophia turned to see what held up the group her heart left her body. He stood on the other side of the parking lot next to the GTO that he loved more than his children and their mother combined. It still had been neglected. There was rust all over it and they could smell the interior from where they stood. It brought back memories of being left in the car with the windows down while he was inside a bar, drinking.

They had to walk closer to get to the RV. Sophia whispered for Bridget to keep her gun ready. He got in front of them when they started to walk, and David put himself between his father and the others. "Why are you here?"

"I came to say that I'm sorry."

Sophia spoke from behind her brother. "Like all the times you said sorry to Mother before beating her the next time you got angry?"

"I'm trying to repent."

"Let me guess, you found Jesus?"

"Is that so wrong?"

"Only that you've found him fourteen times in the last seventeen years and each and every time you find him someone gets hurt."

They started to get back into the RV and he said, "Well you may leave, but I'll still be getting my kids back."

David's whole body went cold, and he whipped around, looking his father in the eye. "If those kids so much as ever see you again, I will kill you. I will kill you with my bare hands."

"You some big man now boy?" he asked, turning into his old self.

David struck his father in the throat. He gasped for air as David shoved him backwards and to the ground. They got into the RV as their father brought a gun out from behind his back and started shooting wildly. He got three shots off before Bridget killed him.

When they were on the highway, and everyone had calmed down they took inventory. One bullet had hit the window, one had hit a book on the shelf, the other had hit Sophia right in the gut.

She didn't even seem to notice. She slowly went to the floor as the others rushed over to her. Bridget tore her shirt open to inspect the bullet wound and Jazz jumped over the dining room table to hold Sophia's head in her lap. "It's okay sweetie, you're okay." Jazz said, clearly trying to hide the tears in her eyes.

Bridget was looking over her stomach, wiping away blood so that she could assess the wound. Tears were clouding her eyes as well as she looked up at David and Jazz. "I..." Words failed her and she shook her head.

Sophia was calm in a way she shouldn't have been. David looked down at her and she seemed to be looking out into the distance, though it was only the ceiling to see. She suddenly turned to look at him and whispered,

"Promise me that you will keep the kids safe."

Tears were falling all around as David nodded. "I will,

I promise...oh Sophie.

The three of them just sat there, Sophie's head still in Jazz's lap as she cried. There was nothing they could do. They had no I way to fix what had been done. Marko sped along the highway crying himself. It seemed like hours passed before they got to the hospital. The doctors sped her into the back while the rest of them prayed.

They got the money, not that it mattered. David sat there in the lawyer's office the entire time in a daze. Signing where he was ordered, thanking God with every breath that his sister was a few hours away, slowly recovering.

The lawyer said that he wouldn't have to do any work or business stuff. His grandfather had long since retired and his various companies and holdings just made him money. They could spend a billion a year and still be rich for the rest of time. It was a month before Sophie was fit to travel. They made it back to Mrs. Kettleback's property. Sophie fell down to hug the twins, tears filling her eyes as she remembered how close she had come to leaving them forever.

One day, as Sophie was doing her first exercises since getting the all-clear, David looked at Mrs. Kettleback,

"How would you feel about a European tour?"

COMICON GIRL

In the whirlwind world of Comic-Con, two souls collide: one timid, one adventurous, both masked by the allure of cosplay. Little do they know, their chance encounter sparks a connection that transcends the convention floor, leading to a serendipitous reunion where love blossoms anew, unmasking their true identities beneath the guise of anonymity.

CHAPTER ONE

CARLY

Carly was walking home, thankful to be done with another year of school. She was taking her books home with her, the novels that she had accumulated in her locker over the past year. She hadn't realized that it had been so many, but she had five in her arms and the rest were weighing down her shoulders and bulging out of her backpack.

She turned around upon hearing shouting from behind her. She instantly got nervous, if this was some sort of fight, she was sure to get her butt kicked. *Oh god, what is happening.* she thought to herself.

"Hey, hold up!"

Carly exhaled with relief. It was only Jesse. The most annoying girl she knew, but still the closest thing she had to a friend. Jesse finally got to Carly, bending over and breathing hard. Jesse usually abstained from any physical exertion that wasn't sexual in some way.

Carly couldn't help but eye Jesse's breasts, though that was certainly the point. She wore clothes too open and pushed them up so that they were one sidewalk trip away from coming out. Jesse was very outgoing, but not in a good way. She was a manipulative, needy brat, and kind of a slut.

"Why were you running?" Carly asked.

"I wanted to catch up to you before you got into those granny pajamas." Jesse told her, out of breath.

"My what?" Carly asked, a bit confused.

Jesse waved that away, like she couldn't be bothered to explain. "That's not important," she said. "I need to ask you something." Carly started to walk. She never got very assertive, but she was starting to get pissed off. "Walk and talk then." she said, a little bite in her voice. "It's movie night and I don't want to be late."

Jesse followed behind her as she walked. "It's so sad that your mom is your best friend."

Why am I friends with her? Carly asked herself. Jesse was mean, mean for sport. She was the kind of mean where you didn't know if there was trouble at home, and you almost didn't care. Carly gripped her books tighter. She felt like she could cry, but she had told herself since second grade that she wouldn't cry in front of Jesse. Not since that bitch had made her cry during a spelling test and then got the whole class to laugh at her.

Carly could see Jesse come up next to her and she tried to shake herself out of that place in her head where she is lost in thought. "I want to go to Comicon this year and I need you to go."

Carly looked at her, she hoped Jesse could pick up on the 'You're a moron' expression, because that was certainly what she tried to project. "You don't even like comic books." Carly said.

Jesse sighed in exasperation. "Dude, it's San Diego Comicon. It barely has anything to do with comic books. There are parties, and guys, and I'd get to wear a costume, and sometimes famous people are walking around."

They stopped in front of Carly's house, just a little normal house in the center of a street, nothing overtly special, yet somehow it was the epitome of home to her. All she wanted was to get inside. "So you want me to go to San Diego so that you can stalk Chris Hemsworth?"

Jesse shook her head. "No...Jason Momoa."

Carly rolled her eyes. "Why do you need me to come? This doesn't exactly sound like the kind of thing that you bring someone like me along to."

Jesse had a guilty look on her face, she groaned. "My Dad says that you have to come. He hopes that with you there I will behave myself."

"I bet that goes well."

Jesse laughed. "Promise to think about it? I'll text you more stuff later, okay?"

Carly considered a moment before she realized that the only way to get Jesse to leave was to agree. "I promise to think about it." she said.

Jesse, all smiles, started to jump up and down. When she finally calmed down, she spoke, "Well I guess I'm going home."

Jesse took off down the street. Carly exhaled a sigh of relief, but she was a bit ashamed to be relieved. What kind of friend was she? "Bye." Carly called halfheartedly.

Jesse was already so far down the street that she shouldn't have been able to hear, but she called out, saying goodbye. Carly headed inside.

Hours later, Carly and her mother were watching some chick flick about a guy whose wife lost her memories or something. Carly got a stream of messages from Jesse, explaining everything about the trip and how if she agreed to go then Carly wouldn't have to pay for anything.

Carly looked over at her mom. She wondered if she should even bother to bring it up. She knew that her mom would think it was a good idea, but Carly didn't want to go. She briefly entertained the idea of just telling Jesse her Mom had said no, but she knew that Jesse would be here withing the hour asking her mom why. Carly took a deep breath, sighing. Her mother looked over at her, concerned. "What's wrong baby girl?"

"Jesse wants me to go to San Diego Comicon with her, but I don't want to."

Carly's mom took a bite of popcorn, never taking her eyes off Carly. When she spoke, she was still chewing. "So why don't you want to go?"

"What do you mean?" Carly asked, a little shocked. Didn't her mother understand why she couldn't go? She would suffocate that far from home, virtually alone, around thousands of strangers, she threw the blanket off her, starting to panic. She stood up and started to pace back and forth. Her Mom, used to this, just ate popcorn and watched with a look on her face that said, 'You need to calm down.'

Carly paced a few more times before she started to speak.

"I can't go, there are thousands of people I don't know, you won't be there, Jesse isn't going to comfort me if I have a panic attack, I just...I can't."

Carly looked at her mother, who was only looking at her, not trying to make any sort of comforting gesture. "Do you need a pill?" She asked.

Carly shook her head. "You know I hate those things."

She put her hands up in defense. "I know, I know, but Doctor Klein said,-"

"Oh, fuck Doctor Klein." Carly said, knowing her mother didn't like bag language or being interrupted. She looked at her mother and saw that she was getting Mom eyes. "Sorry."Carly told her. Her mom pointed from her to the couch, marking the path that she took as she walked over and sat down.

"So why don't you want to go?" Her Mom asked her.

"What do you mean, I just told you."

"Actually, you gave several reasons why you couldn't go, all of which were totally bullshit, but you never said why you don't want to go."

Carly's jaw dropped. She couldn't believe what her mother was saying. "They were *not* bullshit." she said.

Again, with the mom eyes, those eyes that only a woman who has gone through childbirth can give. A look that melts your argument and says, 'We both know you're full of shit.' Occasionally they would say, 'Your argument is invalid because I am Mom and you cannot change that.'

Carly groaned. "I just, I, I don't know."

She felt her mom's hand on her thigh. "I know you don't like new things Carly but, -"

"I like new things."

"You have a panic attack every time we visit Grandma." Her mom countered. "But my point is, you're a writer, how is having a new experience ever a bad thing?"

"Some writer I am. I write for you and I." Carly said, but upon seeing the mom eyes again, relented. "Okay fine, maybe you're right."

Her Mom smiled. "And besides, you'll be in the car for a few days, right? That's hardly any time at all."

"Jesse's Dad is paying for a flight." Carly told her.

"Even better, take some Dramamine and wake up in California."

Her Mom went back to watching the movie. Carly hadn't even realized that she'd paused it. Carly sat there, watching, but she wasn't really paying attention. She was thinking about the mess that she had gotten herself into.

The next day she called Jesse and told her. Within the hour she had been dragged to a thrift store that seemed to cater exclusively to Vagabonds, druggies, and current and former strippers. Carly sat on a couch that had probably seen more than a few porn shoots, talking to Jesse, who was doing most of the actual talking.

"I thought the point of Comicon was to dress like a comic book character." Carly asked through the curtain of the dressing room.

Jesse's voice was muffled as she spoke. "You can dress up like anything you want, you just have to look cool, and besides, I want to look unique."

The curtain came back, and Carly gasped. She had to gulp a bit before she spoke. "Well, you certainly look unique."

"Thank you." Jesse said. She did a twirl, which almost caused her breasts to fall out of the leather bra that was made for boobs three sizes smaller. The vest did almost nothing to cover them, and the leather pants she was wearing were tight enough to put a coin in the back pocket and see if it was heads or tails. Carly found her body reacting to Jesse's new look, despite the fact that her personality was off putting.

"You like it?" Jesse asked. "I'm a warrior princess, I'm gonna find a weapon or something to carry."

Carly was staring, she couldn't help it. "What?" Jesse asked.

Carly felt her face heat up. "I can see your whole boob... like, areola and everything."

Jesse looked down, somehow just noticing her exposed breast. "Huh, look at that."

"Please cover yourself." Carly asked. "I don't have enough money to bail you out for indecent exposure."

"Uh, Carls...those people are having sex." Jesse said pointing.

Carly turned around and saw, in a flash she was looking back at Jesse. "What am I going to wear?" she asked. "You said you wanted to pick."

Jesse started to hop and clap her hands. "You go in there and get naked, I'll hand you things."

Nervously Carly headed to the dressing room. She went inside and pulled the curtain. Instantly it was dark. Wasn't there supposed to be some kind of light? She thought she would pull the curtain open enough to see what she was doing, it was only Jesse after all, but there were people on the opposite side of the store, and she jerked it closed.

Once she had taken her clothes off and was standing in the dark, covering herself despite being alone, a fist full of clothes poked through the curtain and she heard Jesse say, "Put these on."

She started to get dressed in the dark. She fell over and discovered a bench had been there the entire time. She couldn't see what she was doing, but the pants, or what she hoped were the pants, were too tight.

"Are you done?" Jesse asked from outside.

"Almost."

"Put this on." A ribbon came through the curtain. "Tie your hair back with it." Carly did as instructed. When she opened the curtain, she turned and covered herself. "What're you doing? Jesse asked.

"My boobs show."

"We can get boob tape."

"I am not walking around all day with my nipples taped to a dead person's vest...oh my god, I look like Rambo if he'd been a stripper. I didn't even know they made camo this tight."

Jesse threw her hands up in the air. "Then let's try something else!" She stomped off and Carly went back into the changing room to peel off her pants, thankful she'd remembered to keep her underwear on.

Twenty minutes later, when she had finally gotten her next outfit on, she came out, looked at herself in the mirror, and gasped. The top, that she had known was too short, took too short to a whole new level. Most of her boobs were out of the bottom and what was in the shirt strained against it like an animal trying to escape a cage. She looked at her lover half, she hadn't worn shorts like this since she was seven. Thank God she'd shaved, or the entire world could have seen her bush. She was overcome with anger. She turned to Jesse, "Fuck you."

After overcoming her shock that Carly had cursed, Jesse seemed in genuine shock that she didn't like the costume. "What?"

Carly motioned with both hands towards her crotch. "I don't want to have to wear a hair net." She exclaimed, the anger in her voice palpable, to her at least.

Jesse sighed. "Okay, one more and if I can't find something you like, we'll go to a party city and get you a batman mask."

"Please get me something that doesn't look like I'm going to a hell's angels party for a gangbang." Carly asked, hopeful that she would actually listen.

The next outfit was a dress, easy enough to slip into. When Carly came out of the dressing room, she looked at the mirror and was instantly out of breath. The dress was made of a loose tan material that, while still looking beautiful, kept all her secrets in their chamber.

She had a crown of woven sticks and golden metal leaves on her head. Jesse came up behind her, "What do you think?"

Carly twirled around, smiling. "I actually like this one." She looked back at the mirror, still in awe of how great she looked. "What do you think?"

"It's easy to get off in case you meet someone."

Carly roiled her eyes. "Do you ever have a non-sexual thought?"

Jesse thought for a moment, "Nope." She laughed. "We should cover you in body paint, the visible areas, go for the full 'Elf princess' look. It would look awesome."

"Okay. Hopefully it's warm in the building, otherwise I'm going to tear through this dress."

"It's loose enough for a bra, unless you're going for the aroused look, which is fine."

Carly laughed at that one. "Will you go pay? I'm gonna change and then I'll buy lunch."

Jesse shook her head. "I'm buying. You're doing a big favor for me, and I am going to pay for everything."

"Works for me." Carly said as she walked into the curtain. She straightened herself and pulled it back, hoping no one saw her do that.

CHAPTER TWO

T EGAN

Tegan loved Comicon. She was never really a nerd. She liked Star Wars and some of the Commercial stuff, but she wasn't nearly as hardcore as the guy who'd just passed her wearing a nearly five-thousand-dollar Boba Fett suit.

But she loved being weird. She never pretended to be normal or anything, but this large building was a place full of weird people just like her. She liked being one of the undergrounds, the people here just to enjoy what it started out as, comics. Only every few years did Tegan even bother with all the other crap.

"God, I hope weird doesn't become normal." she said, only half paying attention to who was around her.

"Huh? What'd you say?" Theresa asked, shocking her out of her daydream.

"Just that I hope the world stays mostly the same. I mean, the whole straight people who are weirdly pleasant type normal. I hope that being weirdoes like we are never comes in to style."

Her friend looked at her like she had three heads. "Why? Wouldn't it be better if you could be openly you?"

"I am openly me. But I enjoy being strange, standing out. If being weird turned mainstream and was suddenly normal, then you're just like everybody else and we turn into the Capitol like in the hunger games."

Kieran turned around, effortlessly walking backwards while he talked, damned tour guide training. "So, what you're saying, is that you want everyone to be themselves, so long as no one talked about it so it's still seen as weird."

Tegan nodded, impressed. "How do you do that? Just sum up what someone is trying and failing to say?"

Kieran shrugged, "Dunno." He turned around and continued walking. Tegan was about to comment on how he could articulate someone else's point but not his own, when she saw a girl sitting on a bench out of the corner of her eye. She stopped and so did her friends. They were a close group, they had all worn Victorian clothing with metal elements, not quite steam punk, but pretty close. Tegan didn't like the fact that the dress she was wearing covered her tattoos, but the fact that she hadn't had to wear underwear kind of made up for it, that and the super amazing fingerless gloves she had on.

The girl was sitting on a bench, crying. She looked like a beautiful elf or some magical woodland creature. Her skin was painted blue with lines and specks of gold, and she had a crown of woven sticks and leaves on her head, further enforcing the elf princess thing that Tegan had been thinking. "I'll meet up with you guys later, okay?" Tegan said to no one in particular.

Theresa chided her in the fake British accent they had all been using since that morning. "Well, well well,"

James looked to where the blue girl was sitting. "You cheeky girl, don't do anything I wouldn't do."

Tegan smiled, putting her hand to her chest in mock offense. "Why James, whatever would that be?"

Tegan started to walk away when she heard Bianca yell, "Don't come home pregnant!" She laughed to herself and continued on to the bench, flipping her friends off behind her back as she went.

The girl, who was even more beautiful upon a closer look, was hunched over in tears as Tegan walked up. She saw her approaching and straightened up, wiping her eyes. "Sorry, I'm sorry." she said in a hurry.

Tegan tilted her head, going for the confused puppy look. "Why are you apologizing to me? You don't even know who I am."

She rested her hands in her lap. letting loose a small her laugh amid the crying. "You've got a point there." she said, out of breath.

"May I sit?" Tegan inquired of the beautiful elf girl. She nodded and Tegan sat down. "Why is a beautiful blue skinned beauty such as yourself crying on a bench?"

"My friend abandoned me." she said, stammering a bit.

"What an idiot you are." Tegan said firmly.

The girl looked shocked. "Wha...what?"

"I'm sorry, but if you are friends with someone who would abandon you, looking like that, and while you are being as interesting as I find you, then you are an idiot. You should never speak to that moron again."

"Thank you...I think."

Tegan patted the girl's knee, trying to comfort her. "Why haven't you gone off on your own?" Tegan wondered.

The girl looked at Tegan for a second and then seemed to find something very interesting in her lap. "I'm too shy. I get really nervous around new people. I actually have panic attacks."

"Well, I seem to have calmed you down." Tegan told her.

She straightened up, seemingly noticing for the first time that she had calmed down. "I guess you did."

"Why don't you come and have fun with me?"

She looked shocked by this, she started to shake her head so fast Tegan feared it might come flying off. "I can't..., -"

Tegan turned so that she was facing the girl on the bench, she did the same and Tegan took her hands in her own. "What if you stayed in character?" she asked. "My Mom is a shrink and she says it works with a lot of her patients."

"What?" she asked. "I don't understand."

"We won't tell each other our names. We will give each other nicknames and we will let our costumes be who we are...that way you're not shy."

"I'm not?"

"Well, you are, but uh, Ella isn't. She's a bit crazy."

"She is?" Ella wondered.

"Yeah, crazy enough to have an adventure with a stranger."

Ella's face lightened up; she looked like a weight had been lifted off of her. "Okay then, Poppy. Let's go."

Tegan reached out her hand and Ella took it, together they walked back onto the convention floor.

A while later the two of them were walking around with the Frappuccino's Tegan had bought them, when she noticed a comic book sticking out of Ella's bag. "Is that an issue you're trying to get signed?" Tegan asked.

She looked down like she had forgotten it was even there. "Oh that, no. I got scared while I was looking at it and threw it, so then the guy made me pay for it."

Tegan nodded her understanding. She took a sip from her drink and spoke, "Do you like comic books?"

Ella shook her head. "I mean, I don't really know anything about them. So, I guess I don't actually know if I like them."

Tegan felt a light bulb go off in her head. "I know where you need to go."

Tegan was so excited to share these comic books with Ella. She walked over to a big folding table where several dozen titles were laid out and made a 'Ta Da' gesture. "This is where you need to start if you're gonna get into comics." Tegan told her.

"Why?" Ella wondered.

"Because they're independent, they aren't about big bucks or making movies or anything like the mainstream publishers, like Marvel or DC. These are just for storytelling. They're what comics used to be."

Ella's eyes flittered over the table; Tegan wondered what she would go to first. Ella looked at her, "Where should I start?" she asked.

Tegan smiled. "I am so glad you asked."

CHAPTER THREE

C arly

Fifteen minutes later Poppy had her bag filled with almost a dozen books. Carly couldn't believe she was spending the day with a gorgeous stranger. Well, her cheek bones. Because of the masquerade mask that was all she could see of Poppy's face. But there was more to her than that. It was like her very presence calmed Carly's mind and made her into the girl she had been before her Dad died. Daring. Willing, to overcome her fears and do anything. Poppy noticed a line as they were walking down the aisle, and she turned to Carly. "You're gonna love this guy, he's a good friend of mine.

Before Carly could follow, Poppy took off up the line.

Carly wished she could have such confidence. She followed Poppy up the line, apologizing to the people she pushed past, until she heard Poppy yell, "Calm down nerds, you'll get your damned comics signed."

When she finally made it to the front of the line, Poppy was standing there next to a man in his late twenties wearing a baseball cap and a dress shirt with slacks. He held out his hand. "Hi, I'm Bobby."

"Hello." Carly said.

"This enchanting beauty is Ella." Poppy told him.

"Nice to meet you, Ella." Bobby said.

Carly suddenly felt embarrassed, despite her 'Character' not being supposed to get nervous. She moved to get some of the comics out of her bag as she spoke. "I bought some of your comic books," Her bag spilled to the floor. The comics went all over the floor and her favorite book crashed to the ground, adding yet another scuff to the well-worn cover. There was tape on the spine and marks everywhere, she had loved that book for years, almost to death.

Bobby knelt to pick up the book and when he looked at the cover his face lit up. Looking at Carly he said, "Come with me." He started to walk away but turned back to the crowd. "I'll be back in ten everybody." He called out. There were groans from the crowd and he said, "Now now, I will make sure the signing goes long enough to sign everyone's books. Back in Ten."

He turned to the girls. "We'd better hurry or they will hunt us down." He turned and started to walk away. Poppy started after him, and Carly followed.

Carly followed them to the back of the building, behind booths and the displays and to an exit. They entered a stair well and they started going down. Bobby led them through another door and down a long hallway, when they finally stopped,

Bobby knocked on the door. "Come in." An old voice said from inside.

Carly followed the others inside and she saw a man who looked no older than fifty but had an air about him that said he was the wisest in any room. He had on a Victorian suit and fingerless gloves, and on the table was an old coat and an ancient looking top hat. "Hello." He said looking at her.

"Hello." she replied. Something about this man made her nervous yet intrigued at the same time. She turned her head and the breath and courage left her. Standing on the other side of the table, shaking hands with Poppy, was Carly's favorite writer, Arthur Patrick, the guy who'd written the book she always carried with her. He extended his hand to her.

"Nice to meet you."

Carly tried and failed to speak. She was only vaguely aware of the mumbling that came out of her mouth, then she heard Poppy say, "This catatonic beauty is Ella, she's a big fan." Carly felt a pinch on her butt, and she really hoped it was Poppy. She jerked to life and extended her hand to Mr Patrick. "Um, hi sir, I am..well..."

Out of the corner of her eye she saw Bobby produce her book. Mr. Patrick took it and he smiled. "My my, this has seen better days." He said with a fondness in his voice that told her he was thinking of his own favorite book. He looked at her with concern. "Are you alright sweet heart?"

A thousand and one things ran through Carly's mind, her favorite author was touching her arm and he thought she was crazy, did everyone think she was crazy? Of course they thought she was crazy, she was crazy.

Finally, she couldn't take it anymore. She turned and ran from the room.

CHAPTER FOUR

T EGAN

"Wait!" The author guy said. He looked genuinely concerned about Ella, and that wasn't something you saw from a lot of famous people. Tegan appreciated that. He hurriedly wrote something on the book and handed it to Tegan. "Tell her I love her costume." he said.

"Yes sir, thank you very much."

He seemed to forget that Tegan was still there as he went to sit back down, talking to his hot friend in the cool outfit. Tegan got the impression that this guy had no idea anyone was wearing costumes, this was just how he dressed. "Interesting girls." Arthur said to his friend.

"I could tell you stories about this one here." Bobby said.

"Now now, bragging is sinful, don't you know that, Bobby?" He smiled at her.

Suddenly, Arthur's friend let out a laugh. They all looked at him and Arthur spoke. "What are you laughing at?"

"They remind me of some friends of mine." Was all the man said.

Tegan felt like now would be a good time to go, and hopefully find Ella. "Mr. Patrick, thank you for the book. My friend will love it. Bobby, I'll call you. Thanks for this. Mr. coat guy, it was nice to meet you."

The coat guy gave her a two fingered salute. "Likewise." he said.

And with that she left the room. She could still hear them talking when she went down the hall, but she couldn't make out what they were saying. She went back through the door they had come through and was about to go back up the stairs when she heard sobbing coming from below.

She followed the sound of the crying and discovered Ella in the alcove under the stairs, her arms wrapped around her knees, and her head in the crook of her arms. Tegan sat down across from her and put her hand on her knee. Ella looked up at her, a look of absolute panic on her crying face. "I'm so...sorry. I didn't mean to...to embarrass you." She stammered out.

Tegan laughed a little and rubbed her hand along Ella's knee. "Honey, you didn't embarrass me. I thought it was kinda cute. But trust me, after you've gone butt naked down a waterslide and had to walk through the entire park with red marks on your bare ass, you become kind of embarrassment proof."

Ella laughed in the middle of her tears, giving out one of the most adorable snorts that Tegan had ever heard. "Were you drunk?"

"I don't drink, but somebody dared me to throw my swimsuit off the tower and it landed outside the fence, so I had to go down the slide and walk to the street to retrieve it."

Ella laughed again. "An entire water park saw you naked?"

Tegan nodded. "Lots of boys got an education that day, and now my picture is on the wall next to the entrance, so I can never go back."

Ella stopped crying, the most adorable smile spread across her face and Tegan handed her the book. "He signed your book." She erupted into tears again.

"Okay, so maybe don't mention that again." Tegan said.

"I met my favorite author and I...I..." She started crying worse than before. She looked like she was in actual pain. Her face was contorted in agony until Tegan had finally had enough, she couldn't bare such a beautiful thing to be hurt anymore. She grabbed her forcefully and pulled her into a kiss.

She could feel Ella calm down, like all she had needed was a shock to her system to bring her back to life. Tegan was in bliss too. It was more than a kiss; it was like she had found the half of her soul that had been missing. After a few seconds they broke and Tegan asked, "Better?"

"Better." Ella confirmed.

Ten minutes later they were walking arm in arm down the convention center floor when Tegan got an idea. "I have an absolutely wonderful idea." She told Ella.

Ella looked at her, understandably nervous. "What is it?"

Tegan did her level best to smile like the joker. She held out for a few seconds before finally saying, "We should get tattoos!" she squealed.,

Ella started to shake her head. "Oh, no, I couldn't."

"Come on Ella, it will be our way of commemorating the day."

She shook her head again. "I can't get a tattoo, what if somebody saw?"

"Who would care, your parents?"

Ella tilted her head to the side, considering. "No," she said. "My Dad had tons of ink and my mom loved it."

Tegan was curious. She wondered if she slowly broke down all of the excuses if she could get Ella to understand that it was her decision and the hell with what everyone else thought. "Who then, your friends?"

She looked around, as if just discovering that she had no friends around her. "I think that after today I don't really have any friends from home."

"What if we got them in places where only we would know they are there?" Tegan asked. Ella started to say something, but inspiration struck, and Tegan yelled, "Oh, hold on a second." She took out her sketchbook and started to draw.

A few minutes later, Tegan showed the drawing to Ella and her eyes lit up. In the center of the page was a small geometric design, a square with prisms and other shapes inside. Incorporated into it were the names Poppy and Ella.

Ella spoke in a soft voice. "Okay."

CHAPTER FIVE

C ARLY

The Tattoo parlor was not the place Carly would have expected to be at Comicon. It looked like a real tattoo place, but with nerds in it. There was a fat guy in glasses with his shirt off in the corner, crying over and entire back tattoo of the little robot from Star Wars that Carly couldn't remember the name of. But there was also a seedy element that she was not comfortable with. It seemed to her that the ratio of people with switch blades to people without switchblades was far too high. But Poppy seemed right at home. She walked up with pride to the counter and started to show the design they wanted to a guy who had red and black designs covering his entire face and enough piercings to cover the entire earring section at a Walmart.

Carly stood just inside the entrance to the little temporary building, shed, thing, and wondered if she was completely crazy. She was about to get a tattoo from a stranger that had been designed by someone she would have only known about three hours longer than the artist. It was official, she was cracked.

But there was also an element of danger and craziness to it that Carly liked. She felt safe with Poppy. She felt like this person would keep her safe from any real harm, she got the sense that Poppy knew where the line was, and how far she could hang over it without really getting hurt. But Carly also knew from her dad's stories that you found out where the line was by crossing it, and getting hurt.

Poppy waved her over and she came up to the counter, "This guy says that Bones is the artist we need. He's finishing up his last client and then we're up-" Carly gulped and she hoped that it wasn't too noticeable. Unfortunately, Poppy heard it and looked at her with concern. "Are you okay?" she asked. "You don't have to do this if you don't want, I'm not trying to pressure you into anything."

Carly shook her head. "No, I want to...it's just...does it hurt?"

Poppy's face was blank, "Yes. It does." she said honestly. "But only for a little while, then you're gonna want more. It's kinda addicting."

"How many do you have?" Carly wondered.

"Like twenty, but most of them are on the smaller side and they're spread out all over my body."

Carly tried not to look aroused, but she couldn't help it. It was the most outgoing thought she'd had, but she was suddenly overcome with a desire to know exactly where Poppy's tattoos were.

Before she could say anything, the piercings and weird face guy came out and spoke. "I can take you back to bones now."

They started to follow him. Carly took up the rear, feeling very nervous. She saw Poppy put her hand out behind her. Carly didn't like feeling like a little kid, but she took the hand, and they went down the hall. They came into a little curtained off booth, like a hospital room, where a big guy with lots of tattoos seemed to be cleaning up his station. He seemed like one of the more normal people in the place. His arms were like tree trunks, covered in tattoos. The only place that seemed untouched was his bald head., "Who's first?" Bones asked.

Carly swallowed hard and blurted out, "Me."

Poppy looked at her with respect and moved back, motioning to the table. Carly walked over and stood in front of Bones. She motioned to an area on her inner left thigh, just next to her vagina. She figured that since she wasn't sleeping with anyone and her mother hadn't been in charge of her bathing for a number of years, that no one would see it. "Can I get it here?" she asked.

"You're gonna have to take your dress and underwear off." he said. "How old are you?"

"Eighteen. " Carly told him.

"Then we're good."

Carly started to take her dress off, looking around, really uncomfortable, when Poppy whistled. "Come on Ella, show me dat ass!" Bones and Carly both laughed. She finished undressing and laid out on the table. Bones got the colors from Poppy and got ready to start.

"I'm gonna stick you a bit first to make sure you can handle it," he said. "Cause once I start; I'm going to finish. I don't allow anyone to walk around with my half-finished art on them."

"Okay, go for it then." Carly said. He stuck her with the needle and she yelped a bit. It hurt, but it wasn't as bad as she had built in up in her head.

"You good?" Bones asked.

She gave him a thumbs up and he started on the tattoo. She laid her head back on her arm and tried not to look like any more of a baby than she had already in front of Bones. A couple of hours later Bones' needle stopped and he said, "See what you think."

Carly hopped up and went to a full-sized mirror she hadn't noticed was even there before. She loved it. It looked amazing, smallish, but extremely intricate, it was about the size of her palm. She loved knowing that no matter what happened, it would be there forever. She turned around, smiling at Poppy. "It looks amazing." she said. Turning to Bones she added, "Thank you."

"No problem, here." He handed her a tube of triple antibiotic ointment. "Anytime it gets dry, for two weeks. And pat dry after a shower, no rubbing, no baths."

Carly nodded. "Yes sir." She turned to see Poppy get up and she wrapped her in a hug. Poppy laughed. "What?" Carly asked.

"Nothing, just, what an amazing day I'm having, being hugged by a girl wearing nothing but a bra, and I'm about to get a tattoo."

Carly looked down and noticed, for the first time, that she was not wearing anything but her yellow bra. She smiled. She had never been okay with nakedness before, but for some reason, even with Bones here, she didn't mind it so much.

She went over and put her dress back on, thinking better of the underwear. She sat down where Poppy had been and watched as Bones readied his equipment for a second tattoo. "I'm gonna need you to roll your dress down, I can't get to your neck." Bones told her. Carly immediately felt her face get hot.

Poppy just smiled. "Fair is fair." she said, taking the dress off and letting it fall on to her lap so that she was exposed above the waist.

Carly had to fight not to gasp. She'd never really seen anyone's breasts when she actually wanted to. There was the locker room at school, where she found being in a room with twenty naked people awkward, and then there was Jesse, who had shown her her bare breasts, but Carly wasn't even really interested beyond involuntary reactions. Poppy's breasts however, they were magnificent. Carly hadn't met the perfect girl, but she instantly knew that her breasts looked like that. "Sorry, I couldn't wear a bra with it."

"Please," Carly said, trying and failing not to giggle. "Don't apologize."

Poppy winked at her. She sat down on the chair like thing that Bones had set up so that he could get to her neck and spoke. "Let's do this!"

Later that night, as people were emptying out into the parking lot, Carly and Poppy stood in the middle of the throng. She didn't want to leave, but she had to go home, and she knew without a shadow of a doubt that Jesse would leave her on the wrong side of the country. "Poppy, I want to thank you." Carly said.

"No, thank you. I liked the look I got of your body."

"No, I'm serious. This was the best day of my life."

Poppy smiled. She reached out for a hug and Carly met her. It was the kind of hug you don't get every day. She felt like she was going to melt into Poppy. Like if God had come down and said that this was heaven, the two I of them standing there, hugging, then Carly surely would have asked to die, just so she could stay in heaven.

They finally broke and started to walk towards opposite ends of the parking lot.

CHAPTER SIX

T EGAN

"Hey Poppy!" She heard Ella call out.

Tegan turned around and spoke. "Yeah?"

Ella looked like she was gathering her courage. Last brave thing for today?"

Tegan smiled, "Go for it."

Ella pulled down her dress and flashed Tegan her bare breasts. Tegan's face went red, she could feel it. She could also feel her smile on either ear. She knew she'd be smiling like that all the way to ST. Louis. "This day just got even better!" She called out. She saw Ella nod her head in the direction of her bag and Tegan pulled the flap open. In her bag she saw Ella's yellow bra.

Somehow, even though she hadn't thought it possible, her smile got even wider. "I think I'm in love!" She yelled.

"Me too." Ella called out. After a few more seconds, they both knew they had to leave. They turned at the same time and walked away. As Tegan walked through the parking lot, she wiped a tear from her eye.

Tegan thought about Ella for the next several months.

From California to Missouri. Her father had gotten a good job offer, so the entire family had to move. New school for senior year, new practice for her mother, new...well everything.

The new house looked nice enough, but Tegan was still pissed as she took things off the moving truck. Missouri was hot. So hot that she was about three seconds from ditching the flannel and just wearing her tank top.

As she came down the truck her dad stopped her at the edge. "Sit for a second, I want to talk to you."

She did as she was bid, she put her box down and sat on the edge of the truck. "Honey," Her Dad started. Every time he started with honey, she knew it was going to be one of those, 'I'm ruining life as you know it, but try and keep your chin up speeches. "I know you didn't want to leave, and I'm sorry. But this place is gonna be great. I promise."

Tegan looked past him and happened to catch a glimpse of a cute girl walking her dog dog in the street."

She immediately thought of Ella. Ella was the only girl she'd been thinking of for months. "At least the local girls are cute." Her Dad said.

She looked at him. "You know, it's just weird when you say it."

Her dad laughed. "Yeah, I heard it as soon as I said it."

They both laughed. Tegan felt some of her anger go away. There were times when she was mad at her family, but deep down she loved them and didn't stay mad long. They had all been through too damned much to stay mad forever. Tegan sighed. "I guess I have no choice but to get to know the place." she said.

"That's, sort of the spirit." Her Dad said with a chuckle.

He picked her box off the edge of the truck. "Why don't you go for a walk, have a look around? We'll put your stuff in your room for you."

Tegan knew better than to wait around for her mother to object. She hopped off the truck, gave her dad a kiss on the cheek, and walked off down the sidewalk.

Tegan walked around her new neighborhood until she was kinda bored, St. Louis was a smaller city than she had lived in before. It had a small town feel to it but was still big enough that she would need to explore. "Weird city, St Louis." she said aloud to no one in particular.

"You're not actually in Saint Louis you know."

Tegan turned around to see a girl sitting on her front porch, looking at her. "Where am I then?" Tegan asked.

"Bellview Missouri." she said. Tegan thought she was cute. She wasn't Ella, but she was certainly cute. She was wearing jean shorts that stopped just below her knees and a cute blue top with slightly puffy sleeves. She had a look about her that was very Ellie May Clampet, and not in a bad way.

"How did I not know this?" Tegan asked. "I saw the sign for St Louis, and then fell asleep...my dad just said we were here."

The girl laughed. "Most people think of this as St Louis, but the city is actually nearly an hour away. I doubt your dad has any idea he's in an entirely different town."

Tegan started to walk up the porch. "So, is there anything fun to do around here?" she asked.

"I'm not one for group activities. I mostly stay home."

"Mind if I sit?"

The girl motioned to a chair on the other side of a wicker table that was next to her. "Be my guest."

Tegan sat down. She couldn't describe the weird feelings that she was feeling, but the closest thing she could come to it was nervousness. She hadn't felt nervous about anyone since Ella. | Why was she so nervous around this girl? "So how come you moved to Missouri?" The girl asked. "I'm Carly by the way."

Tegan extended her hand. "Tegan." They shook hands and she continued. "My Dad got a new job and he had to move. So, we had to come with him."

"You don't sound happy about it." Carly observed.

"I liked my friends and life back in California." Tegan told her. "But I mean, life is an adventure and I guess moving here counts."

Carly smiled. "I guess it does."

"Can I ask you a bit of a personal question? I don't want to presume, seeing as we just met and all."

"I'd be happy to help. My Dad always said that you should be kind to people until they give you a reason not to be."

Tegan laughed. "I like that very much. What did he say to do once you have a reason?"

"Fuck their shit up."

They both laughed for a while about that. When their laughter died down Tegan spoke, "How's the town's attitude towards the less than heterosexual?"

"What'd you mean?"

"Well, I prefer the fairer sex and I don't hide it, but I wanted to know if this is still the kind of town that burns crosses on the lawn and things like that."

Carly laughed, a bit uncomfortably. Tegan hoped she wasn't ruining the first chance she had at making a friend in this town. "No," Carly said. "They don't burn crosses; I think that was mostly the KKK and they don't live around here. As far as the gay thing is concerned, nobody has ever seemed bothered about me being gay. Even the old biddies are cool with it."

"Really?" Tegan asked, not sure if this country cutie was pulling her leg.

"Swear. Our town is mostly full of hippies that settled down into the conservative lifestyles that they ran away from. They hate democrats, hut they're fine with gays."

Tegan couldn't speak for a minute. She was thinking that she might have found the perfect town. Conservative hippies? what description could possibly fit her better? "You, okay?" Carly asked.

Tegan snapped out of her bubble. "Yeah, I was just thinking that I might love it here after all."

A voice from inside the house called for Carly to come to dinner. "Coming." She yelled back. Turning to Tegan she said, "Wanna stay for dinner?"

"I should probably go home and move into my new room."

Carly nodded. "Okay, see you at school tomorrow?"

Tegan smiled. "It'll be good to know someone on my first day."

They said their goodbyes and Tegan made her way home. That night she was making her room up in the way she wanted, unpacking box after box she thought about Ella, and the day they had spent together, and this new girl Carly.

Tegan wondered if maybe she should move past the girl she'd lost and try to be happy in this new town.

CHAPTER SEVEN

C ARLY

Carly and her mom were watching TV after dinner, well, her mom was. She was mostly staring into space and thinking about Poppy It had been months since Comicon, but she still thought about her every day, and every night. She had never been one to masturbate, though she did on occasion, and the only person she would think about was Poppy.

On her last mandated visit to Dr Klein's office, he told her that he noticed she had become more comfortable in her own skin. He said that she seemed less shy and just a bit more outgoing. Carly attributed this change in her personality to Poppy. She knew it was stupid, but ever since that day with her, Carly had tried to make Poppy proud of her. She tried to act as if Poppy was with her.

She knew it was weird, acting brave to try and impress someone you didn't know what their real name was, and who you would probably never see again, but she did. She tried to be brave for her Comicon girl, as she had started to call Poppy in the stories she wrote.

All this thinking about Poppy and her magnificent breasts was causing something to happen to Carly's body. She shifted in her seat, finally she looked over at her mother and said, "I think I'm gonna go to bed."

"You okay baby?"

Carly nodded. "Yeah, I'm just tired. I want to get some sleep before tomorrow."

"That's probably a good idea. Senior Year. Are you excited to be out after this year?"

"Yes ma'am." Carly said.

"Well, I want to talk with you, but that can wait for tomorrow. Go ahead and head to bed."

Carly got up, kissed her mother good night, and headed up to her room. She hoped her face wasn't red, but she didn't care enough to stop and look in the hall mirror.

When she got to her room, she took off her pajama pants and noticed that she would have to put these ones in the hamper. Her wetness had run down her leg a ways and soaked her through at the back of right thigh. She dumped them in the dirty clothes and did the same with her shirt.

Laying back on the bed she let her mind go to that day, with Poppy. She imagined some bits that hadn't really happened and soon the pressure was building even more, ready to be released.

To the surprise of both Carly and her aching privates, the new girl she'd met on the porch, Tegan, came into her mind. Picturing her elicited a stronger response than Poppy had in a month, which was saying something given what Poppy did to her body. Carly decided to go with it and closed her eyes.

When she was done, wiping herself off with a towel, she ran a hand over her tattoo. She missed her Comicon girl, but she had just thought of this other girl and she wasn't sure how to feel about that…so she did what the doctor told her to do to help cope with all the emotions and things running around inside her head, she went over to her desk, putting on a robe because she had not yet reached the point where she could just hang around naked, even in her own room, and she started to write yet another story that she probably wouldn't share with anyone.

The next day, when Tegan walked into homeroom/English, and Mr. Holinder introduced her, Carly looked up. She thought she looked cute today, dressed in a white sundress that looked amazing under the jean jacket that she had on. When she came down the aisle, Carly looked away. *Oh my god*, she thought. *It's obvious, what I did. She knows I thought about her last night.*

Carly shook her head, she knew she was being ridiculous, but she couldn't help it. She could feel her face growing redder and feel the heat coming off her. "Will you calm down you moron." she said to herself. "Your room is on the second floor, unless she was standing on the roof outside the bay window, she couldn't know. You're being ridiculous."

She did her best to not look at Tegan, who was sitting fourth at the center row of desks, the perfect spot for Carly to look at her. Every time she would look back at Carly, she would get embarrassed and mentally scold herself again, so she did her best to listen to Mr. Holinder speak about Emily Bronte.

After class had ended and everyone was filing out of the room, Mr. Holinder said, "Carly, I need to speak with you for a moment."

Carly was instantly nervous. Was there something wrong with the paper she had turned in on the last day of school? She didn't think he would remember it, but since Mr. Holinder had been teaching Juniors and Seniors for years, she guessed he made it a point to remember even the silly stories that Juniors handed in at the end of the year. She walked up the aisle of desks with a bit of trepidation and sweat on her brow. She really hoped she wasn't in trouble, but then again, what would she be in trouble for?

When she got to the desk Mr. Holinder set her story, still in its orange report holder, on the desk and tapped it with two fingers. "This is absolutely amazing." he said.

Carly gripped her books a bit tighter in her arms. Praise always made her uncomfortable, but then again, what didn't? "Thank you, sir." she said shyly.

"Have you ever written anything more substantial?"

"Like what?"

"A book, a novella, anything above a short story."

"No sir, I wouldn't know how to go about doing that."

He shrugged. "It's easy, just do this, but for more pages." He laughed. "No, I understand. It is hard, but I really think you should give it some thought. You are a terrific writer."

"Thank you, sir."

"Okay, promise me that you will think about it, and you may go."

"I promise that I will think about it."

Mr. Holinder, satisfied with himself, smiled. "Then you may go."

Carly walked out of the room and that is when Tegan jumped out from seemingly nowhere. "Ah, what the hell is wrong with you?" Carly yelped.

Tegan had a smile plastered across her face. "Now? Mostly ADHD and a small case of undiagnosed schizophrenia."

Carly smiled slightly. Tegan raised her arms up and let them flop down at her sides. "Can you help me find my next class? Mrs....something or other, math."

Carly was confused. "Why not ask someone who came out before me? Why wait?"

Tegan spoke matter-of-factly. "Cause you're cute." She smiled, her confidence sort of reminded Carly of the way that Poppy had just walked into any situation, meeting a famous writer, or at the tattoo place, and seemed at ease.

"Follow me." Carly said as she put a strand of hair behind her ear. She took off walking down the hallway and she heard Tegan say,

"Great butt too."

She didn't know if Tegan knew she could hear her, she'd said it more to herself than anyone else, but regardless, Carly wasn't brave enough to say anything. She just smiled to herself and walked down the hall.

CHAPTER EIGHT

TEGAN

Tegan didn't know why Carly had gotten all red upon seeing her this morning, but she thought it was kinda cute. They had taken turns looking at each other like they were in fifth grade. Though Tegan suspected that she had caught Carly looking more times than she herself had been caught.

Tegan didn't have many classes with Carly. So, over the next few months she made it a point to go up to her and talk and flirt and things whenever she had the chance. Carly made her kind of nervous, in a way that no one had in a while.

One day, towards the end of the year, Tegan saw her sitting in the cafeteria and decided to do the same thing she had done periodically throughout the year, take a bit of her lunch. the Carly spoke without looking up from comic book she was reading. "Don't you have a lunch?"

Tegan took another bite. "Yeah, why?"

"Cause you take parts of mine."

"Oral fixation."

That shocked Carly enough to make her look up. "Really?"

Tegan did her best to smile mischievously, hoping to high heavens that she didn't just look like an asshole. "Wouldn't you like to know?" With that she left Carly alone at the table and walked out of the cafeteria, stopping and walking backwards long enough to call, "See you later."

Tegan headed to the library. For such a small town, Bellview had an awfully nice school library. She used lunch to get her homework from all her classes before done, and then used her free period towards the end of the day to get all the homework done that came from classes after lunch. Tegan didn't offer up the fact that she was a hardworking nerd, but she didn't hide it.

CHAPTER NINE

C ARLY

Carly felt a bit weird, being at the pool at night, alone, but she also liked the privacy. She could work out, have a swim, and since the owners were friends of her and her mom, they didn't mind if she stayed late sometimes.

Her cell phone rang, and she saw that it was her mom. Not many other people even had her number. She picked it up and immediately heard, "Where are you?"

"I told you I was going to swim for a while tonight. Don't you remember?"

"Oh yeah, I guess I forgot. Okay, when will you be home?"

"They said I could stay until eight, but then they have to shut everything down for a cleaning, so figure I'll be home around nine thirty."

"Be safe, I love you." Her Mom said, very paternally.

"I will be. I love you too."

They hung up and Carly walked out of the locker room. She kicked her flip flops under the bench, set her towel down, straightened her one piece where it was riding up her butt, and she dived into the water.

And immediately pissed herself when Tegan popped up, grabbing her by the waste and pulling them both to the top. Carly splashed water at her. "You get way too much enjoyment out of scaring me." She started to breath hard, still a bit frazzled.

"I actually scared the piss out of you. I can't believe it; I've never managed to literally scare the piss out of anyone."

"You're lucky I didn't crap on you." Carly said. "Fucking hell that scared me."

"I didn't even know you could curse." Tegan laughed.

"How long were you down there?"

Tegan thought for a moment, "Five minutes I think."

Carly couldn't help but stare in amazement, and confusion. "When I was a kid I watched a special about Navy Seals and it said they could hold their breath for five minutes, so I spent a month training myself to do the same thing."

"Wow. " Was all Carly could say. Tegan popped up out of the water a bit and Carly couldn't help but look down at her cleavage in her bikini. But she got caught, when she raised her eyes, Tegan was looking right at her. Carly looked away, blushing.

"Don't be ashamed. I'm quite proud of what the good lord gave me, and I don't mind having a beautiful girl looking." Carly giggled a little, Tegan came closer, and her tone got more serious. "I'm sorry if I interrupted your private time." she said. "I know that everyone needs some and I'll leave you he if you like."

Carly, despite the cool water, felt her face get hot. "No," she told her. "You can stay. I'd like you to stay."

Tegan smiled. She went under and swam to the other end of the pool. Popping up she said, "Come get me."

And Carly did. The two of them swam and played and just spent time together until it was time for them to go.

That Sunday, as Carly and her mother were going in to church, she noticed Tegan and her family coming up the steps. She whispered something to her mother and when she nodded, Carly did the most courageous thing she had done in ten years, she walked up to someone she thought was cute.

Tegan looked wonderful. She had on a pink dress that made her look beautiful and radiant but didn't make her look like a sister wife. She was beautiful and sexy at the same time. Tegan turned around, surprised to see her. "Oh hey, I was looking for you. Peace be with you."

"And also,with you." Carly said. "I was wondering if you would like to sit with me and my mom today. Assuming that is okay with your parents." Carly could feel her heartbeat in her ears and feared it would burst from her chest.

Tegan smiled. "Is it weird that I love how old fashioned you are behaving?"

Before she could say anything, Tegan patted her father's shoulder and he turned around, "Yes?"

Carly really hoped she didn't sound like a complete buffoon. "Sir, I would very much like to sit with your daughter in church today. Is that alright with you sir?"

Tegan's father had a look on his face that showed he wasn't given this kind of respect every day, but he liked it. "If it's alright with her, it's okay with me. You have my permission."

Carly smiled. "Thank you, sir." she said.

The two of them made their way to the front of the church where Carly's mom was waiting. "That was so cute." Tegan said as they went inside.

Carly didn't have much of a chance to respond, because it was all religious reverence when they stepped inside the ancient catholic church that had been in the town since it first was founded and hadn't really been updated since.

It was called St Mary's, like about a thousand other Catholic churches throughout the world, but it had its own something. The church was made mostly of stone, it had original stain glass windows, except one, from the fifties that had been knocked out when a tree came through during a storm. Electricity had been added in the sixties, far later than most other places. There was a big stone alter in the front of the room, and despite the moderately sized building and the very 'Hunch Back of Notre Dam' feel, the place still felt like a community building, a place where you came to be one with God, one big family.

Carly's Mom made way for them. Tegan went first, making the cross and entering the pew. When they were all in and kneeling, Carly started to pray. *Dear god, I know what the church's official policy is, and I know we have talked about this before, but once again I really hope you don't hate me for asking a girl to sit next to me on Sunday. I really like her, even though Poppy is still out there I think that I should probably try and get over her, to be happy. And I know that you don't hate me. I'm sorry for asking...or thinking that...I love you. But I have to ask, why did you make me so crazy? Is there a reason? There has to be, I just wish you'd tell me what it is.*

Carly opened her eyes and saw that everyone else, including people in other pews, was sitting back. This wasn't the first time she'd been the last one praying, but she still felt her face get hot as she sat back in the pew. Tegan leaned over and whispered, "I hope it was a good prayer. Mine lasted pretty long too, I got up just a second before you did."

Tegan sat back, but Carly smiled. It was nice that someone wanted to comfort her when she felt embarrassed. Normally her mom was the only one who even tried.

The church service was nice. They were up and down so many times that Carly's knees started to hurt. She'd gotten one of the kneelers where the padding had gone out.

When Tegan went back to her family, she gave Carly a brief kiss on the cheek like, as she said, "A proper young lady." Carly and her mom headed home for lunch.

Carly sat at the counter while her mom prepared what would be that night's dinner. Carly ate her sandwich and finally told her mom about Poppy. Carly's Mom handed her vegetables and a cutting board. As she spoke, she went and got a knife. "So, you think that this, here chop those. You think that this girl will be there, at Comicon again?"

"I don't know." Carly admitted. "But I'm hoping she might be."

The two of them cooked in silence for a few minutes before her mom said, "Can I ask you something?"

"Didn't you just?"

Her Mom groaned. "Not that shit again. I swear I curse your father for teaching you that." Carly laughed. Then her mom laughed and before they knew it they both had erupted into laughter. When they quieted down, her mom spoke again, "Have you considered that maybe you oughta focus on the s girl you have here instead of chasing the one that you don't even know where she is?"

"Believe it or not I have." Carly said forlornly. "But I mean, Poppy was amazing. She was the perfect girl."

Her Mom looked at her like she was crazy. "You know what your dad would have said about that."

Carly sighed. "Yeah."

They said it together. "If she was perfect, you wouldn't have lost her." They were silent and then they smiled.

He'd been talking about something completely different, but he said it about almost anything. "You know, Dad was practically a motivational poster." Carly said.

Her Mom laughed again. "Except he was saying that stuff long before those posters were hanging in every shrink's office."

Carly looked down at the vegetables, she had finished cutting them and she wanted to do something. "Do you mind if go sit on the porch for a bit? I need to think."

"Go ahead."

Grateful, Carly went to the porch to think. It was what her dad had done every time he had something to think over. He always said that there wasn't a problem in the world that couldn't be solved with some good thinking on a sitting porch.

CHAPTER TEN

TEGAN

Tegan was thinking of Ella. She was staring out her bedroom window, wondering if she really should move on, when she saw Carly wandering around outside. She jumped up and ran down the hall, took the first flight of stairs in a single leap, landing on the hardwood landing with a thud.

She took the last stairs three at a time and burst out the front door. The door banged as it shut, and Carly turned around in the street. "I didn't know which one was yours." she said.

"Oh yeah, I forgot you've never been to my house." Tegan said as she came off the porch and walked across the yard. "What's up? Is everything okay?"

"Uh yeah, I just wanted to ask you something." Carly said, but then got quiet. Tegan got the sense that she was building up her courage.

"Do you want to sit?" Tegan asked.

Carly shook her head. "I'm sorry. I'm not very brave so doing brave stuff is hard for me."

"Having the courage to walk over here makes you seem pretty brave in my book." Tegan said, still not sure why Carly was here at seven 'clock. "Seriously though, it's getting dark so you might want to come where you can see."

"No, I just want to know if you had any plans for this summer."

"Not that I know of." Tegan said, lying. She wanted to see where this was going.

"Okay, cause I thought maybe you and I could go around and I could show you some of the cool stuff Missouri has to offer."

"Like what?"

"I'm not really sure yet, but I thought we could go see the Arch, I don't know if you've ever seen it..."

Tegan shook her head. "No, I've never seen it."

"Well, there's that, and Branson, I don't know...I just thought maybe you would like to have fun with me. We could go to Lamberts, they throw rolls." Carly sounded like she might cry. Tegan rushed forward and gave her a little hug to comfort her.

When she came away Tegan spoke, "Are you asking me on a date? And to be assaulted with my food?"

"They throw them to you, not at you, and it's more like a bunch of small dates over the summer." Carly said. They were both silent for a couple of minutes before she spoke again. "I really like you; I don't know if I made that clear."

Tegan felt herself smile. "Kinda, did I make it clear how much I like you?" She could have sworn Carly's face was so red it glowed in the darkening night.

"Okay then, I should probably go home. Friday is the last day of school, so I thought we would go for our first adventure on Saturday."

"Sounds good." Tegan said. She was amazed how dark it had gotten in just the last few minutes, because she didn't see Carly coming when she came out of the shadows and gave Tegan a peck on the lips.

"Was that, okay?" Carly asked, nervousness dripping from her words.

"Absolutely."

When Carly went home, Tegan had sat on the front porch for ten minutes trying to decide whether or not she should bring up her new plans to her parents tonight or tomorrow.She ended up deliberating for so long that when she went back inside, her parents and brother had all gone to bed.

Tegan went upstairs and found Ella's yellow bra. She looked at it for a minute. She tried to get her rocks off with it, like she had been doing for the past year. Lately she had thought of Carly more and more when she did it though, instead of Ella. Tonight though, she thought of neither Ella, nor Carly, because try as she might she laid there, unable to actually masturbate. Finally, she gave up and just went to take a shower.

In the shower she thought of Ella, and how the day she spent with her was still one of the best in her life. But she also thought about Carly, the absolutely adorable girl who she liked and who had admitted to liking her.

Tegan came to a decision, she needed to stop obsessing over the girl she had lost, lost out of stupidity more than anything else, and focus on the amazingly smart, funny, great girl she had#. She needed to appreciate what she had before it was gone too. The next day Tegan decided to approach her mother first, hoping to play on the emotions of the family shrink. Her mother was in the downstairs room that they had turned into a joint office for her parents, doing patient hooks, little notebooks she kept on every patient.

Tegan poked her head around the corner. "Hey Mom, can I talk to you for a second?"

Her Mom sat down the composition notebook she was writing in and looked up. "Yeah, what's up sweetheart?"

Tegan came into the room, but she remained standing. She never liked sitting in her mom's office, it made her feel like one of her patients. "I would like to stay home this summer. While you go on vacation."

Her Mom looked at her with the look that she and her brother always called, 'The shrink look,' The look that said, 'I recognize this as an important discussion point, so I'm not going to say no right away, work fast.' "Why?" Her Mom asked.

"Because Carly wants to show me around Missouri, you know, like, little day trips, the Arch, some place called Branson, a restaurant where they hurl your food at you."

"Branson?" Her Mom said.

"Yeah, have you heard of it?"

"I've been there, but not in about twenty years." Her Mom looked off like she was fondly remembering something.

"When did you go there?" Tegan asked. She didn't to get too far off topic, but she kinda hoped this would help her case, that and she was genuinely curious.

"I grew up in Kansas dear, and I went to college here in Missouri. Your father is the city slicker."

"Wow." Tegan said, not sure what else to say.

"And they only throw the rolls, not your whole meal."

"That's only slightly less disconcerting."

Her mom chuckled. "Why do you want to miss a vacation to the Bahamas, to hang around Missouri and spend the summer with some girl?"

"Because I think that I love this girl." Tegan said. She was stunned. She wasn't sure of it, but somehow saying it out loud to her mother had cemented it in her mind. Ella was gone, and she thought she might be in love with Carly.

Her Mom sounded dubious. "You think that you might love this girl? After not showing any interest in, well, any-one, for over a year, you think that you're in love?"

Tegan sighed. "Okay, here it goes." and she told her of Ella, of the day they had spent together and all the feelings that she had had since that day for a girl she didn't really know. She even included the bit about her using something she had learned from her mother to get Ella to spend the day with her. She did not include the tattoo or the bra, but she did try her best to express to her mother just how much she loved that girl, and that was the reason Tegan had been depressive about a lot of stuff.

Then she told her mother about how Carly had brought her out of it. How she had a crush on her since they met on the family's first night here. How Carly made her not quite forget Ella, but she had helped her to get over her, and how she thought

Carly might actually be like, 'The one', even though she didn't know why exactly she felt this way.

When she finished, her mother wiped the hint of a tear from her eye and spoke, "I don't like you missing our family vacation." she said. "But I think that if this girl is really that important, you have to go for it."

Tegan felt a weight lifted from her chest. "Thank you, mom."

"You have to get your father's permission too." she said.

Tegan wasn't even worried, she was just immediately preparing what she would say to her father when he got home later that night. As she got up to leave, thanking her mother again, her mom asked, "What about school?"

Tegan waved that away. "I still want to do what I want."

She reassured her mother. "She doesn't change that. I mean, did Dad change what you wanted? Did Me and Trevor?"

Her Mom had to admit that she made a good point. "No, I guess not." she said. "You all changed how I did it, but not that I did."

"Well, it's the same here."

Her Mom looked at her with pride and Tegan walked out of the room, hoping that when her Dad got home he would agree to let her stay home.

CHAPTER ELEVEN

C ARLY

The final week of school went by fast. The day after school ended, Tegan and Carly got into her dad's old VW beetle and headed for St. Louis.

When they were still ten minutes outside of St Louis, said Tegan said something that she had already three Many times, but still made Carly smile. "I can't get over this car, it is so freakin' cool."

"Thanks." Carly said.

"Did your dad really keep it up from new?"

"He was actually the second owner. He got it from some neighbors when he was in high school and he kept it in great shape up until he died."

"If you don't mind me asking, how did he die?" Tegan asked.

"He was a wildlife guide for rich people." Carly explained. "He took them all over the world, rain forests, swamp lands, he even took them up mountains."

"He sounds amazing."

"He was. He went to the jungle on his last trip, taking some guy who was studying the jungles of the world for a book, I don't know, he was some rich conservationist writer dude. My Dad got bit by a really poisonous snake and he died on the trip." They were both silent for a minute before Carly spoke again. "Please don't tell anyone, but the rich guy actually gave me quite a bit of money, the royalties from that one book. He said it was because my dad saved his life, and that he was really sorry."

"I won't," Tegan said. "But why won't you tell anyone?"

"He asked me not to tell anyone that he did it. He also made sure never to use his real name, but it was easy enough to find it. I'd already read 'Surfing on the edge' and 'Volcano Island'."

"You know, in California, someone would have sued him."

"Yeah, but Mom and I both agreed, even before he gave us the money, that we weren't gonna do that."

"How come?" Tegan asked. She seemed genuinely curious, but also like she was testing Carly.

"Because no amount of money would bring my dad back. And that is what I want. He died doing what he loved, if he had to go, he went how he would have wanted." Carly looked over and Tegan had a big smile on her face, "What?"

"I just officially like you more than ninety percent of the people I met while I lived in California." she said. "I have never understood why people wanted to sue someone over something that wasn't gonna change it. I mean, I know it was awful to lose your kid, but fifty million dollars isn't going to ease that pain. Not if you actually loved him."

"That's how I feel." Carly said as she took the exit heading towards the arch.

The two of them stood in front of the Arch, looking up. Carly hadn't been here in ages, so she wasn't sure about this, not completely anyway. "We're going up there?" Tegan said, sounding just a bit unsure.

"Wait until you see the egg." Carly told her.

"What?"

Carly laughed and took her arm, leading her inside. A few minutes later Tegan was looking at the small white egg shaped elevator, and back at Carly like she might be nuts. "What the fuck is that thing?" she asked. "It does not seem sound."

"Are you scared of heights or something?"

Tegan looked at her, this brave girl who she hadn't seen look even remotely nervous in the year that she had known her, she looked just a bit clammy. "I'm not scared, I'm just not found of them." Tegan said.

Carly gripped her hand, they looked at each other, and they got in the egg. Carly instantly thought to herself that the look on Tegan's face made the trip worth it. There was just this look of childlike wonder and amazement. Carly got the impression that she had never seen any city from so high up.

"This is incredible." Tegan said. "I can't believe they built this...when did they build this?"

Carly went over # to a plaque on the wall and read off the date. "It started in nineteen sixty three and was finished in sixty five."

Tegan looked thoughtful, but also a bit disappointed. "I thought it was like in the eighteen hundreds. Still impressive though, I mean look at it, we're so high, this is so cool. I, this is amazing."

She ran over to Carly and wrapped her arms around her. Carly almost fell down. It was a hug like she had had with Poppy. It felt like she was going to melt into Tegan, like they were two halves of the same person and they had finally found each other.

She couldn't tell Tegan this, but she thought she might love her.

CHAPTER TWELVE

T EGAN

Tegan still didn't know what had come over her when she was up there, but it was like her inclination to stay on the ground had been reversed and she now loved the view from the air. She even considered getting a pilot's license.

On the ride home she thought about that hug, and how it felt just like she was hugging Ella again. But she shook that out of her head. She had made the decision to leave Ella in the past, even though it hurt her, she had to leave her there. So, she decided to learn more about Carly on the drive home.

Funny enough, Carly beat her to it. Just as Tegan, opened her mouth, Carly spoke. "Can I ask you a question?"

"Didn't you just ask me a question?" Tegan said playfully.

Carly laughed. "I guess I did, here's another one, how come you're scared of heights? I mean, I didn't think you were scared of anything."

"I got over a lot of my fears when I was younger, almost dying does that, but my fear of heights persisted until today. Now I'm thinking I love them.,"

"What happened that you almost died?" Carly asked. Tegan could tell she was hesitant to push, and Tegan appreciated that.

"Do you know what Rhabdomyosarcoma is?" Carly shook her head. "It's a cancer in your tissues," Tegan continued. "But it can spread, like mine did. It spread to my muscles and pretty much everywhere."

"That's awful."

"Yeah, I was in and out of the hospital from twelve until I was fifteen. It wouldn't have taken that long normally, but my tumors continued to grow...so when I finally got out, and my three years as a lab rat were over, I decided I wasn't going to be scared anymore."

"That's...intense..." Carly said. "You want to ask me something?"

Tegan thought for a moment. "How come you're so scared? Does it have anything to do with like a mental illness, or did something traumatic happen?"

"It's a bit of both. I was diagnosed with a bunch of stuff like anxiety and panic attacks and some other crap, I never bothered to learn it cause I don't want to let it hold me back, ya'know?"

Tegan nodded. "Sure, sure."

"Mostly," Carly continued, "It was my dad's death. When I was little he always had a way of calming me down, of getting me to do anything wild or crazy just by saying, "Come on Darlin'". So, when he died, I kinda got shoved back into my shell. That was when I got the actual diagnosis, so my mom thought it would be a good idea to see a shrink."

"You don't like shrinks?" Tegan asked.

"No, I mean, they're fine for people who actually need them, but I'm fine. I have my shit to get through just like everyone else. I think too many people use therapy as a crutch."

Tegan nodded, understanding. "My Mom says the same thing, and she is a shrink."

Carly looked over at her like she might have heard Tegan wrong. She didn't know what that was all about, so she continued. "I think it's your turn."

That seemed to jar Carly back to life. "When did you tell your parents you were gay?"

Tegan smiled to herself, remembering the time she had told them. "When I was being wheeled into surgery." she said.

"What?"

"I was being wheeled into surgery and I saw my parents looking worried, so I turned to them, said, "I'm gay!" and then I said, "Wheel me in boys," and they took me to surgery."

Carly looked stunned. "Has anyone ever told you that you have a flair for the dramatic?"

Tegan smiled. "Yes, yes they have."

"Your turn."

"Same question."

"My parents always just knew." Carly said. "My Dad said he noticed when I was a kid, Mom said she knew when I was in about second grade. They said I never showed any interest in boys, I never said they were cute or anything, I only talked that way about girls."

"It's cool that they were so accepting."

Carly shrugged. "They said that it didn't concern them what gender of the person I was attracted to was, so much as what kind of person they were."

"I love your parents."

"Me too." They both laughed. They drove in silence for a couple of minutes before Carly spoke again. "First kiss?"

"This girl I met in Chemo. We sat across from each other, and after a few weeks we got the nurses to let us sit side by side and we talked and played games and stuff."

"Did you guys ever get to go out, like on an official date?"

"No. She uh...she didn't win. Her battle with cancer I mean." Tegan felt the tears start to fall down her face. She hated crying, but she almost always cried when Marie was brought up. Whether it was happiness or pain, she always cried. "I'm sorry." Tegan said/. "I, she was my first kiss and I, _"

"You loved her." Carly finished.

"Yeah. It's not something you ever really get over, holding your first love's hand as they die."

"I can't even imagine." Carly said.

Tegan wiped her eyes. "Okay, new subject. I'm even depressing me."

Carly laughed and the discussion changed to a lighter topic. They talked about light stuff like that for the rest of the drive home.

That Sunday was graduation. Tegan couldn't help but feel pride, not only that she had graduated, but that she had even made it to this age, or her senior year.

Later that same day her family left for the Bahamas. They tried to get her to come one more time, but she assured them that she was where she needed to be, and that she loved them. She didn't see Carly for that week. She said she had to help her grandmother do some things, but she assured her that Branson was that weekend.

CHAPTER THIRTEEN

C ARLY

Carly pulled up in front of the house, eager to take Tegan to Branson and show her some fun. She honked the horn but no Tegan. She honked again, then waited for five minutes, still no Tegan. She started to get nervous. Had she left?

Where would she even have gone? Finally, Carly decided to go up to the house. She found the front door unlocked. She went inside. It was a nice, older house. She if saw a long front hallway lined with pictures, leading into what she presumed was a kitchen in the back. Immediately off the hall was a livingroom with a nice TV and a lot of book cases. Towards the back of the room, closest to the front of the house, she noticed a door that led into another room. She went in checking to see if it was Tegan's, but it looked to be an office.

I'm officially a home invader. She thought to herself. She went back to the hall and saw the stairs, just off the front door, and followed them up to the second floor. She passed a room that was very nicely kept. There was a TV hooked up to a video game system, all the controllers and games organized in a very tidy manner. Carly guessed that this was her brother's room.

The next door, on the other side of the hall, was clearly Tegan's parent's room. A large bed, well kept, clearly a home-owner's room. People who owned the house never had much stuff in their bedroom as they had the rest of the house to put stuff in.

The room at the very end of the hall had the door part way open. Carly peaked her head! in and was greeted by Tegan's naked butt. Her head was jammed into the mattress, her ass poking out. She wasn't so much sleeping under the covers as she was straddling them, like she had to have something to hold on to while she slept.

Carly got a mischievous idea. She gingerly stepped forward, and smacked Tegan's naked ass.

Tegan jerked awake. She flew up so hard she fell off the other side of the bed and landed where Carly couldn't see her. Tegan popped back up. Her breasts looked familiar to Carly.But she hadn't ever seen her breasts, so how would they look familiar? "Interesting way to sleep." Carly said. "Face smashed, straddling a blanket."

"Weird dream," Tegan said. "Ended up sleeping with a blue alien. I was the big spoon."

"You know what, I'm not even going to ask if that's true." Carly said. "I'm gonna hope you're messing with me."

Tegan spoke as she walked around the room, gathering her things to get dressed. Carly noticed that her room was extremely messy. There were clothes on the floor, spilling out of a wardrobe, art supplies covered a desk, this place was a wreck.

"Sorry I overslept." Tegan was saying, "I really did have a bad dream."

"You're fine. Are you always so naked?"

"More naked than most people, does it bother you?"

"No, no, I quite like it."

Tegan looked at her with a gleam in her eye that suggested she might take Carly right then. Carly wouldn't have minded. "Do I have time to shower? I sweated like a pig making babies last night."

Carly laughed. "Yeah, go ahead."

Tegan turned to grab her towel off the door of the wardrobe. "Can you hand me a hairbow?" She asked. "There should be a couple on the dresser."

Carly handed her a hairbow and went back over to one of her walls, covered in drawings. Tegan walked by with her hair up, and Carly caught a glimpse of the back of her neck as she left the room.

"Holy shit."

CHAPTER FOURTEEN

TEGAN

A smack on the ass was a strange way to be woken up, but she did not mind it. She was just glad she'd been smart enough to come up with that Alien story. She didn't want to tell Carly what her dream had really been about.

She had her towel draped over one shoulder and her toiletry bag in the opposite hand as she went into the bathroom. She turned the water on and set her things down. She rubbed her hand on the back of her neck and looked at her sleepless face. She sighed and got in the shower.

The water felt good on her skin. She hadn't been in there for more than a few seconds before she heard the door open. She started to say something, but before she could, the shower curtain was thrown to the side and Carly rushed forward, taking Tegan into a kiss.

Tegan felt an explosion go off in her mind. She knew instantly what was going. She pushed Carly awake gently and the two of them spoke in unison.

"Poppy."

"Ella."

They stood there, smiling like idiots as the water sprayed onto Carly's clothes. In a couple of minutes, they were soaked. Tegan reached behind her and turned off the water. They stood there, just looking at each other, the dumbest smiles on their faces.

"I can't believe it's you." Carly said. "Do you have any idea how, -"

Tegan kissed her. When she came back, she said, "Yes. I do."

They were silent again, suddenly, as if a gun had gone off, they both started to remove Carly's wet clothes. Tegan knelt and looked at her tattoo. She was eye lever with the image that she had dreamed about and thought about. She kissed it. She felt Carly shudder and she stood up, grabbing Carly's hand and leading her back to her bedroom.

Carly slammed down on to the piles of bedding and Tegan leaned down over her, close enough that her short hair still brushed Carly's face. She kissed her again, on the lips, then moving lower. She kissed all the way down her body, stopping every once in a while to do a bit more than kiss.

Hours later, when they had had all the sex they could handle, and a bit more when they went back to take an actual shower, Carly was resting when Tegan came back with a couple of mugs of tea, wearing a big T-shirt that only covered half her ass, which was completely on purpose. "I put your clothes in the dryer." she said as she handed Carly her mug.

"Thanks." She took a sip of tea. "I'm sorry, I just can't get over the fact that we've been right here, together."

"I know." Tegan said. "It's like, I had just made the choice to give Ella up for Carly, come to find out they're the same person."

They kissed again. After a bit of silence, Carly laughed. "I guess the only gay virgin is no more."

"What do you mean?"

"I always felt like I was the only gay person who wasn't having sex. I can't say that now."

Tegan smiled. "You couldn't say that then dear."

"What do you mean?"

"Up until a few hours ago when you, ya know, I was a virgin."

Carly looked genuinely shocked. "I just kinda assum,-"

"That the freedom loving hippie chick fucked around." Tegan finished. "I don't blame you; most people assume that. But I happen to be quite picky. Before you the only person I had ever even thought about sleeping with was Marie."

"I guess I got caught up in the same stereotype that bugs me, you know, that gay people are sluts."

"Yeah, I know what you mean. It happens to the best of us.

They drank their tea mostly in silence. Tegan hoped Carly was thinking of the same things she was, because after Tegan had set her cup down on her nightstand, she decided to bring it up. "Do you love me?"

Carly looked a little shocked by the question. She swallowed her last drink of tea and sat her cup on the table. Just as Tegan was getting nervous, Carly said, "Yes."

And Tegan exhaled a breath she hadn't realized she'd been holding. "That's good, because I didn't want to ask the next question without knowing the answer to that one."

"What's the next question?"

" Do you want to spend our lives together?"

Carly looked like she might pass out. Tegan felt bad for a brief moment, but then she figured that Carly ought to know who she was getting. "Sorry if that's shocking or abrupt," Tegan said, "But I don't beat around the bush."

"That's actually what you did a little while ago." Carly said and they both laughed. "No," Carly began. "I mean, yes it was shocking, but no I'm not like, upset about it. I just...I was getting ready to ask you the same thing."

"You know our parents will probably say we're rushing into this."

"Yeah, still don't care."

"Me neither." Tegan said.

Since her parents were out of town and Carly couldn't just not tell her mother where she was going, they went to her house that night and told her mom about them and their story.

"Wow." Was all Carly's Mom said at the end of the story, which left out the tattoos and copious amounts of sex they'd had that morning.

"So, you don't have a problem?" Carly asked.

"Why should I have a problem? I was nineteen when I married your dad, you're only a few months away from that age."

Tegan turned to look at Carly. "You're older than me? That's hot."

Carly's Mom laughed and high fived Tegan. "There are a couple of things I would like to know. Her Mom said. "Tegan, what do you want to do with your life?"

"I want to be a psychologist." Tegan said. "I really want to help people, the people who really need help... and maybe sell some paintings and artwork on the side."

Carly's Mom looked impressed. "Okay, I like that very much. Carly, why don't you get one of your stories and let Tegan read it."

"But, -"

"If you can't show your wife what you write, how much do you really love her?"

"That's a good point Momma, but my but was about us being in the middle of something."

"Please just go get it."

Carly left the room and her mother leaned closer to Tegan „ "What kind of person are you?"

"I don't think I understand." Tegan said.

"I want to know what kind of person you are."

"I'm kind, or at least I try to be. I'm mischievous, I like to raise some hell, but in a healthy, mostly law-abiding way. I am loyal until death and I fell in love with your daughter twice. Once in a 'Love at First Sight' sort of way, spending a day with her, and the second after getting to know her over the course of a school year."

"Have you had sex with my daughter?"

"Yes, several times, all of them today."

She laughed. "That's the test. I wanted to. see if you would be honest with me. Welcome to my family Tegan."

"'Thank you, ma'am."

Before they could say anything else, Carly came into the room with a collection of papers. She handed it to Tegan and sat back down.

Tegan started to read it immediately. She could not believe how good it was. It was the story she hadn't known, The last year from Ella's point of view. Thinking of her, wondering where Poppy was, what she was doing, if she even remembered her.

Tegan assumed her mom hadn't read this, because there was also some R-rated stuff in there. Nothing that shocked Tegan but still. The overall story was one of longing and sadness with just a little bit of hope.

When she was done Tegan ran her hand over the typewritten pages. She knew that their future wasn't going to be all rainbows and sunshine. There was going to be hard times, sad times, but she knew, deep down, that they were going to be okay, she felt it in her soul, because they had each other. She'd found her Comicon girl, and she wasn't about to lose her, not even in death.

She stood up and walked to Carly's chair, if wiping a tear out of her eye. "It's amazing." she said. ow Carly stood up with a look of gratitude on her face.

She hugged Tegan and Tegan held her, even when the hug was over. "What now?" Carly asked.

"I don't know if exactly, but I know one thing for damn sure."

"What's that?"

"I am never losing you again."

SEARCHING: THE MAKING OF

Embark on a cinematic journey with a group of friends turned filmmakers as they capture the essence of adventure and friendship during a road trip while crafting their very own movie.

CHAPTER ONE

C ash was standing next to where his grandmother had just been put into the ground. He felt like an asshole.

He hadn't been to see her for nearly a year before she died. She claimed to understand though, when they talked on the phone. She had led a life full of adventure, only retiring to Nashville when she had started having kids. Even then she ended up owning a large portion of the city, so the adventures never really stopped.

He reached over and took the hand of his best friend in the entire world, Delilah. She was a slight, skinny thing with a body more akin to a really tall nine-year-old than a grown woman, something that bothered her and came up on nearly every one of the brief occasions that the two of them fought. But no matter how angry she got she was always there for him. He thanked God for her on days like today.

He looked over to where the normal people were standing in morning, under the tent. He saw his cousin Ivy talking to two girls who looked like, wait...was that? "Those are the girls from Nashville Panic." Delilah whispered, finishing his thought for him. "Let's go over."

Cash was about to say that they looked busy, but before he could he was being dragged towards the tent. As they were walking over, he could hear Ivy say, "Well you tell her I'll come see her very soon." He didn't have time to ask, or cough to let them know that they were there, before Delilah had him almost bumping into Amber.

He started to apologize, but Nya was hugging him. "I am so sorry for your loss. You don't know how much your grandmother meant to me."

"Um...thanks?"

She backed up and Ivy introduced the two intruders. "This is my cousin, Cash, and his friend Delilah. Guys, this is"

"We know who you are, I love every one of your songs." Delilah said at a million miles a minute.

"I am also a fan," Cash said. "Just not nearly as hyper."

"You wanna see hyper give this one coffee." Amber said pointing a thumb at her keyboardist.

They all laughed a little but died down as soon as they remembered where they were. "How did you know my grandma?" Cash asked.

Nya went first. "She took me in when my parents kicked me out. I lived above her antiques store and worked there instead of paying rent."

"And she helped my parents buy their club, so she was kind of a surrogate grandmother when I was little." Amber said pointing to two older people off talking to Ivy's Mom. The woman looked like an exact copy of Amber, only about twenty-five years older.

"Oh, before I forget," Ivy said taking an envelope out of her back pocket. "Grandma left this for you."

Cash opened the envelope and found a check for seven thousand dollars. When he opened his mouth the only thing that came out was more akin to a wounded animal than a human, so Ivy continued. "She remembered you saying that Robert Rodriguez only had that much. You've already bought the film, but she said she still didn't want to make it too easy."

Cash loved his grandmother, not for the money but for the fact that she could remember the smallest detail of a conversation they had had months before she died. Ivy had apparently inherited that trait because she had met Delilah all of three times yet knew her name despite all of the amazing things she had going on.

Since his words were still failing him, he tucked the check back into the envelope and put it in his jacket pocket. He hugged Ivy, trying not to cry in front of two famous people. When he came back from the hug Nya said, "What are you shooting on?"

"An Arriflex thirty-five. It's a film camera."

"Oh, dear God." Amber muttered.

Then Nya Reynolds, this famous person whom he had listened to for thousands of hours, spent the entire drive back to the club where the wake was being held talking to him like they were best friends. She asked him about film and lenses and remarked over and over how cool he was for shooting film. Then, sitting on a leather chair in a club, at a wake for his grandmother, his favorite member of his favorite band, asked to write some songs for the film.

"Are you serious?"

"Yeah, I would be totally fucking honored to do that for an old school style filmmaker. I'll give you a P.O. Box and if you'd be okay with it, I'll read the script and we'll work on some stuff."

"Don't curse at a wake." Amber said.

"Oh please, Nan once told the widow of a man she knew that the urn she had her husband was fucking tacky, and then proceeded to tell a twenty-minute story about the man in which she said the word cunty forty-seven times."

Nya laughed for a few seconds and then her eyes started to water. "I'm gonna miss that woman." They all sat in silence for a long time before Nya said, "I'm sorry. I'll go write that down."

She walked away and a thought occurred to Cash. He had seen one cousin but not the other, "Where's Tessa?" he asked Ivy.

"The baby has colic and Jackson has the flu. Poor dear has spent the last week cleaning someone's fluid off something."

"Tell her I said I miss her."

"I will. If it wasn't for Gretchen being sick to she would have been able to come."

The wake died down and soon it was just and endless stream of people that had known his grandmother coming up to him on their way out to say how sorry they were. Ivy was next to him in the family line and would give him a look every time someone disingenuous hugged them. "Fucker hasn't been to see her in twenty years but as soon as a rich lady dies every shit she's ever met comes out of the wood work acting like they were best god damned friends." she whispered after one man in a tacky suit and expensive watch hugged them, leaving them both smelling like cigarettes.

Eventually they were all gone. Nya and Amber gave him the information as they went to an RV, in a hurry to get to a gig in Georgia. Ivy hugged her cousin and said, "I'd love to catch up some more, but I'm the executor of her will and you have a movie to make." she winked at him.

He said goodbye and met Delilah in the parking lot as she brought the car up.

CHAPTER TWO

When they pulled into the driveway of Delilah's house at two in the morning Cash was too excited to go home. "I'm gonna go ask Megan." he said.

"Dude, it's two in the morning. She's gonna hit you."

"No, she won't. She loves me."

"She's loved you since second grade, that's never stopped her from hitting you."

He waved her away and walked across the street to his house, walking around and through the hole in the back fence. He walked to the side of the house and knocked on the window. He saw the lamp go on and Megan get out of bed. She opened the window and ran a hand through her dirty blonde, nearly brown, hair as she yawned. "How'd it go?"

"Okay for a funeral. But afterward Delilah and I met Amber and Nya from Nashville Panic."

She was awake now. "Seriously? Why were they there?"

"I guess they knew Nan. They were friends of hers."

"Wow."

"Guess what."

"What?"

"She left me enough money to actually do a feature, and Nashville Panic is going to do some songs for the movie."

"They are?"

"Yeah. How cool is that?"

Megan yawned again, "Cash, did you wake me up to talk about the movie or your grandmother?"

"Question answer time?"

"Yes."

"The movie."

Megan nodded, understanding. "Okay." She punched him in the left eye. He went down, and she closed the window.

Cash didn't know why he was on the trampoline in the back yard, but that's where he woke up. He rolled off, his face hurting. He walked over to the brick patio, sliding the glass door open and sitting down to his waiting plate of breakfast. His Dad was reading the paper in between bites. He looked at Cash's eye and asked, "Why would you wake her up that late?"

So, he explained to the both of them what happened at the funeral, adding in the fact that they understood why the two of them weren't able to attend, and when it was done his mother said, "I still would have waited."

"I wanted to tell her; I couldn't wait."

His mother exchanged a knowing glance with his dad before asking, "So which movie are you going to do?"

He had been writing films for several years and he wasn't sure which, if any, were good enough to actually be made. He'd gotten rave reviews, but how much could you really count on family and friends for an honest opinion?

He thought hard for a couple of minutes, and then he remembered something he had done a few weeks earlier. "I'm going to do *Searching*."

His Mom looked impressed, but his dad looked concerned. His Dad had tried to make a go of it as an actor a few decades past and he probably thought that Cash was doing it to give him his moment. He said as much and Cash assured him, "I'm going it because I already have a huge scene done and filmed and it was really good."

His Dad thanked him anyway and Cash had him sign a waiver before going to see his friends. "I'm in." Delilah said as she opened the door. She had a bag packed and was pulling on her jacket as he walked up, opening the door for him. She stepped out into the cold Iowa wind and pulled on her shoes as she walked down the front walkway, leaning on him at the end.

"Well, that's my lead then." Cash said.

They walked past his house and through the hole in the fence. They saw Megan in her room, packing her stuff, and they both fell to the ground seconds before her mom came into the room. "This is insane."

"Maybe." Megan said.

"I don't see why you would want to do this."

"Too bad."

"He'll never make it. You're gonna end up living in a trailer, starving."

"It's just a movie mother."

"Well don't come crying to me when this shit goes south."

"When have I ever come crying to you? The only reason I even live here is because I couldn't go with Dad."

Cash knew that one would hurt. Her parents had gotten divorced a few years before and her dad was working a government job that was secret enough that Megan wasn't even allowed to know where he lived, let alone go with him.

A few minutes later Megan was outside holding a duffle bag and a makeup case. She'd been doing the make-up and effects for their films for a while now and she was really good at it. They didn't say anything. She set down her things and hugged Cash, burying her face in his neck.

"You'd better be doing the one I think you're doing."

"*Searching*?"

Megan exhaled. "Thank God. I thought I'd just made myself homeless for a stupid grocery store movie."

"You love Clerks."

She raised up and looked at him. "Yes...but your blatant rip-off, I do not."

"So...Eggby?" Delilah asked.

Megan nodded. "Eggby."

They walked back to Cash's house and stowed their bags before borrowing a car and driving across town to a house that looked more like it should be in Louisiana, overlooking the Missouri River. They ignored the boat graveyard and the customers looking over the salvage, or buying bate, and they walked up the wooden steps to the apartment above.

They knocked for several seconds before Eggby came to the door, shirtless. His alligator tooth necklace hanging around his neck. Eggby looked like a rock star. Night black hair that despite not being cut or, well anything but washed, on a regular basis, looked amazing. He had abbs and muscles from all the scavenging and swimming his day job demanded.

"What is up peoples?"

"I'm making a movie. Delilah is the lead and Megan is in charge of make-up, effects, and making sure I remember to do human things. You in?"

He thought for a moment. "What would I do?"

"Drive, Mic operator, and you'd be the dude in the van."

Eggby looked at Delilah, knowing what that would mean eventually. "You cool?"

"I'm cool." she said.

"Then let me go ask the boss man."

A couple of minutes later they were sitting on the porch looking out into the yard while Eggby followed his boss around the open-air shop, asking for the time he needed off. "No, I need you here."

"For what Ricky? The three days a week I work? Or the other three hours a day I watch the store while you go to lunch and home for a bit? Come on!"

"No Egg, you go, and you're fired."

"Dude didn't you say Alesha was back from school for a while? Surely to god she could use the extra cash."

This made Ricky stop. The other three didn't dare look around, they just stared at the bones of old boats and refrigerators and junk while listening for a yes.

"Fine, but you have to salvage at least two hundred pounds from the east end wreck."

Eggby sighed loudly. "Cash!"

"Yes sir?"

"Are you sure about this?"

"Yes."

"Willin' to bet your life on it? All of you?"

"Yes." They said in unison.

"Okay." He shook hands with Ricky and walked out, telling them to follow him.

They drove a couple of hours North, nearly to Wisconsin. They followed a bunch of dirt roads until they came to the river and Eggby got out. They followed him over and he handed them all scuba masks from a bag in the van. "A couple of yards upriver is a ship that went down, long time ago. We've got to get anything valuable, and at least two hundred pounds of scrap off it. He was undressing.

"Do we have to do it naked?" Megan asked.

"It gets really cold, so I like to have warm clothes to put on when I'm I done. I'll need help."

Cash paused for a moment, but when he saw the girls pulling their shirts over their heads, he started to do the same. He saw Eggby looking at Delilah and she covered her chest with her hands. "I know, I've got nothing," she said walking to the river.

Eggby looked at the other two. "That's not what I was thinking at all."

"We know." they said.

He walked off and Cash turned to Megan, immediately turning his head again. She was in dark pink under things and, though he didn't know anything about boob sizes, he knew that hers took his breath away. He looked back again, out of the corner of his eye, eyeing her middle. Soft flesh and curves, not too muscley, made for holding in someone's arms and planting kisses on. He wiped his head back around. "Am I that ugly?" she asked, covering her middle.

"No...I Uh...let's go." He walked towards the river.

He could hear Megan following him and he wanted to turn around, but he willed himself not to. They all waded into the water and started to swim upriver, their snorkels on their heads and the metal saws Eggby had given them tied to their wrists. "Shit." Delilah said.

"Yeah, that's the other thing." Eggby said and Cash saw that the ship was upside down and sliding at a really dangerous angle. "We have to be careful inside cause if it flips, we're dead." They went under, spreading apart when they were under the ship. There was an air pocket that they could use, and they threw metal down into the riverbed. Cash wanted badly to explore, but he knew it wasn't safe. But he made a mental note about this ship for a later film.

When they had been cutting for a few hours, the ship started to move. Eggby sent the girls to start taking the metal to land and Delilah asked, "Why, because men are better suited to dangerous jobs than some delicate flowers?"

"Actually, it's because your lives are more valuable to us than our own. Isn't that right Cash?"

"Absolutely." he said.

Megan, beautiful and wet, blushed. "Come on." she said to Delilah, who was still eyeing Eggby. They put their as masks back on Megan dragged Delilah to the exit.

The guys didn't work for much longer before they followed, them out. Cash was a strong swimmer, but even so Eggby had to help him along the way he was so tired.

When they came up on the bank and started to climb out of the river, Cash saw Megan on the shore, standing there, jogging slightly in place to warm up. He felt a hand grip him and throw him backwards into the water and cold, freezing water went up his nose. He hit the bottom and stayed there.

Opening his eyes and seeing Eggby in front of him. They both pushed up and broke the surface. "Thanks man." Cash said.

"Any time brother."

The girls were dressed and the scrap in the van when they went back on shore. Delilah claimed shotgun as Eggby pulled his shirt on. Cash suddenly understood the itchy black sweaters that Eggby wore. Megan and Cash however were stuck in clothes that were not doing the job. So Eggby threw them a blanket and the two of them hunched together under it in the back of the van, trying to not let scrap metal impale them every time Eggby took a corner too fast. Cash could feel the warmth coming off her, the water turning to steam as her body heated up. He was grateful the ride was almost three hours long.

CHAPTER THREE

They left the next morning. Camera and sound equipment and everything else was packed into the van, save for a small area that had couch cushions on it, where Megan and Cash sat instead of a back seat.

When they were in Kansas, they found a large stretch of paved back-road and Megan helped Delilah get ready while Cash got the camera set up and Eggby tied the back doors of the van open. They filmed Delilah's sections for a large portion of the film, just her character walking down the road in various conditions, outfits, and from different & angles. Thankfully Kansas looked like much of the Midwest and he could make it look like she was walking in a bunch of different states.

When they had filmed the last walking scene, Cash told Eggby to stop the van. "I need to refresh the Magazines."

"I'll help!" Megan said, jumping in the van as the doors closed. She put the blackout curtain over the front part while Cash did the doors and soon they were in utter darkness. Cash reached over for the next can of film and Megan yelp. "Not the box."

He almost swore that their blushing showed up in the dark. "Sorry." She handed him the film and they got to work.

Outside, Eggby and Delilah were sitting in the grass a ways down the road. "Can I ask you a question?"

"Sure." Delilah said, not looking at him as she basked the sun.

"Do they know how they feel about each other?"

"Yes."

"Okay, I know I haven't hung out quite as much in the last few months, but I swear it wasn't as obvious then as it is now."

"Well, she's told him how she feels every so often since second grade."

"How did I not know that?" he said, unbelieving.

"It's amazing how oblivious being a grade ahead can make you." She looked at him just as he looked away.

"What about Cash?" he asked after a silence.

"I can't tell you. All I can say is that Megan hasn't ever really been sure how Cash feels about her, but she has made her feelings known. Past that, it's a secret."

"Fair enough." he said, laying back and stretching out, their hands not quite touching.

"I'm not quite sure what to do next." Cash said as they were finishing up.

"What do you mean?"

"I want to shoot something good, but I'm not sure if I there are any scenes I can get today that are more, you know, substantial."

"Why don't you move Kevin's entrance?"

"Explain." '

"Well, like, instead of having them meet at the diner, have him pull up and their dialogue be in the van."

"I love that!" He burst through the doors and hurriedly explained the idea to the others. And then they piled the stuff out of frame, in a ditch, and they filmed Eggby pulling up. Then his shot through the windshield as Megan sat in the back, under a blanket, recording dialogue. Then he switched to the back of the van, getting a shot of Delilah looking small next to the full van, shooting it from a few feet away so he got the entire back of the van.

Delilah started her dialogue. "Hi." Pause. "New Mexico." Pause. "I'd sure appreciate it."

Next, they filmed the same scene, but from her point of view, looking up and into the van at Eggby, AKA 'Kevin'.

Next, they drove down the road filming Delilah, AKA 'Samantha's side of the conversation. Eggby backed down the road, they waited for a car to pass, had Megan switch out the tape on the recorder, and they filmed the next part,

Eggby-"So you mind if I ask why a pretty girl like you is walking out here all alone?"

Delilah- "Only if you don't do it like a serial killer pervert."

Eggby-"Sorry, didn't mean it to come out that way."

Delilah- "Fucking hope not."

Eggby- "So what's up? You running?"

Delilah- "More like searching. I'm going to find my Dad. My grandmother said he lives in New Mexico.

Eggby- "I see. Well, I'll get you as close as I can."

And they went on like that for most of the afternoon.

When they were finished and were loading their stuff back! into the van, nearly ten minutes of the film done, a state trooper with his sirens on pulled up Eggby and Delilah instantly put their hands up while Cash and Megan just stood there. He walked up, an average looking man with a menacing stare, and asked, "Can I ask just what in the hell you are doing?"

"What do you mean officer?" Megan asked.

"I just got a call saying you're out here driving forward and backward on the same stretch of road over and over again and just looking shifty in general."

"We are filming a movie." Megan said, seemingly the only one of them able to function and not staring at one of the items on the cop's belt. "May I show you?"

He looked suspicious and placed a hand on the top of his gun. "Alright."

Megan walked over to the open van doors and showed him the film cannisters, opened the camera case and makeup case, she even explained the plot. When she was done the man stood there with a befuddled look on his face. "Really?"

"Yes sir, I promise it's better than it sounds. If you'd like, I will send you some tickets when we get a screening set up." The officer gave her his card and walked back to his car, warning them to make double sure they were careful and to call an officer for any future traffic endangering work.

As he drove away Megan looked at her three friends. "What the fuck? Why did I have to do all the talking?"

"Because apparently cops make me comatose," Delilah said, just now learning this about herself.

"I have no excuse." Eggby said.

They all looked at Cash, "Good, I don't...thanks Megan."

Megan rolled her eyes with a smile. "Just get in the van moron,"

As they were driving, on their way to another state in hopes of finding a suitable location somewhere, Cash whispered to Megan, "I think I got you in a shot."

She was mortified. "Really? Do we need to reshoot?"

Cash shook his head. "Can't really afford it, don't have time, and I don't really want to,"

"What do you mean?"

"Remember when we watched El Mariachi and I showed you the bit with Robert Rodriguez in it, where he was in the bus mirror?"

"Yeah."

"I kind of like the idea of you being the special quirk my movie has"

Megan blushed, smiling. She tried to lean in and put her head on Cash's shoulder for the ride, but at the last second, he moved up to ask Eggby how far out they were.

CHAPTER FOUR

C ash and Eggby were telling the extras they had gotten from the local high school what to be doing in the scene while Megan did Delilah's make up. They had found a beautiful park in Owensville Missouri that would work terrific for multiple scenes, but it was cold, so they had to find a teacher willing to force her students to go to the park.

"Can I ask you a question?" Delilah asked as Megan brushed her face.

"Sure."

"Do you think Eggby might like me?"

Megan looked thoughtful for half a second before saying,

"Yeah, he's liked you since sophomore year."

"Really?"

"Well, he hasn't specifically said that, but I can tell. He wasn't gonna say it obviously, he had his reputation to maintain, but yeah, he liked you."

"A junior liked me...cool."

"Okay," Megan said a bit sarcastically. "You've been out of high school for over two years, why don't you just ask him? It's not like he's still the cool older kid."

Delilah knew she was right, but she sighed just the same. "I know that, it's just...he's our friend and if he doesn't like me I don't want to screw up the group."

Megan sprayed her face and made it look like she was sweating. It was supposed to look like she was freezing, yet hot at the same time. "I've never got that," she said. "I told Cash in the second grade, and then again in third, that I liked him. I've made my feelings known and it didn't screw anything up."

"Well maybe we wouldn't be able to be that amazing." she looked away so that Megan didn't see the secret on her face and Megan because she was an angel, didn't pry when she saw it.

Delilah went over the script one more time before time to film the scene. The movie had a lot of scenes where it was just her character, either not talking, or talking to strangers for only a few seconds. So, she had to think about how to look contemplative and pensive and bunch of other crap, all while still making it entertaining to watch...

So, when her character was walking through this park, watching all of the 'normal' kids doing fun stuff, and she was supposed to be thinking about all the bad stuff, yet trying to be strong, Delilah thought about before.

She walked through! the park, hands firmly gripping her backpack, and she thought about when she lived with her parents. Before salvation. Before her grandmother wrapped her in a blanket and carried her through the snow to the truck that would take her to a real home. She thought about looking through her arms, out the window, to see her grandfather beating the ever-loving shit out of her father, the snow streaked with blood and the holes where her father's teeth had fallen into the snow. She thought of her gramps pointing a weathered fingered at her mother on the porch, promising death to the both of them if they so much as thought about calling anyone.

When she walked into the drainpipe that would be her character's bed, she knelt and started to cry.

Cash called cut and ran over to her, kneeling. "Are you alright?"

Delilah wiped her eyes. "Yeah, sorry. I know I wasn't supposed to cry, but I thought, you know...she's alone, sleeping in a park, this might be the one time she lets herself break down."

Cash exchanged a glance with her, a silent conversation that asked if she really had been thinking that. She knew that he knew she was lying, that she'd made that up, but she could also see that he liked it. "That's really good. Can you do it some more, for the other angels?"

She smiled at him. If it was for anyone else but her best friend..."Yes, I can do it." He helped her up and they reset so that she could go through all of her pain again.

It took them two more days to get all the shots they needed. On the last day they were filming in a general store the town had as part of a museum/tourist thing. Cash scanned the store and turned to the sweet gray haired old woman that ran the place. "I'll have her walk through here, then we'll cut over to you watching suspiciously, and then...oh, we don't have anyone to play the neighbor girl."

Megan raised her hand. "I'll do it."

Cash smiled. "Awesome." He turned back to the woman. "Then she's gonna steal some things knock over the rack and run out."

The woman looked uneasy. Exactly how a sane person would, look if a bunch of young people came in and asked to wreck her store. "And you'll pay for it? The product?"

"Yes mam." He unrolled some bills, "Will that be enough?"

"That'll be fine." she said and stuffed the money into her apron before Cash could realize he'd overpaid.

They filmed the scene twice. It sucked having to right everything only to knock it over again, but they got the shoplifting scene finished just as the woman was losing her patience.

They stopped along the interstate at a gas station. Cash was plotting the next scenes and getting a shot list, changing some things based on an idea he'd had along the way. Everyone else booked showers and bought the best food they could find in the place, eating it at an outdoor table in the cold air.

"What?" Cash asked.

Megan looked at him, incredulous. "Five minutes ago, I asked if you wanted a burrito or something, five minutes."

"Sorry." he said sheepishly. He took a burrito, now cold, and chewed silently. "We need to stop at a post office tomorrow."

"Okay." Eggby said. "Why?"

"I'm going to send in the film we shot so that it should be at the house when we get back."

Eggby nodded his understanding, and they all went back to eating in exhausted silence.

The others were asleep in the back and front of the van as Cash sat up, working by the light of the gas station. Megan looked out at him, thinking of nothing else, and sighed.

She tugged on her jacket, not bothering with shoes, and slugged across the parking lot Cash. She noticed him staring, sitting down across from at his notebook and asked, "What's wrong?"

"I was just thinking of how awful this fucking movie is going to be. It's shitty writing, shitty directing. I don't know why I thought I could do this."

Megan didn't reply to his self-doubt right away. She had seen Cash do this before, and he didn't get out of it right away. But she had too much riding I on this. "You need to stop that."

He looked at her. "I'm just being honest."

"No, Cash, you're not. You are being a whiny self-doubting moron. This is a good movie. Is it going to be perfect? No. But who's first movie is? You are a good writer and a good director. Why else would I have done so many of your shorts?"

"Cause you like acting."

"Nope. I hate it. I have never liked acting. I did it because I liked being around you. I liked watching you work, seeing the passion and drive you put behind a dumb kids movie made in the back yard."

"What are you saying?"

"I wouldn't be here if the movie wasn't good. None of us would be." She reached for his hand and he pulled away. The hurt on her face pained Cash so much that he had to look away. Megan sighed, sounding like she might cry.

She walked back to the van.

CHAPTER FIVE

They were looking for a place to eat breakfast when Cash pointed to a diner off the interstate. "That place, pull over!"

Eggby jerked the wheel, narrowly making the exit. They wound through the streets until they found the right place. It looked like they were getting ready to open. A man was shouting into his phone as he got out of in expensive looking car. "What do you mean they got fired...well who the hell is going to clean my diner?"

The man saw them pull up and hung up the phone. "Sorry folks, we're not open yet. If you don't want to wait there is a Mc-Donald's twenty miles up the road." He was an average looking man in a suit, with slicked back hair and what, even from across the parking lot, looked like knock off jewelry and watched. They got the feeling he probably owned the McDonald's too.

"No sir," Cash said getting out of the van. "I am filming a movie and I wanted to use your diner for some shooting today."

"Like with guns and shit?"

"No sir, they call it that because the camera shoots the scene."

"I don't need you interrupting business."

From the passenger seat window Delilah said, "We'll clean the diner."

"What?" The man asked, looking past Cash at Delilah.

She spoke as she got out of the van. "You need a cleaning crew, right? We'll clean the place tonight. We need to use it at night anyway."

"Yeah," Cash added, "One daytime shot, then the rest is at night."

The man considered for a moment before agreeing, telling them that his niece would be there to watch over them in case they weren't being honest.

With that all set they had most of the day to explore and do nothing. They took a vote and decided to visit some caves in the area where you could either take guided or unguided tours. The caves were a tight fit getting into them but opened up into a space where they could have fit most of their town. A path had been laid out and Delilah and Eggby immediately looked around and, seeing no one, left the path.

Cash was preoccupied by the filming they would do later that night, but even he took time to admire nature's work. The stalagmites grew close together and looked like spikes guarding a fortress, and the stalactites made him think of a trap laid for enemies. But together they looked like the teeth of a giant beast, just waiting for its next meal to wander into the cave. "Can I ask you something?"

He looked at Megan and noticed how beautiful she looked in the light reflecting off the white walls of the cave. "You can always talk to me" he said.

"Why haven't you ever told me how you feel about me? I mean, I love hanging out with you and I still want to, but Cash, I'm getting sick of waiting around for you to man up and talk to me about it."

Cash felt the heat rising to his face. "I just..." He ran a hand through his hair. "Megan, I can't right now." He watched the tears start to come, but she refused to cry in front of him and sucked in a breath.

"I...okay."

She turned and walked away, towards where Delilah and Eggby had gone. Coming around the corner Delilah saw Megan sitting with her back against an enormous rock, her head in her hands.

She looked at Eggby and mouthed, "Give me a minute."

She walked over and sat cross-legged beside her friend. "I don't want to talk."

"Me neither. I thought this was the girl's bathroom."

"Go away Delilah."

"Just a second, I'm not done peeing."

Megan had to look up despite herself. She looked horrified at Delilah. "Are you really peeing?"

"No, but you looked."

"Because peeing in a cave during a tour is exactly something you would do."

"Fair enough." she said leaning closer. She wiped Megan's eyes and said, "Why do you love him?"

"What do you mean?"

"Well, he's my best friend so I get to say this, but the dude is a moron. He is completely oblivious and oddly self-centered for such a caring person."

"You love him."

"Of course I do, but that doesn't blind me to his faults. Cash is my best friend, we've been through some heavy shit together, but I know his faults and he knows mine." She wiped Megan's face with her shirt and said, "The question was, why do you love him?"

Megan put her knees up and wrapped her arms around them. "I don't know. I just always have. Ever since second grade when I saw him get hit in the face with a red rubber ball during gym, I knew I loved him."

Delilah leaned back, sitting the rest of the way on her butt. Her hands locked around her ankles; knees flat on either side. She looked at Megan, so deep in contemplation that it started to scare her. Finally, she said, "Give me some time to talk to him."

Megan started forward, "No, don't please, -"

But Delilah was already up.

Deep into the night, when they had filmed the scene, they needed and were in the middle of cleaning up the restaurant, the niece of the guy they had met earlier in the day told Cash, "You let them clean and come sit with me."

"Um, no thanks. I think I should be doing most of the work since it's my movie.

The niece was on the taller side of average height, had perfectly blonde hair and a rack that, while not quite as big as Megan's, was still pretty great. Delilah hated her for that alone. Why were the super pretty girls so damn upstairs blessed? Meanwhile Delilah had to wear shirts one size smaller just to remind people that she had breasts. Double A was a battery, not a boob.

The pretty bitch had flirted with Cash all night, making sure that she was working next to him, taking any open, and a few not so open, opportunities to touch his arm or chest. Delilah swore she saw the bitch undo a couple of buttons when she thought no one was looking. Her yellow uniform was straight out of a rom com, or a porno. The worst part was Megan saw all of this. The niece would look right at her and flirt with Cash, who to his credit, or idiocy, didn't seem to notice. Delilah hurt for her friend watching this tramp flirt with Cash.

"You know," The niece said at a whisper that was one hundred percent intended to be overheard. "I live in my uncle's guest house, not far from here."

"That's good." Cash said, "It must be a short commute,"

Delilah laughed and the niece shot her a death glare.

Eggby came back out from cleaning the oven just as the girl said, "Do you wanna see the place? I could give you like, a private tour...I'll drop you off to your friends in the morning."

"I'm really okay." Cash said.

They all looked at the door when they heard the bell. They saw Megan walking past the glass front window. Delilah looked at Cash, "You need to go after her."

"What for?"

"Cash, so help me god if you don't go after that girl and tell her the truth, and I mean the whole, unvarnished truth, I will and I will tell her so much more besides..."

Cash got her meaning and made for I the door. As he walked out the Niece said, "What does he even see in that mousey cunt?"

Delilah lunged forward and felt Eggby's hands on her arms, keeping her from choking the slutty waitress.

Megan was pacing the parking lot, trying to figure out how to get out of there, when Cash saw her. "Where are you going?" he asked walking up.

She turned away from him. "I don't know."

"Well, we're almost done, come back and then we'll be out of here."

"I'm not coming with you guys Cash."

"What?" he was genuinely shocked.

Megan turned back to him, furry and tears mixing in her eyes. "I gave up everything for you! Everything! I can't go home! My mother told me that if I came with you, I wasnot allowed back in her house, ever. I came here because I believe in you and I thought that maybe if we spent this time together and you made a feature that you might finally..." She broke off.

"What?"

"Love me!" She screamed. She turned to the hill that overlooked the interstate. She screamed at the top of her lungs and then got very quiet. He could barely hear her when she said, "But you don't, and you never will."

She started to walk away as Cash took a deep breath. "I've always loved you."

Megan stopped in her tracts, not turning around she said, "What?"

"I've loved you since you came and helped me up from the asphalt and held my arm all the way to the nurse."

Megan turned around, "Then why haven't you ever done anything?"

"Because you deserve better."

She looked at him with a mixture of incredulity and anger. "What?" she said, stretching out the word to indicate just how stupid she found his previous statement.

"I've known what I wanted to be since I was seven years old and my dad gave me his old super eight camera. I also know what it's like, slogging to the top, or even to the middle, and I think you deserve better than that.

He took a deep breath. "I also know how obsessive I can be. I see it. You all think I don't, but I do. I think you deserve a guy who will make you his whole world.

Megan let out a laugh that was not joyous at all. It was like she was releasing a pain, like someone had said something she hadn't been able to, and now she knew. "You're such a fucking dumbass."

"What?" he said as she walked closer.

"I don't need that Cash. I don't need a man who will wait on me hand and foot and treat me like his goddess. I just need someone who will be there for me." She got closer, inches away. "Love isn't finding someone who will pull you out of the mud, it's having someone kneel next to you and say 'This is where I am supposed to be'." She kissed him.

It was the sweetest kiss he had ever had. And the only kiss since seventh grade when she had pushed him up against a locker and kissed him because she wanted her first kiss. When they broke, she said, "I would live in a mansion with you, and I would starve in a studio apartment, or on the streets, as long as I'm the second thing. Maybe the first on holidays, birthdays, anniversaries, you know."

"Deal." he said, and he kissed her.

CHAPTER SIX

Megan was putting cut makeup on Eggby to make it look he had been beaten. She was all smiles and had been the last several days. She was so giddy and lost in thought that she at first didn't hear Eggby talking to her. "I'm sorry," she said, "What were you saying?"

"I was asking if you thought Delilah might like me." he said.

"Yeah, she does. I mean, she had a crush on you all through high school."

"Really? I thought she just couldn't get a date cause "you know, she's got..." He made a gesture for her small breasts and butt right as Delilah walked around the corner.

"Asshole." she said and hurried away.

"No, I didn't...fuck." He looked down. "Fuck fuck fuck." he said under his breath.

"Nice going moron."

"Yeah."

Megan worked the camera that day. Cash showed her how to block the scene and they went through what to do, she did his makeup and costume, stopping for several kisses, and they were ready to film the scene.

The alley was lit from a streetlamp as Megan said, "Action" And Cash started to pretend to beat up Eggby. When it was her cue Delilah walked past the camera and chased Cash away. They filmed that scene a few different ways, having to cut down and re-duct tape the mic for each new version.

When they had filmed Delilah walking past the corner and rushing into the alley. Cash called "Cut." And said, "Let's get a room tonight."

They found a decently priced motel, and everyone slogged in, too tired to shower. They designated one bed for boys and one for girls, but Eggby said, "Ima go sleep in the tub." And he left, closing the door.

They got to bed, but Cash couldn't sleep, so he sat up working with his notebook and a script. Delilah kicked in her sleep, landing several shots on Megan before finally kicking her out of the bed. Megan got up, rubbing her sore bottom and said, "I think she's doing that on purpose."

"I promise she isn't." Cash said getting off the bed. He looked in the drawer and found the Gideon bible. Leaning over the other bed he swung back and let fly, smacking Delilah loudly in the ass. He did it three more times before Megan stopped him. Laughing she said, "I believe you...good lord."

Cash let her get in next to him and he put away his things. They lay there for several minutes before, thinking her asleep, Cash asked, "Did she really kick you out?"

Megan turned and he moved so that they were facing each other. "Yes, she did"

"Then you'll come live with me." Cash said, resolute. "To my parent's house and then wherever we want to go."

"I'd like that." she said smiling. And the two of them stayed there, talking and looking at each other as they planned the plannable parts of their future.

CHAPTER SEVEN

When Cash opened his eyes, she saw Delilah's bed empty. He also took note of the fact that his arms were wrapped around a still sleeping Megan. He didn't let go until he heard the snickers coming from the front of the room. He turned over and saw Eggby's wide eyes and an enormous smile plastered on Delilah's face.

Megan turned over, not as asleep as he'd thought as Delilah moved aside and showed them the desk, full of food. "We got breakfast."

The food was unidentifiable in name and appearance, but it was absolutely delicious. Cash dug into what looked like a burrito smothered in a lake of salsa and herbs. It was stuffed with sausage and eggs and, despite looking like something someone had thrown up, was the best thing he'd eaten since leaving home.

While they were eating, Cash decided to brook the subject that they had all been dreading because of the awkwardness. "So, since we have the room, do you guys want to film your last scene together?"

Delilah's gaze nearly set the paper bag in front of Eggby on fire. "If he can stomach being around my disgustingly boyish form."

Eggby tilted his head to the side, "You know, there was a big part of that conversation you missed."

"Oh no...I missed you being an asshole? I am so upset now."

"Let's just do this." Eggby said getting up.

Cash set up the scene and they filmed the part where Delilah bandaged him up, laying him back without a shirt on. They kissed, Cash called out, "Now take your shirt off and Eggby, ask if she's sure."

Delilah peeled off her shirt, exposing her chest to Eggby. He stared at her in a way that she wasn't quite sure if it was for the scene or not. It must be after...what he'd said..."Are you sure?" he asked.

Cash had them hold, moved the camera into place, and was on her as she removed her bra and said, "Definitely."

There was nothing sexy about the scene as they removed their pants, and she covered them up. In the scene it was for romance or something. In reality, it was so they didn't have to be naked. As she moved her hips into Eggby she felt him. They exchanged a glance and she saw his face go red. He leaned forward and kissed her, even though they weren't supposed to in the scene, just so they didn't have to talk. The tension grew and grew as Delilah went faster and faster until Cash called out, "Now flip her."

Eggby took her by the waist and flipped her so that he was on top. Cash moved in and shot her from above, unable to see his lips on camera Eggby said, "I'm sorry." as he started to grind himself into her. They kissed again.

Cash said he was trying to keep it to as few takes as possible, seeing as they were nearly out of film, so they only had to film most of the scene once. Near check out it was time to film the last bit of the scene.

Cash scanned over their bodies as they lay there, fully naked, intertwined so that their hips kept each other's privates from view. Eggby said, "Why don't you come with me?"

Hoping that she got the pause right, Delilah sat up and said, "What?"

"I said, why don't you come with me?

"Because I'm going to see my dad."

"I know, I mean...you're like what, twenty? Why do you need a parent? Just come with me."

She got out of bed and stood, looking for her clothes while she talked. "You know what," She picked up her jean shorts and motioned at him with them in hand. Just because we fucked doesn't mean we're like, in love. I'm going my way, and you're going yours. Just deal with it.

While the camera was away from her, she got half dressed, missing only a shirt by the time Eggby was done. "I don't want to come with you, that's why. We've known each other for a grand total of what...fifteen hours?"

The two of them were lost in the scene. Eggby got up and. looked at her, anger in his eyes. "And you've already screwed me...maybe the reason you're searching for Daddy is that you've got some serious issues."

The camera turned to her, and she looked at him, "Fuck you." She turned, grabbed her backpack and stormed out of the room in her bra.

Cash called "Cut," a smile plastered on his face. "That was brilliant. I loved you leaving like that. It works so much better than what was written."

"Thank you." Delilah said walking back in. She grabbed her shirt and started to put it on as she heard Megan say,

"Uh...Eggby?"

Everyone looked at Eggby and he looked down to see himself still...himself, and his face went red. He scurried into the bathroom as the others broke out in strained laughter.

The other three packed up the van and Cash and Megan went to check out. Coming out of the room Eggby saw Delilah standing in front of the van, leaning on the hood. He tried to look away before she saw him, but she just laughed. "Embarrassed?"

"Why would I be?"

"Cause you aren't exactly...blessed."

"Yeah well, we all have parts of ourselves we can't change."

Cash and Megan walked up. Delilah's face fell as Eggby walked to the driver's side. Cash went to the back and Megan met Delilah on the side of the van. "How did that feel?"

"What?" she asked, thinking that Megan had overheard Eggby.

"Duh, dude was at full salute for you babe, that's gotta be a compliment."

"It was cause of the scene."

Megan shook her head. "The grindy bits were over. That was for you...half naked..." Her tone suggested that Delilah might in fact be the dumbest girl who had ever lived.

Delilah got into the van, wide eyed and thinking of more things than her brain was built for. Did he really like her that much? Could anyone? She spent most of that day staring straight ahead and not really seeing what was coming

CHAPTER EIGHT

They shot a few bits in the desert and headed home after mailing the film off to be processed. Cash slept for hours having only really slept for the one full night the entire trip, he was exhausted.

Delilah stared out the window, watching things pass by her side, thinking. Eggby, one night when it was close to dark, said, "I need to stop guys. And he pulled off the road on to a dirt one, driving along winding roads that got narrower and narrower, until he was just driving through a field.

He moved around, backing up to the side of a lake. The rest of them hadn't thought to ask what was going on, too lost in the strangeness of his actions. Finally, he looked at them and said, "This is my grandparents' farm. I thought we could camp here for a while."

The girls nodded. Megan woke up Cash as Delilah and Eggby got out. Eggby brought up a hatch in the back of the van with a couple of tents, and a trunk that had sleeping bags in it. Delilah started to set them up while Eggby got a fire going. "So where is their actual farm part?" Delilah asked.

"About an hour that way." He pointed into the darkness. "But we were close to this part, and this is my favorite place to camp on their land."

"Wait, they own the whole part?"

"A hundred and fifty acres I think."

Delilah looked impressed and Megan and Cash walked past, done with their tent and headed to see the lake. "So why are we here?" Cash asked.

"Because Eggby thought it would be fun, and I think it would be good for you to hang here a couple of days. You can relax before we get into the movie stuff and you disappear."

"That's probably a good idea." he said, though he sounded unsure.

The area was beautiful. There were trees hanging over the lake and vine like leaves hanging off and between them. It was very idyllic Cash thought. "Let's go swimming." Megan said as he looked out over the lake.

"But we don't-" He turned to see her in the midst of taking her clothes off. She dived into the water, naked, and looked up at him, still on the bank.

"Well?"

"Coming dear." he said lovingly. He soon followed her in.

At the fire, Delilah heard the giggling and splashes of her two friends in love, and she was inspired. Megan had been a ballsy kid her entire life, and in the end, she had gotten what she'd set out for. She felt the heat of the fire on her face as she looked at Eggby and said, "Do you have feelings for me?"

Eggby was so surprised he nearly fell into the fire. "I, uh..."

Delilah's face was already falling, and she started to walk away. "Of course not."

"No," Eggby said. "I mean, of course I do. You just surprised me is all."

Delilah turned around, looking at him through the fire. "What did you say?"

"I said you surprised me.""Duh, I meant before that doofus.""I said of course I do. I've liked you for a long time."

Delilah wasn't yet ready to sit next to him, but her legs buckled, and she ended up directly across from him. The two of them looked at each other through the flames. "I thought you didn't like me because of," She made the gesture that she'd seen him make to Megan.

"I was saying that because I thought you didn't date in high school because all of the guys were too stupid to see how great you are, and they got distracted by the fact that you aren't all busty and shit."

"That's only slightly better."

He stood up, "I know, but what I was going to say is that your body was never what interested me."

Delilah glared at him. "And it's worse,"

"Let me finish.," he said and took a deep breath, though it came out a bit shaky. "I like you because you're confident. You don't take shit from anyone. I like you because you're adventurous and crazy and your personality enters a room ten seconds before you do. I liked seeing a seventy-five pound ninth grader beat the hell out of Duke Evers for picking on a kid in her theater group. Your body is great, D. I am a big, big, fan of your body...but it's not even remotely why I love you."

Delilah looked quizzical. "You what?"

"I love you. Have for a while"

She ran through the fire and jumped, knocking him into the grass and she kissed him. When she came up for air she said, "I love you too."

They didn't end up using the tents. They slept out below the stars, relishing in the quiet and restfulness that they didn't have at home. Long into the night, when he could hear Eggby and Delilah snoring, Cash reached over for Megan's hand and found her awake. "What's up?" she whispered.

"I almost don't want to go back." he said.

"I know what you mean. One way or the other our lives are going to change. Either people love it, or we start having to work really hard to make another."

He couldn't see her in the pitch dark, but Cash looked in her direction, filled with love. If he crashed and burned, she was willing to just immediately start working so that he could make another. He loved her, and he wanted to show her.

Cash leaned over, pressing his lips down, and listening to Megan giggle. "That's my armpit." They both laughed loudly and then looked over to see their friends undisturbed. They turned back to each other, and Cash tried again.

CHAPTER NINE

When the van pulled into the driveway it was three in the afternoon. Everyone was tired so they let themselves in to Cash's house and slept where they fell, Megan on the couch, Delilah on the chair, Cash on the floor, and Eggby on the coffee table.

When he woke up it was dark outside. His mother was watching television, having moved Megan's feet onto her lap. When she saw Cash she said, "Your film was delivered yesterday. We put it in the garage."

His eyes went wide and he jumped up, the sluggishness gone from his bones. He ran outside and through the garage door, eyeing the cans of film, still in their boxes. He felt something looking at those boxes. He felt accomplishment. Whatever happened, whether people liked it or not, or even if they never saw it, he had done this. He made a movie.

He turned on the lights and looked around the garage that his father had long since let him take over. The metal shelves had come with the house, but unlike most houses, where they were filled with tools and every present that you have to unpack when your grandmother visits, but never actually use, his shelves were filled with cameras, lenses, props, and film cans. The small alcove that his dad had built him a ladder to housed his archive of old movies and the ones that he had made. Larger props hung from the rafters and walls, and his projectors took up their own shelf. Save for the one he'd bought out of a movie theater, that one had its own corner of the room. This room was why he never had any money, despite working two jobs on a fairly regular basis.

Cask walked back to the far-left corner of the room and flipped on the massive Steinbeck editing table, moving his smaller editor to the side, glad he'd put it on wheels.

The massive machine, which had taken him three months' pay and several thousand dollars to learn to use, hummed to life. He moved the smaller sixteen-millimeter machine to the other side of the garage and put the film cans in its place. He thought back to the local commercials he'd shot, the neighborhood showings of his shorts, and his other businesses that had helped pay for his equipment, along with his two jobs. It had been a long road to his first feature, a long road and a hard one. But here he was. He unwrapped the first can and set to work.

Cash had been in the garage for the better part of a week. There was a bathroom in there and Megan or his mother brought him his food and drink. No one really bothered him other than one of them would periodically make sure he hadn't gotten some sort of weird artist bug and offed himself.

But Delilah and Megan both agreed when Nashville Panic's RVs pulled up, it was worth bothering him. Nya came down from the second RV and vaulted towards the house. She came at Delilah with open arms before she knew what to do, and soon Delilah was being hugged by a famous person like they were best friends. "Hey Delilah, where's the auteur?"

"In there." she said pointing a thumb towards the garage, eyes wide and extremely conscious of the arm around her shoulder.

"Cool." Nya said walking and leading her back to the RV. "I'd like you to meet my wife, Nickki," A pretty blonde woman walked off the RV with a child's hand in hers. "And this is David."

"Hello." The boy said.

"Uh, hi." Delilah said.

She was taken around and introduced to every one of her favorite musicians. Cash came out at that time, looking bleary eyed and squinting at the sunlight.

Nya rushed back to the RV and got a box out, handing it to him. Inside was a bunch of small metal cannisters and a notebook. "We wrote a bunch of songs, like fifteen, and I thought you could just choose which ones you want to use."

Cash looked at the cannisters, " You recorded on tape?"

Nya's eyes went wide with worry. "You need magnetic tape right, for film?"

"Oh uh, yes. I was just surprised that you would even be able to do that."

Nya smirked. "I know a guy."

Her wife raised an eyebrow. "I know a guy."

"She knows a guy."

Cash, rather rudely, turned his back on the band and walked back towards the garage. "Can I come watch?" Nya asked.

"Sure."

She ran off and Delilah turned to the rest of the band. "Sorry he just walked off like that. He doesn't really think of much else when he's in the middle of a project."

Their faces were blank as they all said, "We're used to it."

Delilah invited them all in and they walked back towards the house. She noticed Megan in the driveway, staring.

"You alright dude?"

"I... you told me, but...You know Nashville Panic?"

"Yep," she said and they all went inside.

The band wasn't doing anything, so they hung around for the next several days as Cash finished up the film. He offered to screen it for them all, but Nya refused. "No, they have to see it at the premier."

"What premier?"

"You didn't tell him?" she asked, looking at the rest.

"I didn't have many opportunities." Megan said. Turning to Cash she said, "We've set up a premier in the city. The band let me tell people they will attending."

"So, we think there will be quite a few people there." Amber said.

Nya leaned in and whispered, "Thank you is a big one in these situations."

Everyone laughed and Cash said, "Thank you."

CHAPTER TEN

The premier was in a park amphitheater, the screen set in front of the stage area. There were only allowed to be around three hundred people in the seats, but a bunch more had taken up spots in the grass, hoping to get glimpses of the band, and the famous guy that was supposed to be there.

The front few rows were taken up by Cash's family. Ivy, and Tessa with her kids, the other cousins and their friends who could come. Megan was taking tickets when Amber walked up to help. "You're famous, you don't take tickets."

Amber's face suggested that Megan might be hating a break down. "It's cool dude, It's not like I'm Angelina Jolie. I just sing."

Amber started to take tickets when a girl rushed up with pen and pad in hand. As if God was trying to make Megan's point for her, this girl was a fan. She was near tears as she said, "I love you so much, you are my favorite singer and Nya's song is my favorite, can I get an autograph?"

"Okay sweetie, are you buying a ticket?"

The girl pointed behind her to a man who seemed nearly invisible in the evening light. "He's paying."

Okay then, after the movie we'll be around, okay? I'll introduce you."

The girl nodded and once Amber gave her a ticket ran to get a seat. The man walked up with another man and a girl the same age as the first. "Katelyn, go get Juno and tell her to calm down." The girl ran after the first and the man paid for the tickets.

When he left Megan looked at Amber, who was equally slack jawed. "Isn't that?"

"Yeah," Amber said. "Dude owns half the city. I live a transient, on the run, life style and even I know who he is."

The ticket taking ended soon after, with two tattooed women getting in last. Megan wasn't sure, but she thought she saw a really cool one on the neck of one of the women. She only caught a glimpse as the woman swatted a bug out of her hair.

Cash saw a man in a Victorian coast walk over and sit behind the really rich guy who's name he forgot. The man took his hat off and waited for the film to start. Cash had practically bitten his thumb off by the time the projector started rolling. Ivy put a hand on his shoulder, and it shocked him so much that he got up and went to the back.

She followed him back and watched as he paced up and down the pathway. "Are you alright cuz?"

"No, I am so fucking nervous I think I may have shit my pants without noticing."

"Trust me, mixing Heroin and Cocaine is the only way you can shit yourself and not notice." That made Cash laugh and Ivy came closer, hugging him. "Each sect of m our family has an artist, that's why we're so fucking nuts. I'm mine and you are your family's. You wanna know what that means?"

"What?" he asked, head buried in her shoulder.

"It means that no matter what happens we keep creating, always. Like sharks, if we stop we die."

"So even if they hate it,

"We keep going."

"We keep going." he said, less confident.

They broke the hug and walked back just as the movie was getting out of the front credits. Ivy leaned in and whispered, "You and I are lucky. We have an excused, the rest of the family is just crazy."

Cash laughed and they went to watch the movie.

It was hard to gage the reaction during the movie. He didn't dare look around, and he didn't hear anything. He saw Delilah's grandparents' cover their eyes and ears at the sex scene, and once both Ivy and Tessa squeezed his shoulder.

But it wasn't until the end that he knew.

As the credits started to roll, he heard thunderous applause from the people around him. Granted that most of it was probably his ears being overloaded by his family's shouting. But when he stood up and looked around, he saw people clapping, shouting, standing up.

And he started to cry.

When the crowd had died down and thinned out, and the band was talking to fans, Cash sat on the stage, next to the screen, and looked out at the mostly empty seats. He could still hear them, and he thought he would probably be able to hear them for the rest of his life. No I matter what happened, in the past or future, here, today, they had loved his film.

Just as he was ready to get up, he saw the rich guy coming over. He was instantly frozen in fear. The man had a gaze more intense than staring into the sun. Though the resemblance ended there. He was a shadow, sucking in the light around him until Cash wasn't quite sure where he was, until he was right next to him. "Hello."

"H..hello."

"Do you know who I am?" Cash simply nodded. "Good. How much did you make this film for?"

"I forget the exact number sir, but it was around ten thousand dollars."

"I see. And do you think that you could do it again? Make more films with such small budgets?"

"I don't see why not."

The man smiled. "Well, as I'm sure you know, I own forty-five theaters around the country and ticket sales are down, but Hollywood prices for movies are going up. So, I've been working on rebranding my theaters as more, art-house, old-school type stuff."

"Movies with feeling, a message. More than a blow it up shoot 'em down titty flick." Cash said.

"Exactly. So, I'm thinking that if they can only be seen there, and we brand them right, then maybe we can carve out a niche."

"I like the idea," Cash said. "But what are you saying?"

"I would like you to make films for me. I'd actually like you to help me build a studio."

Cash didn't hear the next few words because his heart was beating so loudly in his chest. When the man stopped talking, he said, "One condition."

"What's that?"

"Film only, from creation to projection."

"Why is that?"

"Because, and I know I sound crazy, but there is just so much more there. In the feeling, the tactility, there's magic there."

"Deal." he said and held out his hand, giving Cash a look of respect. They shook hands and Cash was given a business card with orders to call Monday.

The man walked away, and Cash was alone, though not for long as Megan and Delilah walked up, Eggby close behind.

"What was that about?" Megan asked after a kiss."Our future, I think."

ABOUT THE AUTHOR

Ethan Thomas has lived in over twenty houses in his life and written stories in most of them. He lives in Wisconsin with his dogs and his beloved Hermes Ambassador that he uses to write his books.